Avens

PRIDEFUL MAGICK COLLECTION
BOOK FIVE

TENTH ANNIVERSARY EDITION

HOLLOW RYAN

Avens

Second Edition

Published by Hollow Ryan

Ebook ISBN: 978-1-968729-13-4
Trade Paperback ISBN: 978-1-968729-12-7
Hardcover ISBN: 978-1-968729-14-1

Cover elements courtesy of:
Vintage Damask by DarkMoon_Art via Pixabay.com
Realistic Smoke Fog by Hakan Kaçar via Vecteezy.com
Flowers by Zenaga via Pixabay.com

Cover Design by Christiana Nehmsmann
Interior Design by Christiana Nehmsmann

Books By Hollow Ryan

Prideful Magick Collection

Ivy

Oleander

Valerian

Hawthorn

Avens

Demon Kin

Demon Kin: The Queen

Demon Kin: The Lovers

TABLE OF CONTENTS

For Faolan

Even if things look like the end, they're often really new beginnings.

Chapter One

REUNITED

I'd forgotten what it was to feel so alive. The second I stepped into the circle, I remembered.

All around me, an electric pulse shot through the barrier, awakening every tiny aspect of the dormant spells. For a moment, I was overwhelmed by the information that swirled around me. Pieces of the past drifted through me, leaving imprints in my skin. As each memory seeped into me, I could feel the weight of responsibility settle into my bones. Upon my return, I took up my duties to this place, and now I could never take them back.

Taking a deep breath, I stepped farther into the fold. Like a rubber band, everything snapped back into focus. Moonlight bathed the circle in a pale glow, lingering over the smaller circle in the center. A brisk, cool wind pushed through the barrier and swirled around me before slipping out again. For that one brief moment, I could almost hear a whispered *"Alexandria"* in its gentle embrace. Fighting tears, I took my place in the center.

It was harder to breathe once inside of it. There was so much history buried in that soil, and much of it was mine. My past life of Mary Sullivan was burned at the stake in this place. I'd found that out during my Wiccaning at the age of nine. On the night of my Ascension, I was witness to my mentor's suicide. Yet another blessing met by a curse. That was the balance of being a witch.

Standing in the midst of the memories, I started to pull back. If I lost myself in them now, I would never find my way out.

With another deep breath, I raised my face to the moon and closed my eyes. I let the power fill me. There was so much of it. More than I had ever needed. Now I had a use for it, and I would make it count.

I let the magick fill me until I could hold no more, then I pushed it out. A dome of it formed around me that slowly grew outward. Farther and farther I pushed it, cataloging every single flicker of life as it encompassed them. As it began to inch over the entirety of Cedar Creek, I felt at peace. All of this was mine, and I intended to claim it.

When the entire town was within my grasp, I sank a pulse into every life-force.

The Witch of Old Grove Road had returned, and now all of Cedar Creek knew it.

When I had first returned to the cottage, I let the nostalgia have me. In the dim light by the fire, I relived every memory, and cried every tear. There was a cost to being home, just as there was the promise of it. Within the shadows, I let the memories have me. Come dawn, I remembered what it was to live for the moment.

Daylight brought responsibility. So, I put on my grungy, paint-stained overalls and a tank top and set to work with a dust rag. Keeping a notepad and a pen in my back pocket, I began to jot down everything I thought I would need. It didn't take me long to realize that there was a whole lot more to be done than my little dust rag and some water could handle.

With a sigh, I finished off the grocery list before I headed out to the garden. As soon as I was amongst the wilderness that had once been a forest of organized chaos, a pang shot through my heart. Not only were the non-native species nothing but compost now, but the carefully trimmed weeds had exploded and choked out many of their brethren over the years. Making the list of what needed to be replaced was difficult enough, but what was worse was knowing how much time it would take to restore it to the glory of before.

For a moment, my mind stalled on that word. *Before.* As if there were stages of my life that were encompassed in simple words like *before, after,* and *now.* Before I left Cedar Creek. After I left. Now that I've returned. The history of Cedar Creek from before was something I didn't need repeated. The after, however, would have to be broken down for me, and the list of people I trusted for that conversation was short.

Shaking the thoughts off, I went inside and grabbed my wallet. Shoving that in my pocket with the grocery list, I started the long walk to the store. It wasn't so bad at first, but a quarter of a mile down Norfolk Street I was wishing I had a bike. One more thing to add to the list.

As I was getting to the business quarter, I was gratified to find that a few new ventures had filled some of the spaces in the older buildings. There was even a café that looked promising. A fact that seemed reinforced by my sudden change of direction once the doors opened and I caught the scent beyond. My stomach growled in pleasant anticipation as I entered the quaint establishment.

It didn't occur to me what kind of reception I could expect. Even though my announcement had hit every living creature in Cedar Creek, it had somehow escaped my notice how it might affect them. As soon as I walked in, however, I was treated to several people performing a double-take. Conversations faltered as I walked past, and I felt my spine straighten in response. Only the barista who took my order seemed ignorant as to who I was.

I had just finished paying her when a bell above the door jangled in announcement of two new arrivals. All at once, my chest tightened and I couldn't catch my breath fast enough. Bracing my hands against the counter, I closed my eyes and let myself get lost in the feeling of security that enveloped me.

The pair stopped almost right inside the door, and I could feel his gaze boring into my back. For several seconds, he neither moved, nor spoke. My brain was short-circuiting and I couldn't figure out what to say or do. Not when the moment I had waited almost four years for was finally before me.

At last, I heard him clear his throat and I raised my head a little. Then a warm, rich voice forced out in a casual tone, "Only one girl I know would wear those overalls in public."

A wide smile spread across my face as I stared at the wall behind the counter. After clearing my throat, I remarked, "Only one girl you know has enough pride not to care what anyone else thinks." When I'd finished speaking, I turned slowly in place. The second my eyes met his, everything in the world felt right.

There was another moment of silence as we smiled at each other. Even that seemed right. Just like old times. Then our eyes broke apart and we scanned one another, noting all of the changes and taking stock of what the years had stolen from our sights.

It looked like he'd finally stopped growing, though not before he reached six foot one. His brown hair was cut shorter than the last time I'd seen it, and no longer fell into his emerald eyes. What little baby fat had clung to his face when we were fourteen was gone now, leaving his features in sharp relief. Opposite of this occurrence, the rest of his body had filled out with the ropy muscle common to teenage boys. In four years, the gangly teenager had vanished and a man had replaced him.

"You're home," he mused.

"I'm home."

Nathan wasted only a second before taking three long strides toward me and I rushed to meet him. I threw my arms around his neck in the same instant that his arms wrapped around my waist, pulling me off the ground in a crushing hug. Both of us laughed like giddy children, unaware or just unable to care about the people watching us. My hold tightened as he swung me around and I squeezed my eyes shut in order to absorb the feel of him. As had happened with Matt, every memory of my time with him came flooding back.

There was my first day of school when we were introduced. The day I first traveled down Old Grove Road and passed through the gate into Morgan's garden. I could almost feel the ghost of his hand on my arm from when he'd dragged me out. All at once, countless memories of bus rides, shared classes, and shopping trips fluttered through my head like the pages of a book. Those images blurred together, adding up to the time where we barely spoke, but kept each other's secrets.

Then the memories hit a speed bump on the day I'd met Matt, and they trickled into the strange phase our friendship had taken prior to Morgan's suicide. At last, I was forced to relive every second of our time together following my Ascension. Tears filled my eyes as I found myself remembering the last time Nathan's arms were around me. The hourglass scar inside of my wrist throbbed as I was forced to relive the moment we had said goodbye.

Before I could stop myself, my body spasmed with a small sob and I felt Nathan easing me back to the ground. As soon as my toes touched the tile floor, I loosened my arms and brought my right hand up to scrub away at the tears trying to make an escape. This was neither the time nor place to be crying.

As my left arm was slipping down his shoulder to rest on his forearm, Nathan released a choking sound. Before I had time to wonder what that was about, he grabbed my hand and straightened out my arm, examining it in the light. Unable to look at the scars magickally burned into my skin, I watched his features instead. Remorse was written across his face, but I couldn't bear to ask him about it. There would be time for that later.

"Oh, Lex," Nathan whispered in a voice low enough that only I could hear it.

Working to catch his eyes with mine, I forced a sarcastic grin into place. "It's not as bad as it looks. Not anymore."

"Uh, Nathan, I'm just gonna–" Mark took a step back toward the door before I ever realized he was there.

Nathan turned toward him, but didn't release my hand. "Sorry, man. Get yourself something to eat. I'll drive you back once lunch is over."

Mark looked between us for a long moment. Then he offered me a timid smile and said, "It's good to have you back, Alex."

Before I could reply, I heard the barista calling out my order. For the third time. All at once, the world seemed to snap back into place and the present popped the bubble that had surrounded us. Forcing a smile, I shot Nathan a look that said 'give me a minute' before my hand slipped out of his.

Once I'd picked up my order, I motioned to a table and Nathan was quick to follow. The second he dropped into the seat beside me, all else was forgotten. All that mattered was that we were together again.

There were so many things to say. So much that I needed him to know. More than what I'd been through or the things I'd done, I wanted Nathan to know that I essentially hadn't changed. I was still the proud, stubborn, smartass little witch he'd always known. I was still his best friend.

And of all the things I wanted to say ... I didn't say a word.

Neither did he.

We reveled in that. The old camaraderie where we could sit side by side and not speak a word. Not about our pasts or presents. Not even about how dreamlike this all still felt. No questions. No answers. No words. Just us.

Staring into his emerald eyes, it was all I could do to stay in the moment. There was time for the heavy, and we had it now. All of it. For the rest of our lives, Nathan and I could deal with having lost each other. That didn't have to start the second we were reunited.

A smile pulled at his lips and I knew we were thinking the same thing. Even so, there was one memory neither of us could ignore. The one that meant the most to both of us. When the world was black and I was in his arms as he asked me to come home. Finally, I had listened.

Because of Nathan, I had returned to Cedar Creek.

Chapter Two

ADRIFT

A sandwich dropped onto the table in front of Nathan before Mark strode off to find a seat in the corner. I almost smiled as I saw him pull out his cellphone and begin to text someone. For the time being, at least, he was leaving us alone.

Shaking his head, Nathan began to pick at the sandwich before his eyes raised again to mine. I could hear every unspoken question behind it when he asked, "When did you get back?"

"Last night."

"And you didn't come to see me. I feel neglected." His grin implied that he was teasing, but there was a darkness in his eyes that suddenly had me worried.

"You didn't come to me," I rejoined.

He at least had the good grace to look chagrined. Especially since we both knew that when I made that announcement, it was for him more than anyone else.

For a moment, we simply stared at one another, making the promise to hash it all out in a more appropriate setting. Then he asked, "So what's the plan? Going to transfer in to finish out your schooling?"

I snorted. "No. I have the credits to graduate and my parents know where to mail the diploma. In that regard, at least, I am free."

It was Nathan's turn to scoff, "How the hell did you manage that? Matt said you skipped most of your freshman year."

"I've been to six schools in the past four years. Between their scheduling differences and credit requirements, I had enough to graduate last semester."

"Really?" he asked, a hint of censure in his voice. Again, I could hear the rest of the questions lingering behind that single word.

I lowered my voice a little as I assured him, "I would have been home sooner, but ... life happens."

I could see it on his face that he was desperate to ask, and knew by his clenched fists that we were experiencing the same level of frustration. This was not the time nor the place. While part of me wanted to grab his hand and take off in order to unburden ourselves, it didn't feel right. We would have time for him and I, but this moment wasn't it.

As if in testimony to that fact, Mark appeared at his shoulder. "Hey, sorry to interrupt, but we've got ten minutes to get back."

At once, our eyes locked and I knew we were both feeling the sinking sensation that preluded a goodbye. Even if it was a temporary one, it was asking too much of us. And yet...

"I've got to drive Mark back to school. Then I'll head straight to the cottage."

"Nathan, don't worry about it." It felt like pulling a tooth to get the words out, but I managed. "I'm going to be running errands and cleaning all day. Just stop by after school."

"But you just got back," he muttered.

"And I'm not going anywhere. I promise."

For a few more seconds, we sat at that table and performed an intense staring contest. Neither of us really wanted to be apart. Even for only a few more hours. But we couldn't live our lives pretending that we would vanish if out of arm's reach for three seconds, either. Our new normal had to be created now, before we warped it with our dependence on one another.

"Fine," he sighed, rising to his feet. As soon as I stood, Nathan pulled me into another tight hug. In my ear, he whispered, "I've missed you, Lex."

"I've missed you, too," I murmured back.

As he let me go, Nathan made sure to catch my eye as he vowed, "I'll come by tonight."

"I'll see you then."

It was easier than an actual goodbye, but it was still difficult to pull my hand from his. Once more, his eyes traveled over my arm and I could feel the remorse fill him. All of a sudden, his emotions were shoved into that same damn bottle he'd always hidden them away in. Just like old times.

I kept my eyes on him until I couldn't see them through the windows anymore. Then I sighed and resumed my seat. My untouched tea had become lukewarm, so I poured a little magick into it to bring it back to a drinkable temperature. And while my interest in the bagel had evaporated, I forced myself to rip off pieces to nibble on.

In all that time, no one suspected how hard it was to remain seated. They didn't know that it took every ounce of willpower I possessed not to run after him. Without him, I felt bereft. Adrift. Like something vital had been torn out of my body and walked off. The only consolation I had was that I was home now. And I would be able to see him, touch him, and hear him every day.

Swallowing the last of my tea, I pitched the rest of the bagel and marched out into the bright daylight. Beginning at the Post Office, my day of errands had officially begun. After setting up a box, I bought a postcard and wrote my address on one side and mailed it out. It would only take a day or two to reach Grant. Just in time for my parents to return from Colorado.

The bank was my next stop before I finally made it to the grocery store. As with everywhere else, I got a few sidelong looks, but overall was left to myself. Thanks to the list, it was a simple procedure to get in, get what I needed, and get out.

Yet, nothing was as surprising as going through the line and having the cashier smile widely at me and wish me a good day. Especially since she was wearing a pentacle pendant on a black velvet choker.

When I'd made my announcement last night, I'd felt them throughout the town. For some, there were distinct signatures that marked them as being something akin to me. Others just seemed to emanate a certain knowledge that brought them into a familiar sphere. Yet, in one way we were all the same. Witches.

It was something I had avoided thinking about because it bore a lot of thought. I wasn't ready for that yet. I didn't want to dive into their motives or expectations or methods of practice. They were not relevant to me. All I wanted was to enjoy coming home. Later, I would worry about building a life for myself ... and the child. When that occurred, then I could give the witches my full attention.

Before I knew it, I was back at the cottage. Pushing those thoughts aside, I let others take me as I set about cleaning the house. When I fin-ished, I took myself out into the garden. After deciding on a general layout of what I wanted, I set about settling some of the chaos into order. Thus, when four o'clock struck, my knees were buried in dark soil while I pulled weeds.

As soon as I felt him approaching, I took the first deep breath in hours and a smile tugged at my lips. With each step he took, my heart picked up an extra beat and I could feel the loneliness retreat a fraction at a time. This was what being home felt like.

Shaking my head, I forced myself to continue pulling weeds as I monitored his journey. It was odd that he was taking the path through the woods that led from my old house instead of coming down the road. Still, I didn't care where he was coming from, as long as I got to see him soon.

When he reached the edge of the garden, he lingered in the trees. Watching me. Taking it all in, I supposed. The same as I was doing. Just breathing. Listening. Waiting. Wondering. Hoping. And fearing that it would all somehow turn out to be an illusion.

"I dreamt of you. Sometimes, I'd swear I could even feel you. As if you were standing right in front of me."

My breath caught as I remembered every incident he was talking about. All of the times when I had been at my worst and the numbness had faded beyond all measure of recall. In those moments, I had reached for him. For some small piece of him that I could cling to in order to keep me sane. In that moment, it felt like a lifetime ago.

"And I remember standing in a world that was all black, begging you to come home."

My head snapped up and my eyes locked onto his. "You did not *beg*. Your exact words were, 'Come home, Lex. Come home.' *Both* times."

The corners of Nathan's eyes crinkled as a slow, sly smile spread across his face. "So, they weren't just dreams."

Staring at him, I released a breath and shook my head. "You never thought they were."

Silently, Nathan wove between the plants along the overgrown path and came to sit beside me in the soil. I didn't hug him this time. Nor did he touch me. A fact that made my throat close with how natural it was. As if we'd seen each other every day for years instead of just reuniting.

He didn't look at me as he played with the leaf of one doomed plant. Then he asked one simple question that encompassed everything. "Why?"

I bit my lip, not sure which answer to give him first. In the end, I knew it was best to start at the beginning. Taking a breath, I stripped off my gloves and held my left arm out to him. Then I moved my tank top aside so that he could see the trail of ivy leaves that started near the Ascension scar on my left breast.

"This one was the first. I burned it into my skin at midnight on the day we left."

Once I'd started, I couldn't stop. Day by day, I took Nathan through the calendar in my arm. Each leaf and flower represented a twenty-four-hour period that I had survived. Another day that I'd spent away from home. And I knew every single day that they stood for; even the ones that found my flesh during the five months of endless dark. When I'd finished, silenced descended. It wasn't the complacent kind.

At last, Nathan murmured, "Matt told me about that—you being in a coma. I had nightmares every night. I wandered that damn blackness screaming your name until my voice was hoarse, but you were never there. Then ... there was the anniversary..."

My stomach dropped and tears filled my eyes. Only twice did I see Nathan whilst in the midst of my coma. In all that time, I'd hoped that the first time was just an illusion. A memory to help me cope with the anniversary of our separation. However, the second he took hold of my wrist and ran his thumb over the hourglass scar, I couldn't hold back the sob.

Nathan didn't bat an eyelash as he pulled me against him. As I'd done before, I cried into his shirt and clung to him like my life depended on it. Half an hour later, when all the tears had dried, we still didn't release one another. We weren't prepared for that. Letting the silence fall around us, Nathan and I allowed one another to feel exactly how much we were missed.

Chapter Three

MEANT TO BE

"So, what took you so long? If you had enough credits to graduate last semester, why did you wait until now?"

My breath hitched as the thoughts lurking in the back of my mind leapt to the fore. The presence I had pushed to the side to deal with another day was now pulsing like a heartbeat. So young and new and fragile. It was hard to imagine that each day she would grow stronger, more present, and less surreal. At some point, I would have to come to terms with the reality of my pregnancy. But not yet.

Until I could wrap my own mind around it, there was no way I could tell him.

I forced a smile and said, "That's a conversation for another day, I think."

Nathan raised his eyebrows at me. "But you will tell me?"

"Every last detail that you or I can handle. Promise."

"You're making a lot of promises today," he remarked.

"Only to you." And only the ones I knew I could keep. Shaking my head, I looked up at him and said, "Alright, now it's your turn. What happened while I was away?"

A few seconds passed before he responded. When he did, he told me everything but what mattered most. Not that I could blame him. Sometimes the heavy was best left for later.

"A lot has changed since you left," he forced out. "Aunt Sarah moved. Set her kids up in private schools and all that and she's kicking ass at a big law firm in the city. Mom went back to school right after Tyler started college. She is now a registered midwife. I got a job doing a bit of property management for a local investment company. Dad sort of switched gears and does all of their accounting now, too. Let's see, what else...?"

Well if he wasn't going to talk about himself...

"The witches?" I prompted with a sarcastic
grin.

"Ah, yes. The witches," he pretended to sigh.
"Well, the first one showed up about two months
after you left. She called herself Luna Moonchild—which everyone thought was ridiculous—
and she set up an occult shop downtown. Half
the town threw a fit about it and she was gone
within four months of getting here. The funny
thing is, about a month later, another witch
moved to town. Her name is Caroline Rook, and
she's fit in a lot better. She set up a candle shop
right above where Moonchild's store was. People
were skeptical of her at first, too, but when she
didn't try preaching to them and they caught a
whiff of those candles, they were calmed down
pretty quick.

"After that, they just started arriving. One or
two at a time. Some setting up businesses, while
others just melded into the community. It's weird
in a way, because you can feel the stasis around
them sometimes. As if they're waiting for something to happen all the time, but none of them

know what it is."

I was going to hate myself for asking this... "Do you know what it is?"

Nathan's smile was patronizing. "Of course I do. They're waiting for you, Lex."

"I was afraid you'd say that," I sighed.

"What's so bad about that?" His grin was incorrigible.

"Do you know why they're waiting for me? Because I'm afraid that those poor delusional people showed up here to stand with the thirteen-year-old girl who survived her very own New England witch trial. And that's something I can't handle. While I'm better than I was before, I still have no doubt that I'm not in a position to deal with them. Not now."

Nathan took hold of my left hand and squeezed. "No one said you had to, Lex. Deal with them whenever and however you feel like it. Whatever you choose, Cedar Creek will back you."

That caused my head to tilt to the side as I looked at him. "What does that mean?"

He tried to shrug it off but eventually sighed, "There's another reason for their stasis. You see,

I've come to learn that Cedar Creek accepts the Witch of Old Grove Road. She's part of Cedar Creek, and we've never really been without one. But other witches coming in when the reigning witch is absent... Luna Moonchild wasn't driven out because she was ridiculous or preachy. She was kicked out because she was invading your territory and no one was having that. Caroline and the others got to stay because they made it clear that they were waiting on you. In a lot of ways, Lex, you mean just as much to Cedar Creek as it does to you. It's not always the easiest or most compatible relationship, but it is an inseparable one. And almost everyone in this town recognizes it, even if they won't admit it."

Damn straight they wouldn't admit it. None of us would. They didn't need to know that I was coming home to Cedar Creek as much as I was coming home to Nathan. And they didn't have to pretend to like me for me to know that I belonged here.

Leaning back on my hands, I let my gaze drift toward the dusky sky. The sun was sinking beneath the trees, leaving splashes of pink and purple painted through the clouds. My lips pulled into a tiny smile as one of our silences descended on us. It was a moment to savor, sitting in my garden and watching the sunset with my best friend.

When dusk began to fade into gloom, Nathan cleared his throat and asked, "Have you had dinner yet?"

I shook my head and he pushed himself to his feet. When he offered his hands, I let him pull me up.

"Good. Then you can come back to my place and I'll feed you. Give the cottage time to air out," he added with a knowing smirk.

For a moment, I seriously considered accepting his invitation, but I didn't want to be around anyone else. Not even his parents. Not yet.

As if he knew every reservation I had, Nathan offered me a smile and said, "It'll be just us. I promise."

I couldn't argue with that, and he knew it. "I need to clean up first."

"Shower at my house. You can even spend the night if you want."

"Why would I do that? I have a house right over there."

"And the whole place smells like cleaner, for one. For two, it's not going to hurt anything. Come on, you can think on it over dinner."

"Fine," I sighed, turning toward the gate.

Nathan surprised me once more by grabbing my hand and leading me toward the path through the woods. Catching my confused expression, he grinned and said, "Couldn't let it get overgrown."

We both knew that wasn't even close to the reason for this trip, but I wasn't complaining. It had been too long since I walked this path, and I was even more grateful that he was beside me for it. For a moment, it felt like we should have had Matt with us. At the same time, I didn't want to share Nathan even with him. Maybe when the euphoria of coming home wore off I wouldn't feel so jealous of his time.

The whole walk was spent in a comfortable, familiar silence. Only the sounds of our shoes padding over the soft soil broke it. With how peaceful it all was, I was almost sad to reach our destination. Then Verity Lane opened before us and my breath caught.

Nathan left me in the middle of the road as he moved to stand before the gate to my old house.

Glancing over his shoulder at me, a tender smile pulled at his lips. "You know, a lot has changed since you left. But not everything." Pushing open the gate, he announced, "Welcome home, Lex."

It took a few seconds for me to process what he just said. Once it clicked, I marched across the road and smacked his arm. "Nathan Richards, don't you dare tell me you bought a house with your trust fund!"

"Hey, relax! I didn't buy anything."

His gaze traveled back to the house and I couldn't help but mimic him. It was just as I remembered. Three stories of aged brick coated in a tremendous layer of ivy. The leaves were a dark green that gave way to lighter shades with splashes of red coating them near the roof. Several chimneys rested atop the building like a crown, giving a sharp new reality to rest overtop my old memories.

The words fell from my lips in a familiar whisper. "This is how a house in New England should look."

Nathan glanced my way and smiled. Then he looked back at the house and asked, "Do you remember Mrs. Donahue?"

"Our landlord? A little."

His smile drifted toward the sly side. "Except she wasn't."

"What?"

"Mrs. Donahue is the property manager for an investment company that's kind of prominent in our county. Turns out, this company owns most of the historic houses throughout the area, as well as almost all of the commercial buildings in downtown Cedar Creek."

A new suspicion cropped up in my head and I narrowed my eyes at him. "Is this the same investment company you work for?"

"It is," he confirmed.

"Okay, I'll bite. What's the name?"

"Oak Grove Investments."

Shaking my head, I couldn't help feeling exasperated and amused all at once. "Morgan."

"Her family's company, as it turns out. Lex, do you remember what Aunt Sarah told you about Morgan's will? About Morgan leaving you everything?"

My stomach twisted into a violent knot. "No. She didn't. She couldn't. I never saw... No one ever... No, Nathan. She didn't."

Because if she did, that would make me more than well off. That would put me near bloody rich status. And I'd never once been approached about any properties I might have owned. I had the cottage, the woods, and the lake. That was all I'd ever taken responsibility for. It was all I knew about.

"Not all of it," Nathan said. Again, he looked back at the house. "I didn't get a trust fund from Morgan. I got a share in the company. You own about fifty percent of it, and my mom and I share the other fifty. Morgan set it up that way so that Mom could run things while you were gone, and I could add my support if it was needed."

All of a sudden, I was looking at the brick house with new eyes. "If that's true, then that means..."

"It's ours."

I was speechless.

"When your lease was up for this one, I knew I couldn't rent it out anymore. It felt too personal, I guess. With all that's happened here and all of the memories... I couldn't share that with other people."

A new revelation made its way through my

mind and I smiled at him. "So you moved in," I mused.

"On my eighteenth birthday."

I couldn't even be mad. He was right. Too much had happened in that house, and I couldn't imagine strangers having the run of the place. Nathan living there seemed right. As if it were meant to be.

Chapter Four

BETWEEN

I followed Nathan up the walk to the colonial front door, feeling my chest tighten as every memory of this place came flooding back. While I loved my cottage, it would always feel like Morgan's to me. This house, however, felt like mine. It was here that the most significant moments of my life had been endured. With that feeling of nostalgia hovering inside of me, I was even more grateful that it was Nathan's and no one else had lived there. And as we walked through the front door, I realized that this was the last missing piece of my homeward bound puzzle. Now that I was in this place, it felt like a weight had been lifted off my shoulders.

The minute we crossed the threshold, I released a long, slow breath. My eyes lingered over the familiar hallway, latching onto the cupboard beneath the stairs where I'd thrown my backpack almost every day. To my left, the family room was set up the same as before, but with a newer TV in place. In the room to my right, nothing had changed. Every inch of the parlor remained the same; including Alyssa Rice's grand piano. Swallowing hard, I moved down the hallway so that I could prop open the kitchen door and take a long look at the rest of the ground floor.

Nathan hadn't followed me. When I turned back with a sheepish smile, he was leaning against a doorjamb, smiling slightly at me. "It must be hard to be a guest in your own home," he observed in a soft voice.

I let my fingers trail along the wall as I walked toward him. "Especially since nothing has changed. It still doesn't feel real, you know? Part of me wonders if I'll wake up tomorrow and find myself still in Grant."

"I've been wondering the same. Except, I don't dream anymore. Or if I do, I don't remember."

My heart stopped. "You're in the blackness?"

"Not like before," he said, shaking his head.

"It's more like I've drifted to sleep for a second and wake up immediately. The only way I know I've been to sleep is because I feel rested."

I paused at the doorjamb opposite him and leaned against the wall. "Same. I've only had one dream since the coma."

"The other night," he said with a wry grin. "Same."

I lowered my eyes to the floor. "I'm sorry, Nathan. I didn't want this for you."

"Lex, there's nothing to be sorry for. I didn't want this for you, either, and it still happened. We survived it. There's nothing left for us to worry about. You believe me?"

With every fiber of my being, I wanted to believe him. But I knew better.

Forcing a smile, I agreed, "Yes, we survived it. Doesn't mean you should have been a part of it. I'm sorry for that. For dragging you into the dark with me."

The smile fell from his face and his voice took on the faintest hard edge when he said, "What makes you think I wasn't already in the dark? You didn't drag me anywhere, Lex. I met you there."

There was nothing I could say to that. I could barely process it. While I knew what had shoved me into that place, I couldn't understand what could have put Nathan there. All this time, I thought it was because I was clinging to him so tightly that he didn't have a choice but to follow me. If what he said was true, however, then that meant more had happened with him than I knew.

Before I could ask, he forced a mocking smile into place. "Conversation for another time. I promise. Now, come on. I'll get you some clothes to change into while you shower, and then I'll get dinner started."

Without waiting for me, he shrugged off the wall and took the stairs two at a time. I hesitated for a second before following after him. Nothing seemed stranger to me than when he ducked into the master bedroom. It would take some getting used to, realizing that that wasn't my parents' room anymore, and was his instead.

Nathan emerged a second later with folded up men's pajamas. "It's all I've got for now. The bottoms might be too big for you, but they have a drawstring waist, so it shouldn't be an issue."

My eyebrows rose a little. "You know I can go home and get my own clothes, right?"

"It'll save you time," he insisted, handing me the clothes.

I tilted my head to the side a little. "Nathan, you do remember that I can teleport, right? It would literally take me two seconds."

For one brief moment, I saw some of the darkness flash through his eyes before his emotions found a way to contain themselves once more. "Lex, that's not something I could ever forget." Without another word, Nathan headed back downstairs.

Trying to breathe past the knot in my chest, I slipped into my old bedroom and hopped in the shower. When I got out, I threw on the baggy t-shirt and tied the bottoms in place. Then I followed the scent of cooking burger down to the kitchen.

When I pushed the door open, I paused to watch him for a bit. Somehow, the sight of him moving about the kitchen wasn't as shocking as I thought it'd be. It was one more of those natural occurrences that almost felt inevitable.

"You gonna stand there or you gonna set the

table?" he asked without looking up at me.

"It's just the two of us, right? Do I honestly need to set the table?"

Nathan shrugged. "Old habits. Dad usually sets it while I'm cooking and Mom's assisting."

"They eat here a lot?"

He laughed. "All the time, anymore. Our kitchen is a lot bigger than theirs, and Mom keeps your herb garden in top shape. She's been teaching me to cook, but sometimes I like to try new things."

My throat tightened a little. "She's the one that taught me how to cook, too. After Morgan..."

He glanced over his shoulder and offered me another tender smile. "I know. She misses that, by the way. Have you gone to see her yet?"

"No. I'll catch up with her tomorrow while you're at school. Figured today was a good one for you and me."

"Was that the plan?"

"What do you mean?"

Nathan shrugged. "Just wondering what your original plan was—if we hadn't run into each other earlier."

There was just enough of a tone in his voice

that made me wonder what he thought of me. Did he think I wouldn't come to him? That I could last a full twenty-four hours at home and not seek him out? Was he unable to realize that I wouldn't be able to survive that?

"I was still trying to figure that out, actually," I admitted. "One plan was just to wait for you when you got out of school. I played with the idea of leaving a note where we could meet. There was a brief consideration of a scavenger hunt, but that would've been way too much work. Afterward, of course, we would have gone to the cottage or the lake and spent hours relearning who we are now."

Nathan took the burger off the stove and busied himself with something else. His back was to me when he remarked, "Who are we now?"

I wasn't sure how to answer that. After a moment, I grinned and said, "I'm the Witch of Old Grove Road, now. I'm a little more battle worn. A lot less pissed off. I like to think that I'm okay now. Oh, and I'm still pretty sure that I make a decent best friend."

He tried to fight the smile and failed. Then he nodded and said, "I'm less of a caretaker, now.

I'm a little more focused. A lot more ambitious. Less patient than I used to be. I have a shorter temper now, though I'm pretty sure yours could still outstrip it by a mile. But I like to think I still make a damn good best friend."

"You do."

"So do you."

"Thanks."

"Hey, Lex? Since you're making all these promises, can I have one more?"

"What?"

"Promise nothing else is going to come between us."

I wanted to say that nothing ever had, but that would've been a lie. What I could say was, "I'll promise if you do."

"It's a deal."

After a minute, I found my eyes scanning the room once more. They locked onto a picture on the fridge. My eyebrows rose a little and I asked, "Who's the girl?"

Nathan looked utterly confused until I pointed it out. "Wow. Totally forgot that one." Then he proceeded to pull it off the fridge and toss it into the trash.

"I take it she's an ex."

"From a month ago," he chuckled.

"Did it end that badly?"

"Nah. Just didn't mean that much. What about you? A team of exes crawling out of the woodwork?"

"There was a team?" I teased. His face went scarlet and I chuckled. "No. There have only been two for me."

"Matt and..."

"And that's a story for another time."

Nathan glanced at me over his shoulder. "I don't get to even know his name? Was it that serious or that casual?"

"That serious."

"Recent?"

A sarcastic laugh left me. "We broke up yesterday."

Nathan nodded for a second before he went back to cooking. His back was to me when he asked, "Do you love him?"

What hit me first was his use of the present tense. Even though Grey was my ex and I was home, Nathan had the presence of mind to consider that I still might have feelings for him.

That intrigued me.

"I think I did. Once upon a time."

He responded with a nod. Then he shot over his shoulder, "So are you going to set the table or not? This is almost done."

Rolling my eyes, I let my magick do the work. Since he'd left everything pretty much as it had been, it was easy to locate the necessities and spirit them from their cabinets and drawers and arrange them neatly on the dining table. Nathan turned his head to catch some of the display, a smile creeping across his face.

A few minutes later, we were sitting at the table and he was adding food to my plate. I waited until he served himself before I asked, "Do you love her?"

The smile slipped a little as he thought about how to answer. "No, I don't."

My curiosity got the better of me and I blurted out, "Did you love any of them?"

A wry smile pulled at his lips when he shook his head. "No. I've never been in love with any of the girls I've dated."

We left it at that. Both of us let each other believe that we wouldn't find out in the end. For a little while longer, our secrets could stay with us. Just not forever.

Chapter Five

MORNING LIGHT

After dinner, we sat up on the couch in the family room, talking late into the night. At some point, we both drifted off at the opposite ends. A fact we weren't aware of until the morning light streamed in through the window and my eyes opened to meet his.

A stupid smile spread across my face and I slowly stretched out my body. At the other end of the couch, Nathan mimicked me.

Glancing at the clock beneath the TV, his expression turned petulant. "I don't want to go to school. I should just skip."

"Don't you have finals coming up?" I asked, pushing myself up from the couch.

"So?"

"Uh, so you might need to attend class to prep for them," I chuckled.

"It's the same crap they've been pounding into my head all semester. I can survive one day without it."

"But why bother? I'm just going to be running more errands this morning. Then I'm heading straight to your mom's."

"After you have lunch with us," he amended.

"Us?"

"Mark and Rebecca might join us."

It took me a minute to realize that Rebecca and Becky-my very first acquaintance in Cedar Creek-were the same person. She must have decided sometime in the past four years that the nickname was too childish. A sentiment I did not disagree with.

"Do they normally eat with you?"

"Typically, yeah. Rebecca was sick yesterday, but Mark said she would make it if she could today."

Talk about the unexpected. Yet, if they were willing to show up and see me, I'd give them the benefit of the doubt. After all, I knew well how much a person could change in four years.

"Fine, I'll see you then. You coming by the cottage after school?"

"Depends on the temperature. Might meet you at the lake instead."

I grinned. "Now that sounds like a plan."

By that time, we'd reached the top of the stairs. For one second, we took a moment to study one another before our days took us in separate directions. Then Nathan surprised me by reaching out and pushing my hair off of my face. In a low voice he said, "Not a dream."

"Not a dream," I repeated.

Then he let me go and we both headed for our bedrooms. Once the door was closed, I removed the pajamas, grabbed my own clothes, and hopped from one location to another. After I changed clothes, I laid out the food dishes for the growing number of cottage cats and slipped out of the house—leaving the door cracked so the felines would be able to come and go as they pleased.

As I began my walk, I made another mental note to obtain a bicycle. Or at least borrow Nathan's. He had to have one, and I doubted he was using it since he got his truck. For a second, I considered teleporting, but I had time to kill before the bank or records office opened anyway. After Nathan's little revelation last night, I was eager to figure out more about what other responsibilities Morgan might have left in our laps.

When I'd made my first trip to the bank, it was merely to add my savings from my travels to the savings account my parents had set up for me when I was nine. It was in that account that the personal funds Morgan had left to me had been deposited when I was fourteen. Which was why I made sure to ask for the current records of any business accounts that my name was currently on. It took them some time of pouring over my ID to make sure that I was the Alexandria Ryder on those accounts, but once the process was complete, three blue folders were handed to me with the most up-to-date records over the past few months. At last, I took my homework and left the bank.

The stop at the records office took longer for a different reason. It wasn't hard to find the properties associated with Oak Grove Investments. Our issue was in sorting them all. There were the commercial business properties that were somehow different from the commercial rental properties. Then there were the houses. Historic homes counted separately for some reason, while others were lumped into the regular rental category. Then there were those that were deemed homesteads by those of us involved with Oak Grove Investments: my cottage, the house on Verity Lane, Anne's house, and another in the next city over which I had to assume was Sarah's new place. Even though she wasn't left a share in the company–Morgan had followed her wishes about staying out of her life–Anne had seen fit to provide her powerhouse twin a place to live. She also got a family discount on the rent, but Sarah had insisted on paying the taxes for it. Considering it was one of the historic houses she was living in, it was a solid deal on our end.

By lunchtime, I was loaded down with paperwork and my head was spinning. In order to get a more in-depth idea of the company I apparently owned half of, I'd have to go to Anne and her husband, Josh, for more details. Or Nathan, considering he'd taken on the role of a property manager.

I arrived at the café before the others did, and

I even got to get my food without interruption. Since it was possible we'd have more people with us, I chose a larger table near the back corner. Not five minutes later, the three of them walked through the door.

After they got their food, they made their way to the table and took their seats beside me. For a moment, none of us spoke as we stared around the table at each other. When Rebecca met my eyes, I was surprised to see her smile.

"It's nice to see you again, Alex. It's been a long time."

"Four years." The last time I remembered seeing her was the day I got arrested for murder. After that, the only two classmates I'd kept in touch with were Nathan and Matt.

"Somewhere around there," she admitted. "Hey, listen, this is going to sound awkward and weird, but I wanted to apologize for being such a brat to you all the time. We were just kids, but that doesn't excuse my behavior toward you. I'm sorry."

I was stunned. "Thank you," I said when I found my voice. "Most people wouldn't admit that."

Her smile took on an ironic twist. "Oh, I know. Which is why I've made it my mission to be better than I was yesterday."

"Not all of us can be so noble," Mark said with a wry smile. Then he reached for her hand under the table and I couldn't help but note how cute they looked together.

"I agree. I couldn't do it. Not in the way you mean it."

"What way is that?"

"You're trying to be a better person every day. I'm okay with just being better than I was."

"Why is that?"

I was careful not to look at Nathan when I said, "I've survived the worst I had to offer, and that took years to do. As long as I'm better than I was, I've already done the world a favor. No need to overcompensate."

As I spoke, I casually rested my left arm on the table. Then I leaned back so that the light could hit the scars just right. For a second, everyone stopped eating to stare at my arm. Nathan was the only one able to keep his gaze averted, while Rebecca was quick to look elsewhere.

"Holy shit," Mark said with a low whistle.

"Why...?"

At once, Nathan shot him a quelling look, but I placed a hand on his arm and answered, "I was lost for a long time. These helped me keep track of what I was leaving behind, and reminded me what I was coming home to."

Nathan turned to face me, offering that same comforting smile I remembered from before. Back when my life was going to hell and that smile was all I needed to stay sane. Some things never change.

I was still looking at him when I said, "Speaking of coming home, I have to go see your mom. If I wait much longer, she might just cook me for dinner."

"While you're there, ask her what we're having tonight. Get me a list and we'll go shopping after I get out."

I grinned as I stood up. "Should I meet you at the gate with an envelope of money, too?"

He pretended to glower at me. "You're not becoming a hermit, Lex. I'll burn the damn cottage to the ground first."

"Pfft! You'd have to make it past about thirteen layers of fireproofing spells. Including one of mine.”

“I’d find a way.”

I rolled my eyes before I turned to say goodbye to Rebecca and Mark. When his gaze met mine, I left him with a wide smile and the promise that I would see him when he got out of school. Then I headed toward my other mom’s house.

It didn’t take long before I was standing before the front stoop to the small house that Nathan and his brother had grown up in. A smile spread across my face as I mounted the steps, and just as I raised my hand to knock, the door was pulled open. Without a word, Anne stepped forward and wrapped her arms around me.

“Welcome home, Alexandria.”

Chapter Six

REST OF FOREVER

My heart felt like it was about to burst. While I'd felt at home from the moment I set foot on Old Grove Road, there was something about reconnecting with my lost family that made it so much sweeter. This was it. This was the treasure I'd been seeking all this time. At last, it was within my grasp, and I would kill to keep it that way.

Anne's grip began to loosen and she pulled away. Her hands lingered on my shoulders, holding me at arm's length as she performed a thorough study. After a few seconds, she smiled, shook her head, and dropped her hands.

"Come on inside. We'll have some lemonade."

I followed Anne into the house, traveling behind her down the narrow hallway to the last doorway on the right. Stepping into her small, intimate kitchen, I understood why Nathan hosted a lot of family dinners at our house. It was hard to imagine her navigating this space with her husband and two growing boys.

"How does it feel to be home?" she asked as she removed a pitcher from the fridge.

"Indescribable," I answered at once. "And a little exhausting. In a good way."

She glanced over her shoulder at me. "Did you keep my son up all night?"

I shrugged. "We were sitting on the couch talking, and next thing I knew, we were waking up."

Setting the glasses down on the table, she motioned me to have a seat. As I did so, I smiled a little. "I missed you."

"I missed you, too." Anne placed a hand on the table with her palm up. I laid my own hand in hers, accepting the comfort she was offering. Her eyes never left them as she asked, "How are you doing, Lex?"

I knew what she was asking. "I'm better. I'm back where I belong, with people I care about. This is all I've wanted, and I'm enjoying every second of it," I assured her.

"Every second?" she asked with a knowing smile.

My eyes narrowed. "Okay, there may have been a couple of moments where I was less than euphoric."

"Which were?"

"Oak Grove Investments."

Just like her mother, Anne didn't appear the slightest bit remorseful about this secret. "Did you even read your copy of my mother's will?"

I shook my head. "Things like juvie, murder trials, and packing sort of made it slip my mind."

Anne rolled her eyes. "Things like grief and avoiding your responsibilities made sure you never looked at it."

There was no arguing with that one. I automatically started rubbing my left arm. As soon as she noticed, Anne reached out and grabbed my hand.

"When Morgan died, she left my dad's possessions and money to Sarah and I. We wondered, at first, why there was nothing left to Freyja, but Nathan told us what you'd told him." I flinched. "Anyway, it explained why so much was left to you. You see, Oak Grove Investments was her family's company and it's been passed down through many generations. When she died, it was almost sad knowing that it was going to you. What shocked us was how much she left to me and Nathan.

"And when her administrators began explaining the responsibilities of my position, I understood why. You and Nathan were both still minors, and there needed to be at least one person able to sign their paychecks on a regular basis. When I became responsible for the company, I realized how much was accruing but how little was being done with it. That's when Josh came aboard and we started growing the company a little more. Because Nathan was here, it was easy for us to make legitimate decisions without you present or aware.

"It wasn't that we meant to keep it secret from you, Alexandria. We just had it under control. Everything was thriving. The bills were all being paid. And you didn't have to deal with yet one more thing my mother dropped on your head. I'm sorry if you feel like we cut you out. That wasn't our intention."

"Relax, Anne. I don't feel cut out. It just made it real easy for Nathan to spring his big surprise on me."

A wide smile pulled at her lips. "He does have a flair for the dramatic, that one. You know we let the boys skip school on their birthdays every year? Well, this year Nathan told me that he intended on skipping and it was no big deal. I thought it was going to be more of the same and he'd sleep in until noon. Well, it got to be around twelve thirty and I hadn't heard a peep out of his room. So I made lunch for us and knocked on his door. No response. I waited a little bit and knocked again. No response. Finally, I opened the door and slowly looked in.

"His bedroom has never been so clean in the eighteen years of his life. When I opened that door, the floor was vacuumed, the shelves were dusted, his bed was made ... and most of his stuff was gone. I freaked out and was in the middle of dialing his number when I saw a sheet of paper on his bed. The letter said, 'Dear Mom, I moved out. Here's my new address. Let's go out tonight to celebrate. Pick you up at seven.'"

I busted out laughing. "He didn't!"

"Oh, he did. The worst part was I had no clue when he could have done it. He must've been moving things out a little at a time while I was working. And the cleaning ... who knows when he did that because I could have sworn I was the only person in my house who knew how to operate a vacuum cleaner."

"How'd you get back at him?"

"The next day I printed off a three-course dinner menu and told him his father and I were making reservations for his house at seven, and we liked our steaks medium rare."

"Did he do it?"

"Of course he did. If I'd done that to Tyler, I would have gotten a bowl of instant noodles for my trouble. But Nathan put candles on the table and played soft music."

She wasn't kidding about that flare for the dramatic. Too bad I'd only experienced a fraction of it. But I had time, now, to learn the full extent. I was home. I had the rest of forever.

"So, what were your plans today? Other than visiting me?" she asked, taking another sip of her lemonade.

I shrugged. "That was about the extent of it.

Dropped by the bank and the records office this morning to figure out some stuff with Oak Grove Investments, but you were my priority today."

A sly smile pulled at her lips. "Good. Let's go for a walk, shall we?"

For a moment, I was suspicious, but I couldn't help but agree. With ease, we headed toward downtown Cedar Creek in the same kind of silence I usually shared with Nathan. While Anne didn't appear in a hurry, I soon realized that she had a specific location in mind. Once we turned onto Main Street, I got a pretty good idea what it was.

"I knew there were witches, but I didn't think they were like this," I muttered, letting my eyes travel up and down the street.

Halfway down the street, I caught sight of the hanging sign for *Rook Candle Company* right beside a sign for *Mystic Manuscripts*. Closer to me was *Basil's Sweet Retreat* and across the street was *Tea Leaves*, which advertised that there was a psychic in residence willing to read palms, auras, tea leaves, and tarot cards. Every single one of those shops was owned by a witch.

Beside me, Anne nodded. "Yeah, there's been

a new acceptance for them going around. Of course, it might have something to do with your classmates becoming more intrigued in their way of life."

"Really?"

"Oh yes. These stores wouldn't survive if it wasn't for those of your generation. Then again, some of the older folks might object to *Rook Candle Company* going anywhere. Helps that Caroline appears a little less eccentric than some of the others."

I had to smile at that, thinking of the cashier with the pentacle on a black velvet choker. "You mean she doesn't wear the black fingernail polish and dark veils? Whatever shall we do with her?"

Anne chuckled. "Basil is another who is gaining rapidly in good opinion. Most natural kitchen witch I've met in decades, and her pies are extraordinary. Of course, her husband is a green witch and he provides all of her spices, herbs, and produce. A clever partnership, that one."

Glancing askance at her, I had to ask, "Do they know who you are?"

"Me? No. Not really. But Sarah was a source of some attention."

That made no sense to me. "How come she was and you weren't? It's not like you can miss the family resemblance."

She chuckled again before it turned into a sigh. "Do you remember when I told you about the spell Freyja set for us? The one that allowed us to remake ourselves in the eyes of Cedar Creek?"

I nodded.

"Well, like all spells, it has parameters. I never broke them, and so the one surrounding me is as potent as it ever was. However, when Sarah claimed Morgan as her mother in that courtroom, it began to tear at the edges of her spell. People who only knew her as Sarah were unaffected, but those we grew up with began to remember pieces of her as Faylin. When the other witches began to arrive, it was with the knowledge already in their heads that she was Morgan's daughter—thanks to the papers. Thus, they only saw Faylin.

"In the end, she was losing the life she had fought to create for herself. When a job opportunity arose outside of Cedar Creek, she jumped on it. I helped her any way I could. Considering how many witches there are now, I'm glad she left when she did."

"So am I," I assured her. "Neither of you wanted this life, and you shouldn't be forced to live it just because others expect it of you."

This time, she glanced askance at me. "What are you thinking, Lex?"

I shrugged. "I'm thinking that I am here to live my life how I wish to, and I have no intention of letting other people pile their own expectations onto me. The rest of them will learn that as needed."

Chapter One

NATURALLY

Anne and I stopped at *Basil's Sweet Retreat* before we headed back to her house. She got a sundae that filled up a cereal bowl and I got a cupcake the size of my face. And as we sat in a corner to enjoy our treats, I kept a careful eye on the woman behind the counter. Even though I could tell she was a witch with a decent drop of power, she never looked twice at me.

"Okay, kid, spill. Why do you keep looking at Basil like that?"

Looking back at her, I whispered, "Can you feel it?"

"Feel what?"

"My magick."

Anne's brows pushed together and her eyes

became unfocused as she tapped into those closed off reserves that contained her birthright. After a minute of intense searching, her eyes snapped back to mine with sharp clarity. "What did you do?" she demanded in a voice tinged with panic.

My expression turned smug. "I learned to hide it. Took me a while and a lot of practice, but until we came on this walk, I wasn't sure if it was working at all. But because Basil didn't seem aware of it, I figured that it must be."

"You can hide your magick?"

I didn't want to lie to Anne. I didn't even want to boil it down to bare facts and half-truths. Yet, I hadn't told Nathan yet, and it didn't feel right telling her everything before I told him. So I broke it down into what I could.

"Near Yule I met a witch as powerful as myself. She could hide her magick, and she liked to use the reveal as a kind of sucker punch to the senses. It's taken me until now to figure out how she did it."

"That's incredible, Lex."

I smiled, but for two separate reasons. One, because of the compliment. But the other reason was because she kept calling me 'Lex.' To most people I went by 'Alex.' Alexandria was a mouth-ful, and I liked that there were so few people who used it. Yet, 'Lex' was used for those I deemed part of my family. I'd never asked Anne to call me Lex, but it had happened anyway. Naturally. And it was perfect, because she was my other mother and I loved hearing the nickname in her voice.

When Anne and I had finished our after-noon snack, we tossed our trash and headed back out into the bright New England day. Un-consciously, I settled a hand over my stomach and grinned at her. "You know, I was supposed to ask you what we're having for dinner tonight, but I don't think I can think about more food after that."

"I'm sure. So maybe we'll try a slow cooker recipe and a light, fruity dessert for tonight."

"Sounds good to me. And if Nathan gets hungry before then he can have a PB&J."

Anne laughed. "He's a teenage boy, sweet-heart. It'll take more than one PB&J to tide him over until dinner."

When we arrived back at her house, we delved into her cooking folders and found a couple of recipes that would do nicely for the evening. I wrote out a shopping list for the ingredients while she promised to deliver copies of them to the house later that afternoon. At last, I said goodbye and began my walk to the high school.

By the time the final bell rang, I was stretched out in the back of Nathan's truck watching the clouds. I had my ankles crossed and sticking up in one corner so that he knew I was back there. Not that he needed the hint. While Nathan had never embraced his magick, it had forged enough of a link with mine to ensure that we were always aware of each other.

A few minutes later, he leaned against the truck. "Hop in. You got the list?" Without waiting, he climbed into the driver's seat.

Grinning, I scrambled out of the bed and got in. I almost didn't notice the group of people staring at us from the doors of the school. When I did, Rebecca raised a hand and waved. Automatically, I waved back.

Then I turned to Nathan and asked, "Who are they?"

He glanced back at them for a second before

a smirk pulled at his lips. "Your fan club."

"Shut up. That is so not funny."

"It's worse because it's true." He saw my aggrieved expression and laughed. "Those kids are the reason *Blue Moon* and *Tea Leaves* stay in business. They're learning, Lex. Because of you."

I wanted to look back at them but we were already pulling out of the parking lot. "Those are the same little shits that tormented me in school, and now they want to be just like me?"

"Jealousy makes people lash out."

"Why is this funny to you?"

"Because you're trying to pretend that it's not."

"It's not."

"Go ahead. Tell me you're not enjoying the irony."

"Shut up," I muttered again, turning my head to hide the grin.

When we got to the store, I pulled out the list, tore it in half and handed one to him. It felt like old times when we each grabbed a cart and split up. Since it was a small list, we met back at the registers within ten minutes. This time, the cashier with the pentacle choker was nowhere in sight.

It was a peaceful shopping trip right up until we pulled into our driveway and found Anne waiting for us. She was leaning against her driver's door, her arms crossed and her expression caught somewhere between concerned and angry. My stomach knotted when her eyes locked on mine.

As soon as I got out of the truck, she thrust her cell phone at me and almost snapped, "Call your mother."

I flinched as I took it from her. Nathan walked around the side of the vehicle and asked, "What's going on?"

"My parents weren't home when I left," I muttered.

"Oh shit."

"Yeah."

"Come on, Nathan," Anne said, grabbing a few of the grocery bags. Nathan picked up the rest and they both disappeared into the house. All the while, I bounced the phone on my palm, trying to work up the nerve to call. At last, I bit the bullet and dialed my mom's number.

"Ryder Housing. Melanie speaking." Just by

the shakiness of her voice, I knew she was counting on it being me.

"Hey Mom," I said quietly.

"Oh Lex!"

It was all she could say before the phone was jerked out of her hands and my dad's voice snarled, *"Alexandria Marie Ryder, what the hell were you thinking?"*

Following that was a lecture on how I obviously wasn't thinking and that I must've hit my head to think that some silly little note and a damn postcard were acceptable ways to tell my parents I'd split. Almost made me want to tell them about what Nathan had done to Anne, but that would've proven his point.

When his lecture devolved into cursing, my mother retrieved her cell from him. "Oh Lex, how are you? How long have you been gone? Why didn't you call us?"

Instead of answering her questions, I said the one thing that meant everything, "Mom, I'm home."

There was a short pause before she replied, "I'm happy for you, Baby Girl."

With that out of the way, I sighed, "I've only

been here a couple of days. I left on the second. I ... couldn't wait anymore, Mom."

"You weren't running?"

Of course I was running. From Crone's Crescent Coven. From Grey's family. From them, even. What I said, however, meant far more than the secret I was harboring.

"I had a dream."

Silence greeted me, and I was grateful for it. Part of our mutual forgiveness had been the agreement between my parents and myself to tell each other everything. They knew that I hadn't been able to dream since those five months I was in a coma. For me to have a dream now, she would know that that was enough to send me on my way.

"About?" she finally asked.

"Home."

"Okay."

"Okay?"

"Okay, here's your father. Love you, Lex."

"Love you too, Mom." As the phone traded hands, I took a breath and prepared to face down my dad.

What I got instead was, "Your Mom and

I put in a bid on a house just outside Colorado Springs. It's a little ranch style that needs some minor repairs and some sprucing up. The yard is a pretty decent size, but it's all grass that needs to be cut. Your mom will email you some pictures so you can get an idea on what you want to do with it. You can discuss your budget with her."

"Wait, wait, wait. So, we're still doing this?"

His voice sounded a bit smug when he answered, "Well, I didn't fire you and I'm not finding a resignation letter. By the way, you need to get a phone. And call us when you can come to work."

"Yes, sir," I said with a grin.

"Good. Love you, Lexi Girl. See you soon."

"Love you, Dad. See you soon."

The line went dead.

At least I hadn't cried on the phone.

Chapter Eight

WORK OF ART

"How was it?" Anne asked when I walked in and handed her the cell phone.

"Not as bad as I was expecting, actually."

"So, what happened? Why didn't they know you'd left?"

"They were in Colorado looking at houses."

"And you couldn't wait until they'd gotten home? Or called to tell them?"

"You know, I could have sworn I just had this conversation," I told her with a smirk.

For a moment, Anne looked between me and her son. Then she sighed and muttered, "Birds of a feather, you two. At least when he took off, it was a few streets over. Not states away."

"To be fair, they knew right where I went, too."

She rolled her eyes at my argument before turning back to the two recipes we'd chosen for that night. Sliding one piece of paper to Nathan, the other was passed to me. "Nathan's on dinner. Lex, you're on dessert. Dinner will take about two hours in the slow cooker and the dessert can use that time to chill."

"Yes ma'am," Nathan said with a grin, setting down his recipe and turning to get the slow cooker out of the cupboard. I followed his lead and went in search of a shallow cake pan.

It wasn't too long after Nathan had started the slow cooker that the phone rang. He took one look at the Caller ID and sighed. "Robert. Again. Be right back," he said as he walked out of the room.

"Who?"

"One of the renters. He lives a few streets over and he is constantly nitpicking everything in the house. Nathan says he wishes he won't renew his lease, but that's still six months away."

"He says?"

A sad smile tugged at the corners of her mouth. "The truth is, he wouldn't know what to do if someone didn't call him with some problem or another. He likes to stay busy. If it isn't the tenants then it's girls or something else. It's almost like he's afraid to stay still for too long. As if everything he's running from is going to catch up the second he stops for air."

He was surviving. It wasn't the same way that I did, but it was similar enough that I could recognize the signs. While I knew what being away from him and Cedar Creek had done to me, I hadn't imagined what that kind of separation could do to him. I'd known before I left that I wouldn't be able to stand having Cedar Creek without Nathan, or vice versa. Now I wondered if the same was true of Nathan. Did he need me as much as I needed him? Was that the pain he'd been trying to dull?

As I was still considering it, Nathan walked back into the room and hung up the phone. Shaking his head, he told his mom about Robert's insistence that Nathan be responsible for lawn care. I didn't bother to pay attention as I finished the dessert and put it in the fridge.

As I closed the door, I took a moment to admire the photographs held in place by advertising magnets. When my parents and I had lived here, we hadn't done the photos-on-the-fridge thing. Mom had passed on her neatness requirements to me and I normally wasn't fond of things that seemed like clutter.

These weren't clutter. They were pieces of history that I missed. Mark and Nathan wearing lacrosse jerseys on the school field. Nathan leaning against his truck, with the 'For Sale' sign hanging limply in one hand. There was another picture of him and Anne standing side-by-side as he showed off his new driver's license. He even put up a picture of his family at Tyler's high school graduation.

My favorite picture, however, was of the lake. No one was in the photo and the sky was lit up with the faint orange and deep pink of sunset. While the trees hid the skyline, the reflection on the water was beautifully captured.

"Earth to Lex," Nathan said with a laugh.

My eyes jerked away from the pictures and I shot a look around the room to find that Anne had gone. Nathan was leaning against the counter, smiling at me. "What?"

For a moment, his eyes flickered to the pictures before darting back to me. "I was saying that this Saturday is prom and I've got two tickets."

"Okay."

His expression flickered again and all of his emotions fled from my awareness. Then he asked, "Would you like to go with me?"

For a moment, I couldn't say anything. I could barely think. Somehow, from the moment I left Grant, I had sort of lost any connection between myself and school. My diploma would be mailed and I had skipped out on things like prom and graduation. Those didn't seem to belong to me anymore.

But here was Nathan saying that I could have a piece of it back. If I wanted it.

I was surprised by how much I did want that. One night to get dressed up and celebrate ... something. It was one night to simply enjoy myself since I'd been home. How could I pass that up?

"I don't have a dress." Rather, I didn't have a dress that didn't make me think of Grey and the entire melodrama that was Homecoming.

All of a sudden, a wide smile spread across Nathan's face. My eyebrows rose a little as I asked, "What?"

"You're about to say yes."

"I thought that's what you wanted?"

"It is, Lex. It definitely is."

For some reason, I felt the urge to blush and quickly turned to clean up my mess. "Okay, then it's a yes. I will go to prom with you."

After I had agreed to Nathan's request, I truly began to worry about the dress situation. prom being two days away had pushed me into calling Anne. I was told to arrive at her house at ten in the morning; she claimed she had this covered.

"Right on time," Anne remarked as she opened the door. "Come on in. There's something I want to show you."

Curious, I followed her into the living room. My eyebrows rose as she went to a black garment bag draped across the back of the couch. Anne unzipped the bag and I caught a glimpse of emerald fabric. The second she pulled the gown free, my mouth dropped.

"That's your ritual gown, isn't it?" I breathed.

"It was, once upon a time. I was your age the last time I wore it. Hell, I was your age the last time I could fit it," she added with a smirk.

There was only one defining characteristic to a ritual gown crafted for those under Morgan's tutelage: it was handmade. From fabric selection, cut, and stitching, it was all done by the skill of the witch meant to wear it. Which was why mine was basically a black sack.

Back when Anne was known as Morgan's daughter, Fiona, she'd made a gown meant to exploit the beauty of the natural world. The dress was a brilliant emerald green with an empire waist. Across the chest and belt, she had added a painstaking amount of beading. Not delightful little swirls, either, but white, orange, and yellow flowers. It was an absolute work of art.

I started shaking my head without ever taking my eyes from the dress. "I can't wear your ritual gown, Anne."

"Yes, you can, Alexandria. It wasn't a request."

"But—"

"It's practically calling to you. Stop arguing and go try it on."

Even if I had wanted to argue more, I couldn't make myself. Gingerly, I grabbed the dress and took it into the bathroom to change. As soon as it was against my skin, I knew it was perfect.

At once, I returned to the living room to get Anne's opinion. A wide smile answered me and she motioned for me to spin so that she could see it all. Then she stood up, grabbed my hand, and dragged me into the master bedroom to place me in front of the mirrored doors of her closet.

"What do you think?" she asked in a low voice.

I said the first thing to come to mind. "It's the color of his eyes."

Something shifted in her expression, as if she were reliving a tender memory. "It should be. I had to dye it three separate times to get it the exact color of Josh's eyes. I was so happy when I realized Nathan had inherited those."

"Me too," I murmured. Then I met her gaze in the mirror. "Anne, thank you."

I wasn't just thanking her for the dress. I was thanking her for Nathan. For treating me with respect. For being on my side through everything. For teaching me and treating me like I was her own daughter. There was a lot I wanted to thank her for, but I wanted her to know that I was grateful for the woman she was. She was the kind of woman any young girl could aspire to be.

Her smile suggested she knew everything that 'thank you' meant. Leaning in to kiss the side of my head, she said, "No need to thank me, Lex. This is what family is for."

Most of all, I thanked her for that.

Chapter Nine

VOLUNTEER

For the rest of the day, Anne and I went shopping. My supply of makeup was low, and we were determined to find the perfect shoes to match the dress. At last, however, we made it back from our trip victorious. We then voted on pizza for dinner. Anne bought two larges: one for her house and one for ours. Nathan was thrilled that he didn't have to cook.

"This should be a regular thing," I suggested. "Every Friday night we have pizza and watch movies. Sound like a plan?"

He grinned at me. "I can live with that. So, what do you want to watch?"

Nathan and I spent fifteen minutes going through his minuscule collection before he revealed that he usually rented them. Five minutes later, we climbed in his truck and drove into town. As we passed by Main Street, my whole body jerked as the magick snaked down the street.

"Lex? What is it?"

I shook my head. "Nothing. Just witches being witches. Gathering of some kind. I'll keep an eye on it, but it looks harmless enough."

"Hey, you didn't come back here to play babysitter."

"I also didn't come home to find a handful of witches ruining my town, either. If they get out of line, they'll be out of town the next day. You can be sure of that."

Nathan offered me a smile as we pulled into the video store. "Hey, the rest of us have been doing this a little longer. Let us have our fun. We've even got pitchforks and torches. The whole bit."

That caused my eyebrows to raise. "How many times have you done an expulsion?"

He took a moment to think about it. "Six times now, I think. Luna you know about, but there were a few fanatics after her. One wanted to start a coven up, and that idea didn't take. Oh, there was this one that wanted to do nothing but preach, and she about blew a gasket when she realized that not all of the witches here are Wiccan. I swear the whole town breathed a sigh of relief when I escorted her out."

"You escorted her? Personally?"

Nathan ran a hand along the back of his neck. "Yeah. It's ... kind of what I do."

"What does that mean?"

He forced a grin that I was having none of. Finally, he sighed, "It means I was your proxy. I told you that Cedar Creek accepts one witch. Well, you weren't here. I was. When other witches started showing up, there were more than a few people asking me what I was going to do about it. After I asked Luna to leave, it became my place, in a way, to validate the witches that came here. So every time one shows up, I interview them. Let them know that this is a trial period and all that. Then, if I have to knock on their doors again, it's not going to be pleasant."

My idiot best friend was interviewing witches to join my town and kicking out potentially vile bitches ... and he didn't even use his own magick. He was going to give me a stroke. Was this payback?

"Do you know what they could have done to you? Just for threatening them?" I demanded through clenched teeth.

"Do you know what would have happened to anyone who touched me?"

I looked Nathan dead in the eye and sank every ounce of truth into my words that I could. "If anyone touches you, Nathan, I will burn them alive from the inside out. That's the least of what I am capable of. I promise."

He offered me a placating smile. "And that's why no one has ever touched me. Relax, Lex."

I shook my head. "You can't tell me to relax, Nathan. After what I've been through and the kind of shit I've seen... Having other witches here makes me paranoid. Knowing that the whole town has been using you as a liaison pisses me off. That ends now. I'm home and I'll handle my shit. I'm done putting it on you."

"What makes you think I didn't volunteer?" he snapped.

That made my head jerk back. Shaking his head, Nathan looked around the video store parking lot for a few minutes, trying to settle his agitation. It didn't seem to be working.

At last, Nathan turned to me and held out his hand. "Let's go to the lake."

I didn't even question it. I laid my hand in his and we were transported in a blink. As soon as we arrived, Nathan released me and ran his hands through his hair.

Turning his back on me, he asked, "Do you remember the last movie night we had together?"

It was a rhetorical question, but I smiled a little when I answered, "You mean the one where we got bored and you, Matt, and I all ended up right here?"

He glanced at me over his shoulder, "And we overheard your parents saying you were going to leave once it was all over."

That hit me like a punch to the gut. Closing my eyes, I nodded.

"That's when I volunteered," Nathan informed me. "Right then, when I realized that you were going to be gone in a few months or a year, I knew that someone would have to take care of things while you were gone. I was that someone. I knew the cottage. I knew the house. I knew the lake. Hell, I knew the town. Everything that needed to be taken care of, I could handle. Just until you came back."

With every word the bitterness in his voice grew stronger and more acidic. I didn't want him to keep going, but I also knew that I had earned this. Nathan knew what I had survived. I needed to know what it cost him.

Taking a deep breath, Nathan released it slowly. "I knew when you let go of me. When it became too hard to hang on and move on. That was the same day that I stopped sleeping over at the cottage on that couch you hate. It was the day I realized that I had to do the same. I'd already spent two years keeping everything stable enough for you to come home to. While I could still do some things—like kicking out the wayward witches and feeding the cats—there were other things I couldn't anymore.

"That's when I started dating. That's when I started getting involved with the company and Mom started teaching me how to cook. I tried moving on, Lex. Really, I did. But that doesn't mean that I wasn't here or that I stopped taking care of everything.

"I knew what I was signing up for that very night. I volunteered for this. So don't say shit like you dumped it on me or that I'm being used, okay? We both know I could have walked away at any point. And we both know I never would."

I wanted to call him an idiot. I almost told him that he should have walked away. I could have told him that it felt like I was using him. And because I knew he was right, I kept my mouth shut.

Crossing the distance between us, I wrapped my arms around his back and leaned my head against his shoulder. At once, his anger seemed to vanish and he pulled me closer to him. I reveled in the contentment that flowed through us. Then, without warning, I took us back to the video store parking lot.

It was the first time I'd been back to the lake since I came home. It was the first time I didn't see any ghosts gliding into the water since I'd learned they were there. I couldn't decide if that was a good thing or a bad thing.

Chapter Ten

LOYALTY FOR LOVE

My patience was wearing thin as I sat in my old desk chair and allowed Anne to do my makeup. It felt like an hour had passed, even though I knew it was only half that. During most of it, I amused myself with thinking about the vanity covered by a sheet in the attic. At least if I looked into it now, I knew Alyssa Rice wouldn't be staring back at me.

"There. Finished," she announced, setting down the mascara. Then she held up a mirror to me and I smiled.

"Does that mean I can come in now?" Nathan asked from the other side of the bedroom door.

"No," Anne decreed.

"Why not? We're going to prom, not getting

married."

"Because I said so," she shot back at him. "Now go downstairs and tell your dad we'll be down in a few minutes. He can go ahead and start getting pictures of you." Turning to me, she added, "We'll get a few singles of you tonight, too. That way you have some to give to your parents."

I wasn't about to argue with that. It was the least I could do, considering all of the experiences I'd cheated them out of. Sweet Sixteen. Prom. Graduation. The least I could offer them in recompense were pictures.

Once the desk was cleaned up, I followed Anne from the room. At the top of the stairs, she motioned me to a stop. "Wait here." When I gave her a questioning look, she sighed, "Indulge me."

"Isn't that what tonight is all about?"

"Absolutely. Now wait here."

I did as she asked. Leaning against the wall, I listened to her voice mingling with Josh and Nathan's in the parlor. After a minute, I could hear them walk back into the hallway. Then Anne called my name and I suddenly understood why she kept us separated.

Nathan looked damn good. My eyes widened

as I took in his tall frame, clothed in the deep black of his tux. His brown hair was slicked back, making it appear almost black. The small, knowing smile on his face was the kicker, however. It was that one touch of familiarity that made me comfortable.

The camera flashed a few times as I made my way down the stairs. I was going slowly enough, since I was wearing new stilettos and didn't want to sprain an ankle. When I neared the bottom, Nathan held out a hand to me, steadying me as I made it down the last few steps. For one second, we were allowed to savor that moment.

"Okay, hold out your hand," Anne instructed. I raised my eyebrows a little and she held up a corsage for me to wear.

My grin widened. "Make him do it. I am his date," I teased.

Nathan rolled his eyes. "If I try to put that on you, I'll crush it. Mom made it herself and there's no elastic band."

As evidence, Anne turned it so that I could see the carefully woven roots that would hold the bundle of flowers to my wrist. My mouth fell open and I extended my right hand so the she could slide it onto my wrist. Once it was in place, I couldn't help running a finger over the tiny petals.

"Avens flower. They're what I designed on the dress. Thought they'd be fitting," she murmured as she somehow tightened the corsage so that it wouldn't shift.

"It's beautiful," I murmured.

"Okay, come on. Let's get the rest of these pictures taken so you can be on your way," Josh suggested, moving into the parlor. Anne grinned and followed her husband.

Before Nathan and I joined them, I pulled gently on his hand. "It's your call," I whispered. When he appeared confused, I looked pointedly at my arm. "I'll hide them if you want me to."

I was still looking at the burns in my skin when Nathan reached out and placed a hand beneath my chin. He tilted my face up and held it there until I met his gaze. The intensity in his eyes stole my breath.

"I will *never* ask you to hide any part of yourself, Alexandria. Never."

It was one of those promises I would keep with me forever. It was one of the few in this world that I knew would never be broken. Nathan was okay with me as I was. Until that moment, I hadn't realized how much I was still waiting on his forgiveness for the scars. Now I knew I had that.

"Thank you," I murmured.

Then his mom called for us and we both took a deep breath and strode into the parlor.

When Nathan had first told me that we would be sharing a limo with Mark and Rebecca, I'd been hesitant. He'd been insistent. The reason for which became apparent when Rebecca announced that the prom theme was 'Hollywood Awards.' Which meant a line of fancy cars and limos pulling up to a red carpet in front of the gym and depositing their occupants a couple at a time. There were even people staged on the edges with cameras to act as paparazzi.

The minute our limo pulled into position, I insisted that Mark and Rebecca go ahead. Then I leaned close to Nathan and hissed, "What have you gotten me into?"

He grinned at me and got out of the car.

Shaking my head, I took the hand he offered and let him help me out onto the red carpet. All at once, everything stopped.

At once, the would-be paparazzi lowered their cameras to gawk at me. This caused the students ahead of us to turn and stare. My stomach knotted and my hand automatically went to my scars. Nathan grabbed it just in time and started pulling me along toward the doors. It was the spell-breaker everyone needed as time resumed moving.

Once we were inside the gym—which was decorated like a banquet hall—Mark and Rebecca dropped back to walk alongside us. She smiled a little at me and said, "We'll hide you as much as we can."

I shook my head. "They already knew I was home. Now they get to see it for themselves. Let them look."

Nathan squeezed my hand and shot a grin at me. Then he pulled me out onto the dance floor. For at least half an hour, he wouldn't let me stare back at those watching my every move. In point of fact, he did his best to make me forget anyone was looking at all. And it worked.

At last, we were both out of breath and he led me to an empty table before he went to get drinks. I was there all of thirty seconds before a pretty girl with wide, chocolate eyes sat down beside me. It took me a second to realize she was the girl from the picture on the fridge.

"You know, as his most recent ex, it's sort of my duty to warn the next girl."

My eyebrows practically shot into my hair. "Warn them about what?"

She shrugged a little before she said, "The usual warning is simply, 'Nathan will never tell you he loves you.' Of course, I was affronted when Megan told me. Just like she was pissed when Gabrielle told her. But the thing of it is ... it's true. Nathan never said 'I love you' to any of us. He couldn't. Can't. Because Nathan doesn't say things he doesn't mean."

"Who are you?"

She glanced at me and there was a sarcastic kind of smirk on her face. "Does it matter if he never told you?"

That one hit home. Because that was how he said it when he tossed the picture. Like it didn't matter at all. And that was ... sad.

Shaking my head, I sighed, "So this is my warning?"

"No. No, I can't warn the one person we were all warned against."

Any sympathy I felt for her died in an instant and my voice was cold when I asked, "What does that mean?"

"It means that we all knew he was waiting for someone." Once more, her eyes found Nathan through the crowd and my stomach knotted when I saw the tender expression. "I've never seen him so happy."

For the first time, she turned her full attention to me. "On second thought, I do have a warning for you. Don't break his heart, Alex, or you will answer to every woman who has tried to earn it."

"You don't know what you're talking about."

"Yes, I do."

Shaking my head, I told her, "You're confusing loyalty for love."

"Is there a difference?"

It was my turn to look for Nathan across the gym. He was on his way back and he looked more than a little surprised to find his ex beside me. I tried to look reassuring.

"Love is an emotion. Loyalty is a choice." Returning my gaze to the girl, I said in a low voice, "The difference between them is that you can't control who you love, but you can control how you love. Nathan and I are part of each other and we will always be loyal to that. You are worried that I will break his heart, but I can assure you that I am not capable of it. I would let the world burn first."

Her eyebrows rose a little before she stood up. Looking down on me, she said, "You are the only one capable of it, Alex. No one else has as much of him as you do."

Then she was gone.

Chapter Eleven

HAVEN

Late that night, I began the solitary walk home. Nathan tried protesting at first, then attempted cajoling in order to get me to stay the night, but I was in that place between wide awake from excitement and feeling as if I were daydreaming. The only cure for that was a walk. So, I slipped off my heels and slid into the shadows of the trees.

As I neared my house, I shifted the shoes from one hand to the other, relishing the feeling of the cold, hard-packed dirt against the soles of my feet. So much for that pedicure Anne made me get. Once more, as soon as I thought of my other mother, my hand went to the flowers on my wrist. Like many things in North America, avens was a European flower that had migrated and combined with local fauna to make a home here. Considering its use in magickal applications was for blessings, it made sense why Anne would design it on her ritual gown.

My mind was still drifting when I reached the border between the forest and the garden. It was on the edge of both places that the avens grew well here. Now that I was taking a closer look at it, I noticed that it was almost a continuous line. As if someone had created a wall of blessings to surround the cottage.

As soon as the thought hit me, the white mist shot up over my eyes.

I was kneeling in the soil beside one of the newer oaks that made up our grove. The attention being provided to the sapling would spill over onto anything planted near to it, or so was my wish. Were it not to be, then I would have to provide the little avens plant with whatever attentions I could spare.

"What use does this one possess, my love?"

I felt my heart leap into my throat as my husband fell to the ground beside me. Before I could catch my breath, his arms were around my middle and his lips were at my neck. Had I not known for certain that no others were about, I might have scolded him about such a display.

Perhaps not.

Clearing my throat, I said to him, "This is wood avens and it is said to guard against poisons and rabid dogs."

"And what use does it hold for you?"

It never failed to make my heart swell when he spoke with such ease about my abilities. More women had died for the fear of their husbands than I cared to think of. Few were there who could trust entirely the man they loved. In all of Cedar Creek, I knew myself to be the only witch with a husband knowing and accepting of his wife's talents.

"In the ways of my people, it is used for the exorcism of vile spirits and creatures of the dark. If no such ill deeds need be done, it is used for purification. As it is the cousin of the rose, it is also said to be a flower which could provoke the love of another."

William smothered his laughter against my shoulder. "No man has been in less need of provocation when it comes to my love of you," he promised.

Wiping my hands upon my skirt, I leaned back into his embrace and allowed my eyes to close. "Nor *have I used such wiles to obtain your love. However, if there had been a need for them in order to call you my own, I cannot say that I would have abstained from their usage. You were always meant to be mine, William Sullivan. If it took my craft to make it so, I would not have let you walk away from me."*

Once more, my husband kissed my neck. Then, with my body pressed firmly against his, he bore us to our feet. I did not protest as he swept me up in his arms and turned toward the cottage. The last my garden had of me that day was the laughter I left behind before William kicked the door shut.

The following morning, Nathan's dad gave us the task of going through the prom pictures and deciding which ones we wanted printed off. After half an hour of digging through them and deciding which ones to divide between parents and houses, Nathan and I headed for the print shop in town. After putting in the order, we decided to go for a walk along Main Street while we waited for the phone call to pick them up.

As soon as we turned onto it, I had to take a deep breath. The magick wasn't as potent as before, but there was still a steady stream trickling throughout the shops. Enough to set my teeth on edge.

"You're hopeless," Nathan sighed. "Go introduce yourself. To one of them, at least. Buy something. Talk witch. Enjoy having company, for crying out loud."

"I have company. Unless this is your way of trying to get rid of me."

"This is my way of trying to get you to break the ice. They're all sitting on eggshells now that you're back. Set some of them at ease, at least."

"How do you know?" There was no way for that to not sound petulant.

"Liaison, remember? Did you really think they'd stop talking to me once you arrived?"

I glowered at him for a minute as we kept walking. "I don't want to deal with their baggage, Nathan. I've got enough of my own to get over."

"Why do you think they're going to just lay all of their problems at your feet?"

"Call it a hunch," I remarked in a dry voice. He gave me another pointed look and I sighed, "I'm stronger than them. In so many different ways, I'm a separate entity from them. Do you get how that feels? Even amongst those like me, I'm still on the outside. A Titan amidst the Gods. It was one thing when I was the only active witch in Cedar Creek. Now I feel like I have to mark my borders and chase off intruders. This was supposed to be my haven. With them here, it doesn't quite feel like that anymore."

Nathan shook his head. "You're a pain in my ass."

"Excuse me?"

"Lex, do you remember what it was like when we were kids? Your little high-n-mighty personality literally pushed away anyone not stubborn enough to stick with you. And you're doing it again. It's not that you're some lone wolf cast aside by everyone else. It's that you're a prideful little shit that likes being the outcast.

"Now, I've literally sat down with every single witch that came to Cedar Creek. Do you think, for one second, I would let any of them stay if they weren't functional adults that could take care of their own crap? Yeah, you're strong as hell. But no one in this town will give a crap because we don't know how to measure that kind of stuff.

"There are people here who do now. And you want them all to run away with their tails between their legs because you're a big badass who doesn't need anyone. Well, that's not how this works. So, deal with your shit and go make friends."

With that, Nathan literally gave me a push toward the street. Across from us was *Mystic Manuscripts* with *Rook Candle Company* above it. Considering Caroline Rook was the first witch to make her presence stick, I decided to start with her. For a moment, I considered keeping my magick masked—a new habit I'd developed once I learned how to do it—but in the end I decided that if they wanted to know who I was, they ought to have a clear picture.

With a sigh, I unleashed my magick and it flared around me in a pulsing array. Then I crossed the street and headed up the stairs to the second-story shops. To my left was a door with a frosted glass window bearing the store's logo of a black bird with its wings enfolding the name of the store. Only the pale gray beak on the creature distinguished it from its cousins the crow and raven.

Through the glass, I could see the distorted images of shelves full of candles of various reds and oranges. A smile pulled at my lips as I sensed the announcing spell placed upon the door. As soon as it opened, the proprietor of the shop would know they had visitors. Clever.

Not willing to waste another moment, I pushed open the door and entered Caroline Rook's domain. Real surprise floated through me once I was able to take a good, long look at the space. Several wooden shelves took up the wall to the right, showcasing a rainbow gradient of jar candles. Little gold placards were used to declare the scents of each candle. On the same wall as the door, another section of shelving held another rainbow of pillar candles in various sizes. Shelves beneath the large windows on the left wall held the specialty candles used for specific rituals. Including ones shaped like body parts that I couldn't help but smirk at. In the center of the room, six wooden tables were responsible for displaying more decorative items. A variety of candle holders displayed tapers, pillars, and tea lights.

The far wall was obscured a bit by the countertop with the register perched on it. Behind it, the shelves held the bulk of the incense supply, colored tapers, and diffusers. Inside of the glass case were the smaller items such as the scented melts, tea lights, and even sealing wax. All in all, it was a very impressive setup.

In the few minutes it took me to take note of the shop, a robust woman in her mid-to-late thirties made her way around the counter. Planting herself in front of the window, she adjusted the cream-colored shawl around her shoulders and folded her hands. Around her pulsed a faint aura of magick. At once, mine was trying to smother it.

Pulling my power back into me a bit, I slapped a smile on my face and approached the woman. I held out a hand for her to shake as I said, "Hello. My name is Alexandria Ryder. I am the Witch of Old Grove Road."

The woman took a few seconds to study me before she took my hand. "Caroline Rook at your service," she intoned with a slight bow of her head.

For a moment, nothing more was said as her eyes traveled over the space surrounding me.

Either she was reading my aura or my magick was distracting her. Probably both.

Her voice was low and tinged with awe when she remarked, "I have never felt magick equal to yours."

My stomach knotted. "I have."

Curiosity sparked in her brown eyes as they lowered to mine. "Truly?"

I felt my lips twist into a sarcastic smirk. "Oh yes, I have. And she was my opposite in every way that mattered, except where it mattered most."

Azure had called us Titans, and she was right. There were probably a handful of witches in the whole world who could hold magick as we could. We were few, and we were volatile. In comparison, the other magick users were many, and they were determined. Which was why she had cautioned against us going to war. Now I had to live with the fact that there was one less Titan in the world, and I was growing more outnumbered as the days passed.

"Where does it come from? Which deities do you pray to?" Her voice was still low, but there was a drive behind it that determined she would get an answer. Had it not been for the direction of her questions, it would have been amusing.

As it was, I raised my eyebrows and waited for her to meet my gaze. As soon as she did, I delved into her. Not just her mind, but into the very cells of her body. It was the first time I'd ever considered someone a chakra witch, but that's what she reminded me of. Where Azure's magick and mine were built into every single cell and molecule of our bodies, hers was nowhere close. Instead, it attached at several key points along her spine. While it seemed good at reading others and detecting spells, I knew in an instant that it could never do an energy working on its own. If she wanted real power, she would have to ask for it.

Shaking my head, I let her see the truth in my eyes. "I do not call on Gods to lend me power. I am power. I call on people to lend me their humanity."

"Is that why he never strays from your side?" she asked with a pointed look out the window.

Following her line of sight, I found Nathan sitting on a bench across the street. He had the local paper open in front of him, but too often his eyes were trained on the storefront. There was no way for him to be less obvious.

I smiled to myself as I said, "Yes. He is the bridge between us. He is the reason I remember who I am, and learn to distinguish that from what I am."

"And what are you, Alexandria?"

This time, I included her in my smile. "A witch, Caroline. Just like you." Then I turned and headed for the door.

I may not have made a friend, but it was a start.

Chapter Twelve

IMPORTANT

On Tuesday, I started really going to work on the garden. Between trimming back the conquerors and spacing out where new plants would go, I had my work cut out for me. It really didn't help that I'd slept in much later than normal—and I still felt weary—so I was working at a frantic pace, trying to get something accomplished before Nathan got out of school.

Right as I was picking weeds out of the herb patch, I felt my stomach seize and the urge to vomit worked its way up into the back of my throat. Sitting back on my heels, I took slow, careful breaths as I tried to banish the feeling. At the same time, I carefully scanned my garden for any hint of ginger. Because this was far from over.

After twenty minutes of coming up empty, I caved. Teleporting from the cottage garden to the one behind our house, I found the ginger plant inside of a minute. Then my heart sank as I realized it wasn't far enough along to do me any good. Which meant I would have to face Anne or go without. Or use magick.

There wasn't even an option. No way was I about to face my other mother. And even if I waited it out today, the nausea would just return. So, I heaved a sigh and reached out for one of the tiny ginger plants. Pouring the spell into it took more magick than I anticipated, but it was worth it when I removed it from the ground and found a large, healthy ginger root. If my stomach wasn't rioting, I would have leapt for joy. As it was, I immediately took the plant home and prepared it for tea.

By three o'clock, I was nausea free and back to work in my garden. I was just beginning to contemplate calling it a day when my cell phone rang. Ripping off my gardening gloves, it took me a minute to fish it out of my pocket and flip it open.

"Alexandria Ryder speaking."

"Why do you answer your phone like that? Who else even has your number other than me and your mom?" Nathan scoffed.

"Your parents both have my number. Both my parents have my number. And the bank has my number. Oh, and Matt. So you see, plenty of people."

"And my name shows up on the Caller ID."

"It's cute that you actually think I look at the Caller ID before I pick up."

"You should. It's how you avoid people you don't want to talk to."

"I avoid that by not giving them my number in the first place."

"Whatever. Are you coming over or not?"

"Nathan, I have been over there literally every night since I got home. Why would today be any different?"

"Good. Then I'll see you soon."

"What's the rush? Wait, it's not my night to cook!"

Nathan chuckled, "Thinking take-out tonight. Mom and Dad are having dinner at Mom's friend's house."

"So, what's the rush?"

"I'm bored," he sighed. "And I don't want to sit here and work on stupid equations."

I rolled my eyes. "I'll get cleaned up and be there in about twenty minutes."

"Just bring a change of clothes and shower here," he insisted.

I took a moment to look down at my clothes crusted with drying mud and at the streaks coating my braid. While a bath would be lovely, a shower would actually get me clean.

"Fine. See you in a bit."

It was still twenty minutes before Nathan actually saw me. The difference being I appeared from upstairs instead of through the front door. I felt him in the office and moved to place myself in the doorway.

As soon as I looked into the room, my jaw dropped. The place looked like a tornado hit it. Manila folders were piled on the desk, stacked on the bookshelves, and there were newspaper clippings pinned on a few cork boards hanging on the walls. Some of them bore my picture.

"What the hell?"

Nathan glanced up from his desk before following my gaze to the cork board. He waited until I met his gaze before he said simply, "Research."

Before I had to ask, he started typing into the computer. Then he beckoned me over to take a look at the screen. As I approached, he explained, "I had my history teacher for my senior project. So, I kissed a little ass."

The website on display was the color of aged parchment and the bold title looked like a headline from a colonial newspaper. As soon as I read the title, I understood what he meant by kissing ass. *History of Cedar Creek* was a website devoted to documenting facts related to our town spanning a few centuries. And a tab for the 1600s started it all.

My hand shot to the mouse and I clicked on the link. As soon as the page loaded, my breath caught. The first and largest image on the screen was a portrait of a young woman. She had pale skin, dark brown hair, high cheekbones, and piercing blue eyes. But that wasn't what got me. Beneath the picture was a small caption; similar to one I had seen beneath another ghostly photograph.

Portrait of Mary Sullivan, accused witch c. 1686.

Photograph provided by the Cedar Creek Library, est. 1893.

"Nathan, you found her."

It all came rushing back. The light of the full moon poured over the circle while a cold, frigid wind whipped over the exposed ground. My arms were bound above my head. I then pleaded for my life, and all it bought me was a death sentence.

Even with my back to the stake and the wood gathered at my feet, I did not use magick to defend myself. I'd had a greater purpose for it. Every last ounce that I possessed went into a spell to protect the one I most cherished: my daughter. My last act as a dying woman was to erase my child from everyone's memory.

Mercy.

I gasped as I once more took stock of my surroundings. And as I pondered the meaning of the single word, a hand dropped to my stomach of its own accord. Because I knew what Mercy meant. I knew who Mercy was.

"Found who?" Nathan asked, breaking into my reverie.

My hand shot away from my stomach as

if it were burned. A shiver rocked my body as the adrenaline from the memory began to fade. Shaking my head, I cleared my throat and pointed at the picture.

"Mary Sullivan. My past life."

His eyes shot to mine. "Your past life?"

I nodded and answered the unspoken question hanging between us. "She was a witch who was burned at the stake here in Cedar Creek."

"I'm almost afraid to ask how you know that," he remarked.

A wry smile pulled at my lips. "You should be. My first memory as her was of the burning. It happened during my Wiccaning when I was nine. In the circle where Morgan died."

Nathan closed his eyes as a pained expression settled over his face. "Please, tell me you didn't..."

"I did," I whispered, reaching out to take his hand. He was shaking.

Suddenly, Nathan stood up and wrapped his arms around me. His embrace tightened until it felt like my spine was going to crack. Even then, I didn't tell him to let go. Instead, I rubbed his back and leaned my head against his shoulder.

At last, he let me go and took a step back. "Sorry. I just..."

"I know. I would've done the same. It's not something you can really imagine until you've lived it, but I appreciate the sympathy. Now, can I ask you something?"

"Anything."

"Did you see my Ascension?"

I'd always wondered if he dreamt of the lightning strike that left the scar over my heart. When I'd called to tell him about Morgan, I'd had a vision of him picking up the phone. His breathing had been ragged and a sheen of sweat had coated his skin. As if he'd woken from a nightmare.

Nathan's jaw tightened a second before he nodded. "Yeah, I saw it."

"All of it?"

"Right up until the moment you called."

So, it had started then. That very night. Our minds had connected to the point where I dragged him through hours of hell. And it had never dissipated.

"Were you in my head? Or were you outside?"

"Jeez, Lex, why does it matter?" he snarled,

sitting back in his chair and running his hands over his face.

"Trust me, it does."

"Outside," he sighed. "Like being in the blackness. I was standing right there when it all happened."

The blackness. Exactly what I thought. "What is it that makes us so connected?" I wondered aloud.

"Morgan," was his immediate response. But his emotions fled into that damn bottle as he said it.

I shook my head. "It's been a long time that we've shared more than Morgan."

Why are you the most important person in my life?

I almost asked the question. I wanted to ask, but I couldn't force the words to leave me. For some reason, I wasn't sure I was ready for the answer.

Nathan forced a smile, but his eyes were nothing close to amused. "You're right. We share Matt, too."

He wanted to change the topic, so I let him. There was still a lot more heavy for later. With how much we had missed, we probably wouldn't find an end to it.

Looking back at the computer screen, I forced my tone to be lighter when I asked, "What else have you found about her?"

Nathan's attention also redirected to the screen. "Not much. She married her husband, William Sullivan, when she was sixteen. And the only reason I know that is because William was a business partner of Henry Vaile. William was a seasoned fur trapper and had good relations with the Natives, while Henry went into business selling and trading the furs brought into him. Between the two of them, they made a decent living in their time. It's why Mary could afford to have a portrait done of herself. Henry's family, too."

His eyes raised to meet mine. "What do you know about her?"

I sighed. "Less than you. I know she betrayed a witch named Margarite, so the coven burned her at the stake. I know that William knew she was a witch and he accepted it. And I remember when William and Mary met." That last bit brought a smile to my lips. It was one of the few good memories I'd encountered during my coma, and I treasured it as such.

At once, Nathan sat up straight. "Margarite? You're sure the name was Margarite?"

"Nathan, she burned me at the stake. I'll never forget that bitch for the rest of eternity."

Leaning his head back, Nathan released a sarcastic laugh to the ceiling. Then he spun around in his chair and reached out toward the nearest bookshelf stuffed with manila folders. "Do you know why I decided on doing the town history? Because four years ago I started tracking my family tree. Just the one side. And it led me all the way back to..."

As he spoke, he pulled a handful of pages out of the folder and began to lay them out on the floor. It didn't take long before the last sheet fell into place. I saw three separate names and wanted to scream.

Margarite Jean Vaile was the High Priestess of Cedar Creek Coven when Mary died. She was also the mother of Margarite Vaile II and Francesca Vaile. My murderer was the ancestor to my best friend ... and my daughter.

Chapter Thirteen

LEFT BEHIND

It felt as if I had only just managed to drift to sleep when a soft whimper impeded on my rest. For a moment, I waited to see if more was to come. Alas, it seemed as if my child could sense my awakened state, for her whimpers grew to a mewling screech that I had learned to interpret as her hungry cry.

William was away on a hunt; thus he did not immediately take his daughter into his arms and pass her to me as he had done for the past three weeks. Thus, it was left to me to crawl from my bed and approach my child's cradle. Taking her into my arms, we retired to the rocking chair so that we might both be comfortable while she nursed.

Some time passed before Mercy ceased her feeding and soiled her cloths. It was as I was applying a fresh cloth to her that a soft knock sounded on the door. Gathering the infant close, I placed her into the cradle.

When I opened the door, I was relieved to find Margarite Vaile standing upon the threshold. "Have we come at a bad time?" she asked, looking between her two daughters and myself. "I have kept them as long as I could, but they insisted on meeting the babe today."

"I have just set her in the cradle, but she is not yet asleep."

This announcement was all the little girls needed to hear. At once, five-year-old Margarite II—Margie—sprinted past me. Three-year-old Francesca toddled behind her as they made for the cradle. Margarite and I laughed in indulgence as I welcomed her into the cottage.

"Would you care for some tea?" I asked, moving toward the hearth fire.

"Oh, do be sensible," she admonished. "Take your rest here in the chair. I do believe I have been here often enough to know how you like your tea. Girls, be careful! She is a bare three weeks and has not the strength you are blessed with."

Having not the energy to argue with my friend, I sat in the rocking chair and watched as her daughters cooed over mine. I do not know how long I enjoyed the scene before sleep started to creep across my vision. There was but one moment when I realized that Margarite had begun to wash the soiled cloths that I tried to fight the exhaustion.

"Nonsense. The greatest gift one mother can offer to another is the charity of shared housework. I am sure when I am laid up again, you will return the favor. And so I shall when you bring your next into this world. Thus the cycle will continue across the ages."

These words I almost failed to hear, for the weariness crept into my bones once more and my mind slipped into sleep.

My hand shot out to steady myself against the desk as the memory faded. A vile taste crept into my mouth as my stomach twisted. This time I couldn't be sure if it was due to my womb's current resident or the fact that Mary had once been friends with Margarite. The thought made me shudder.

"Lex? You okay? What's going on?" Nathan asked, holding onto my other hand to steady me.

I shook my head. "Oh, you know. The usual. I learn something about the past and my brain gets hijacked."

"Come on, sit down. What happened?"

After sitting in his chair, I waved my hand at the family tree spread out on the floor. "As soon as I saw Margarite's name, I had a memory. I'd just given birth to Mercy. She was three weeks old and I was still so tired. Margarite arrived with Margie and Francesca. They wanted to see the baby. Margarite started cleaning the cottage and I fell asleep in a rocking chair. We were friends, once upon a time. Before she killed me, we'd been friends."

What could have happened? What could change things so drastically that two women who were so close could turn on one another? Why did Margarite believe Mary deserved to die?

"Write them down," Nathan suggested, finding me an empty sheet of paper and a pen amidst the chaos of his office.

"What?"

"All of the questions you have. Write them down. Then we can try to find the answers for them."

I nodded and began to do as he suggested. In the meantime, he began picking up the family tree. It was then that I once more noticed Francesca's name written in his blocky handwriting.

It hadn't immediately clicked when he said Henry's last name, but now that I knew, I felt like an idiot. Vaile was never a common last name, and the only time I'd heard it spoken before was in another's memory. The same one where Francesca cast it off and declared herself a Walker. And I knew if I traced Grey's line all the way back, she would be the beginning of his family.

My best friend and my child shared an ancestor. And I couldn't tell Nathan. Not yet.

"So, you've only had three other memories as Mary before coming home?" Nathan asked as he returned the folder to its rightful place.

"No. The first was my Wiccaning, but I had others at the lake. Minor things, mostly. For some reason, I can't remember more than watching Mercy learning to swim. Then there was one during the coma, one after prom, and now this."

"Prom?"

"Yeah. It was the avens that set it off, I think. When I crossed from the woods into the garden, I remembered planting avens near an oak sapling there."

Nathan's lips parted and his eyes narrowed in on me. After a minute, I demanded to know what his problem was. Shaking his head, Nathan sighed, "Think about what you just said, Lex. Where did Mary plant the flowers?"

I rolled my eyes. "On the border between the trees and the garden."

"Which garden?"

"Uh, my garden."

"At the cottage?"

"Yes..."

"Damn it all, Lex, Mary lived at the cottage! Morgan's cottage! *My* family's cottage."

I squeezed my eyes shut and muttered, "I'm an idiot."

Nathan chuckled. "Some days," he agreed. Then he reached over and added a question to my list. *How did Margarite's family end up in the Sullivan cottage?*

"This is some mystery, isn't it?" he asked, reading over what I'd already written.

I shrugged. "Longest running in the history of Cedar Creek, I bet. Not as well-known as Alyssa Rice, though."

He snorted. "The only person more famous

than her in this town is you. Nothing will change that."

My eyes raised to the newspaper clippings of me hanging on the cork board. "No, I don't think it will. But I'd be happy if it did."

Nathan reached out and took my hand. "Hey, everything happens for a reason, right?"

He had no idea.

Nathan agreed to help me search for answers on one condition: I let him graduate high school first. Considering I was doing enough to distract from his studies, I could agree to that one. Not that his ability to earn good grades mattered much. Like me, he hadn't applied to a single college. Instead, he was going to jump straight into his work with Oak Grove Investments and work on expanding the company's projects. Somewhere in between those responsibilities, he was supposed to help me.

In the meantime, I was given homework of my own. Nathan wanted me caught up on his own research so that I would know which was excess material versus fresh facts. It was then that he gave me the totally unnecessary house key. Only because it was unnecessary had he forgotten to give it to me before, he claimed. Still, it felt nice to get the key. Like it was official that the house was really ours.

For the next week, I developed a nice new routine. I'd go to bed early and wake up late. Then I'd brew myself ginger tea that I kept in a travel mug. It was a sip-as-needed beverage, so I tried to keep it on hand wherever I went. Most of where I went was Nathan's office or the town library. Once or twice, I even found myself back in the records office. If there was one thing we could count on being recorded in that era, it was property lines. By the time the weekend rolled around, I was eager to show Nathan what I'd discovered.

Come Monday morning, that routine was shot in the foot. I'd run out of ginger on Sunday night and wasn't willing to risk boosting another plant. If I left them be, their natural healing arts would prove more potent than any that suffered with my interference. However, I hadn't thought myself dependent on the soothing plant until I lurched out of bed and rushed to the bathroom.

For almost an hour, I sat beside the toilet and emptied everything from the day before into it. Even when I had nothing left to purge, the taste lingered in the back of my throat and my stomach seized violently. No matter what I did, the nausea wasn't going away.

As dawn crept across the horizon, I knew that I wasn't going to last much longer. Pushing myself to my feet, I brushed my teeth for a solid five minutes before I threw on some clothes and vanished. I arrived on the sidewalk in front of Anne's house and barely thought to scan the house for others. Relief flooded me when I realized that Josh was already gone to work, leaving Anne alone. Hoping she wasn't still asleep, I made my way to the front door and started knocking.

"Lex?" she asked in confusion when she answered the door. I barely let her step aside before I rushed past her into the house.

Before I could even get a word out, I had to place a hand over my mouth for a few seconds. When I felt like I could breathe, I was quick to ask, "Do you have any ginger? I'm out and I'm in desperate need." Once more, I clapped a hand to my mouth and leaned back against the wall.

"Lex? Come sit down. I'll make you some tea," Anne said, pushing me into the kitchen.

The second I was settled in a chair, she leapt into action. Desperate as I was, the second she filled the kettle and set it on the stove, I brought the water to a boil. She barely had time to add a few tablespoons of ground ginger to a mug before I added the water. By the time she handed the mug to me, I'd already lowered the temperature enough to make it easy to drink.

Sitting opposite me, her expression was nothing short of shocked when she asked me, "Lex, honey, what's going on? Is it a stomach bug? The flu?"

I leaned back in the chair, grateful to feel the ginger begin to work its magick. When the nausea began to dissipate, I opened my eyes to look at her. Making my voice as strong as I could, I shook my head and said, "No. Morning sickness."

Silence.

Minutes passed by and Anne's expression hadn't changed. Stunned wasn't a strong enough word for what she was, but it was the most accurate description I could come up with. And as

I waited, I sipped my tea and prepared for the inevitable.

At last she said, "Morning sickness. That means you're..."

"Yes."

"How far along?"

"Technically I'm four weeks. But if we go by date of conception, I was two weeks yesterday."

"Have you taken a test yet? It might still be too early," she added to herself.

I shook my head. "I haven't even bought one yet."

"But you're sure?"

"Sure as any witch can be." My eyes lowered to my mug before I muttered, "I'm sorry, Anne. You shouldn't have found out like this."

When she waved that away, I knew the shock was wearing off. "I was going to find out one way or another. Sooner rather than later is my preference." All of a sudden, her expression became speculative as she looked me over. "Who's the father?"

At once, my spine straightened and my body went rigid. In a deadpan voice, I announced, "Someone I left behind."

She wasn't having any of my defensiveness. "Does he know?"

"He does."

"And? What did he have to say about it?"

I wasn't going to tell her that. I didn't have it in me to tell her that Grey told me to leave. To get as far from his family and coven as I could. She didn't need to know that he was sacrificing his second chance at being a father so that he could ensure his daughter's freedom.

"I left him, Anne. Even though I carry his child, I wasn't staying with him. He knew that, and he didn't fight it."

"What about his rights?"

"He can have them back when the baby turns eighteen."

"Lex..."

"Stop, Anne. Please?"

"For now," she conceded. Then she sighed, "I'm going to go take a shower. Drink your tea and be ready to go in half an hour."

"Where are we going?"

She rolled her eyes. "One thing you never buy in a small town is a pregnancy test." As she was leaving the kitchen, she paused in the doorway. With her back to me, she asked in an almost timid voice, "Does Nathan know?"

"No."

Anne nodded once and left the room.

Chapter Fourteen

RIGHT THING

I had been sitting on the bathroom floor for upwards of an hour. I couldn't look. I didn't want to see it. Didn't want to know. As long as I didn't see it, I was still me. Still the arrogant, prideful, young witch who had just returned home. For as long as I sat there, I didn't have to become someone else. So I sat there, staring off into space and wondering what changes I would make if I could go back to Beltane.

In the end, I couldn't change a thing.

Slowly, I reached for the little white stick lying on the floor in front of me. My body was shaking so badly, I had to hold it with both hands and brace my forearms against my raised knees in order to read it. I only needed a glance to know.

There, in clear, concise little lines was my positive answer. Pregnant. It was official.

All of a sudden, the protective fog I'd wrapped that word in vanished. In its place it left piercing, painful knowledge.

A wild, desperate sob escaped my throat and I hurled the test at the wall. My body shook with terror as I began to cry. Curling into a ball, I let the pain thrust through my mind in vicious stabs.

Grief consumed me, and I allowed it. With this confirmation, I had to pop the bubble I'd been living in for the past two weeks. I had to admit that they had been a fantasy. That the whirlwind of activity was just a beautiful delusion I was allowed before I was forced to face reality.

In that reality, I had to transform. After two short weeks where my life was exactly as I wanted it, I now had to become someone else. Because of this, I had to become a better person.

It terrified me to think that I couldn't do it. I didn't know how. I'd never wanted to try.

But I had to. For the baby, I had to become the woman she needed me to be.

I'm a mom.

It seemed to take forever, but the grieving did pass. When it did, I was left as an empty shell lying on the bathroom floor. Some dim part of my brain cursed the valerian period that allowed me to stay like that. Half an hour was spent in the numbness while I stared at the little white stick that had fallen on the floor. At last, I was able to push myself to my feet and reenter the real world.

The first thing I thought as the numbness faded was, *How am I going to tell Nathan?*

It was a question that haunted me all the way back to Anne's. As soon as I stepped foot in the house, Anne directed me to the couch before she set a plate of food in front of me. It was almost funny how she tried to describe how helpful and necessary everything was even while I was wolfing it down. When I'd finished, she handed me a list of grocery items, telling me to keep them all on-hand throughout the pregnancy, and to try eating more frequently, instead of in large quantities.

Every time she said things like 'pregnancy' or 'trimester' my head wanted to explode. I'd accepted that I had a tiny being growing inside of me and that meant I had to change my ways. That didn't make me ready for the homework. My brain hadn't caught up enough to grab more information than 'take the vitamins and read the magazines.'

We were in the middle of going over an article when I felt Nathan's truck pull up in the driveway. At once, my eyes widened and I gasped, "What's he doing here?"

Anne appeared solemn as she gathered the magazines and slipped them back into the shopping bag. "I told him to come here after school."

"Why?" I snarled.

"Because when you finish telling him, one of you is going to storm out and the other is going to need a shoulder to cry on. At this point, I don't know which of you it is, but I know who the shoulder is going to be."

As I opened my mouth to argue further, Nathan bounded through the front door. My heart squeezed just seeing him so carefree and happy. Knowing how what I had to say was going to affect him, I was tempted to leave. But he deserved to know.

Before he could even greet us, Nathan took one look at my face and his expression fell. "What's going on? What's wrong? Lex? Mom?" he demanded, striding into the middle of the living room.

Anne rose from her seat and looked down at me. The expression was supportive, but her eyes held a sadness I hadn't wanted to see. When she turned to her son, I could almost see the defeat settle into every line of her body. Without a word, she left the room.

When Nathan looked back at me, his emerald eyes were whirling in panic. My throat closed as I recognized that expression. The last time I'd seen it, I was being arrested for murder.

"What's going on, Lex? What's wrong?"

For one endless moment, I opened my mouth and no words came out. My thoughts darted around inside of my skull, careening off the bone to shout the same message back into the center of my brain. How could I tell him? What would he think of me? Then a snide little voice in my head asked, *How could you keep it from him?*

"I'm pregnant, Nathan."

As soon as the words were out of my mouth, I released a long, heavy exhale. It was the first time that word had passed my lips since I told Grey. Yet, this time felt infinitely harder.

Nathan looked as if he'd been kicked in the stomach. For several seconds, he stood in the middle of the room without twitching a muscle. In his eyes, however, I could see a storm brewing. Details were starting to emerge in his head; all he needed was confirmation.

All too soon, lightning flashed and his voice came out like a crack of thunder. "How long have you known?"

Swallowing hard, I answered, "Since the morning after it happened."

"Is that why you came home when you did?"

"Yes."

Nathan's nostrils flared and his teeth were set on edge as he redirected his glare at the couch. It felt like a slap when he spat, "You should have told me."

If I hadn't felt so ashamed, that might have gotten my back up. As it was, I said nothing in response. Not that he gave me a chance.

"You should have told me. You've known you were pregnant for two weeks and didn't say a word. Why?"

"I took the test this morning—"

"No. Don't go there. You knew right when it happened. You came home the very next day. Why didn't you just tell me then? I'm sure you told others."

My mouth snapped shut. As soon as he saw that, he shook his head and said, "Yeah, that's what I thought. Who all know? Your parents? My mom? Matt? Your ex? Who all knew before me, Alex?"

The second he called me 'Alex' my fuse was lit. I understood that he was upset, but he didn't have to hit below the belt.

"Really? You think there's a pecking order? If there is, then you can bet your ass that my ex was the first person on the list. Yes, Nathan, he knows. He was the first person I told. And up until today, he was the only one who knew. Anne still wouldn't know if I hadn't needed her help. That's it, Nathan. No one else knows. Not even *my* mother. And you better believe I will never live that one down."

Nathan took a step forward. "The father knows?"

It was like he hadn't heard a single word after that. "Yes."

All at once, his anger was redirected. "And?"

"And what?" I snapped.

"Where is he?" he sniped back.

"It doesn't matter."

"Of course it matters! You're carrying his child. He should be here. He should be doing something. Is he even planning on doing the right thing?"

"He did do the right thing," I snarled, nice and low. This was dangerous ground and I was doing my best to broadcast how quickly he needed to back off.

Nathan either didn't notice or he didn't care. "Then tell me what the right thing is. What has he done that I should applaud him for?"

"He did the right thing by letting me go. He did the right thing by telling me to leave. To come home."

"How is that the right thing, Alex? Abandoning you? Telling you to go? Not owning up to the responsibility he has toward you and that baby? What kind of man does that?"

My arm shot out in a quick, deliberate slap across his face.

"Don't you *ever* talk about him like that again. You don't know how hard it was for him to tell me to take his child and abandon *him*. And you don't know what it will cost him to know that he will never watch his child grow. Think what you want, Nathan, I can't stop you. But you will not talk about him like that to me or to his child."

Without another word, I stormed out of the house, throwing my shoulder into his as I passed. If he wanted to make amends, he knew where I lived. And I would not be the one to apologize.

Chapter Fifteen

BACKUP

My body moved mechanically to get me home. With my mind so disabled by the anger, it was a relief not to have everything shut down as I seethed. Of course, once I was within the boundaries of the cottage, I let the bicycle drop at the edge of the driveway and stumbled toward the bench. Shaking with rage and a strange exhaustion, my legs refused to cooperate any further, so I just sat there, staring at the face etched into the stone.

It was my face. Carved into the stone by Morgan's eldest daughter, Freyja, when she was just a girl. She'd had an affinity for stonework, and she'd helped both of her sisters shape the gargoyles that now stood guard at the gate. Somehow, years before I existed, she'd taken this stone and shaped my face into three separate images: Maiden, Mother, and Crone.

I was in the middle of the transition from Maiden to Mother, but I suffered no delusions. I wasn't there yet. The woman in the stone, with the swollen breasts and bulging stomach, was smiling in contentment. As if she had learned something precious about life, and no one could take it from her. Staring at her, it amazed me to know that I would one day be her. Someday, I would have that smile, and I would have that secret.

Slowly, my eyes drifted to the pale irises of the Mother. As soon as they did, my vision blurred and a new scene appeared before me.

Nathan sat on the couch in his mother's living room, his elbows balanced on his knees with his head in his hands. For a second, my chest tightened and I tried to figure out the helplessness that surrounded him. He looked ... heartbroken.

As soon as he felt me watching, his head jerked up and he turned to look around the room. "Lex?"

My breath caught as Anne walked in and

asked, "Did you say something?" Her voice was low and soothing.

I watched his expression grow distant when his eyes seemed to find mine. In an equally distant voice, he answered, "Nothing."

A short silence fell as Anne eased farther into the room and took up her previous position on the loveseat. For a few moments, she did nothing more than sit and watch her son. I wondered if she thought he was staring off into space, or if she somehow knew that we were locked in a kind of staring contest. As if he were trying to see me in the same way I was seeing him.

"You have a right to be upset; angry even," Anne began in the same tone.

My ire rose at the same time that Nathan's eyes flashed to her, growing harder in his irritation. "Don't. I don't want to talk about it."

At once, her expression became even more compassionate. "If that were the case, you wouldn't still be here."

Nathan's jaw clenched and I could feel the anger rolling off him. Suddenly, like the flame of a candle, it was snuffed out. Making a point to look away from me, he let his head fall back into his hands.

It was then that I first tried to break contact. Tried to pull back into myself. Protect us both from what was to come. Both of us counted on our ability to talk to Anne and know that our words would go no further. Curious as I was, I didn't want to be the one to violate that pact.

But he wouldn't let me go.

Our bond was too strong. With our minds so inexorably linked, it was impossible to retreat while one of us clung to the other. Even though we were pissed at each other, I could feel him still hanging onto me. Almost as if he feared letting go.

"Things were going so great. I should have known something would screw it up." His voice was careful and I knew he was well aware of my watching. Now, every word would be chosen with care so that I wouldn't overhear anything not meant for my ears.

"I'm sorry, Nathan," Anne whispered.

He shrugged. "So am I." There was a moment of silence before some thought sparked his anger and he sneered, "You know, of all the people I thought this could happen to, Lex was nowhere near that list."

With that one remark, he confirmed everything I feared about telling him.

Anne swallowed and looked away before muttering, "Everything happens for a reason."

Nathan's head snapped up and his eyes bored into hers as he spat, "What was the reason for *this*?"

"I don't know, Nathan. I really don't. And you're right: I never thought this would happen to her. But things do happen that we can't change. Even things we don't want to change."

"You wouldn't change this if you could?" he demanded.

Anne looked sympathetic again. "I don't think Alexandria would. Nathan, despite what this will mean for her, Lex has already accepted that she is a mother. Not that she *will be*; she already *is*. At the point she's at, Nathan, I don't think she could even imagine life in another reality."

Nathan sighed and shook his head. "Well I have imagined it. Not once did I think she'd come home like this."

"You think she did? Nathan, she came home

the day she realized she was pregnant." I watched him flinch on the last word. "She knows that this is where she belongs. You know that better than anyone, how much she wanted to come home. How much she needed to be here. Do you honestly believe that she wanted to come back like this? With a pregnancy only she could be sure of, and no one the wiser except for the man that let her go?"

"Idiot," Nathan grumbled and I could hear venom drip from the single word.

Anne didn't hear him and continued, "Alexandria came back pregnant and alone."

"But she's not alone!" Nathan snarled. For the briefest second, his eyes flickered to mine before he turned his glare on his mother. "She's not alone. She's got me. And you, apparently. Why didn't she just tell me?" The last came out in a weary sigh.

"Because she needed the proof," Anne said. He opened his mouth to argue and she held up a hand to forestall him. "She needed it, Nathan. It had nothing to do with you. Lex needed that test in order to make it real for her."

"That doesn't explain why she told you and

not me."

"A few hours apart," Anne added in a dry tone. "And if you think you found out in a bad way, you should've been here this morning. Girl shows up on my doorstep, white as a sheet, and asks if I have any ginger. I ask her if it's a stomach bug and she replies that it's morning sickness. Just like that."

Nathan fought the smile hard, but I could see it forcing its way through his pissed off attitude. "No one can ever accuse Lex of being subtle."

Anne snorted. "She might want to learn that. Especially when she tells her parents."

At once, his smile faded and he dropped his head into his hands again. "That's right. I can't believe she didn't tell them."

"When was she supposed to get the time to do that? Nathan, she took that test a couple of hours ago. And the first person she told after it became real to her was you."

I was pleased to see how hard that hit him. As if he finally understood that he wasn't the sixth person down on some imaginary list in his head. He was my backup, in all things. And I needed him to have my back in this more than anything else.

His eyes shot to mine for a second before he stood up and said, "I have to go see Lex."

Anne nodded. "I think that's a good idea. There's a lot you two need to discuss."

Nathan's jaw set and he purposefully kept his eyes away from me. "Not now, Mom."

"Fine," she said. Standing up, she wrapped her arms around him in a maternal hug and wished him luck. Then the vision faded.

Nathan came through the woods after dropping his truck off at home. I hoped, for both our sakes, that he had grown calmer with his walk. It wouldn't do us any good to keep fighting.

I was still sitting on the bench when he entered the garden. My throat seemed to grow dry at his approach and I refused to raise my eyes. I didn't know what to say, so I said nothing. Nathan must have been in a similar predicament, because he made his way silently to the bench and sat on the Crone's side, leaving the Mother uncovered as I did.

Minutes passed and some tiny portion of

my brain kept track of each second. I couldn't understand how they could feel so long when I knew they were ticking by at a steady pace. In five minutes, it felt like an hour had gone by before the silence was broken.

"Why didn't you tell me?" His voice was quiet. Almost forlorn.

His gaze had risen to my face, but I kept my eyes trained on the bench. "Because it wasn't real yet."

Nathan shook his head. "Not good enough."

My jaw clenched and my nostrils flared as my Ryder Pride spiked. Raising my eyes, I leveled a glare on him. "How the hell do you figure?"

For a moment, his stubborn expression matched mine. His voice was under complete control, however, when he said, "Because I'm your best friend. Even if this was just a pregnancy scare, you should have told me."

"Why would I do that, Nathan? Why would I put you through even a suspicion? Suppose it had just been a scare. How is it fair to make you worry about something that didn't exist?"

"How is you dealing with this by yourself fair?" he shot back. "How is it fair leaving me out of it? You could have come to me, Lex. You *should* have come to me. Even if only to have someone tell you it's going to be okay. Instead, you chose not to. Why?"

"*You know why!*" I suddenly exploded. "You know why, Nathan! How could I admit that to you, of all people? How could I come home and see you for the first time in years and blurt out that I had gotten knocked up the day before I came home?"

Tears were pooling in my eyes and I used a fist to scrub at the escapees.

"There are so many things I have to be ashamed of from the moment we said goodbye. In these last couple of years away, I was hoping that there would be just one thing I wasn't ashamed of telling you. So how could I admit to you that I was irresponsible, and reckless, and stupid? Of all the people I love and respect, it's your opinion that matters the most. I can't stand the thought of you thinking so little of me, Nathan. Not you."

"My God, Lex, is that what you think?" Nathan's expression was horrified. "How could I think less of you for this?"

At once, the words he said to his mother

darted through my head. "Don't you?" I challenged. "You never thought this would happen to me."

His expression shifted as he realized what I meant. "Lex, I didn't mean it like that."

"Then how did you mean it?"

"I... Of course I didn't think this would happen to you. You're cautious and critical and paranoid about everything. You're the kind of person that studies other people's lives as if they're cautionary tales and then you avoid their mistakes." With a sigh, Nathan reached out and took my hand. "But you're also passionate, fearless, and damned impatient. I don't think less of you because you're pregnant, Lex. I could never fault you for that. But I am upset that you didn't tell me."

"Why? Why does it matter so much that I waited until I had proof to tell you? What would you have done, Nathan?"

His features remained perfectly solemn as he said, "Well, for one, you would have had someone to hold your hand while you were waiting on that test. And you would have had someone to hold you while you cried about it."

A fist squeezed my heart and my lungs couldn't remember how to breathe. Seconds ticked by as I tried to find something to say. At last, I whispered, "Why do you think I cried about it?"

Nathan's lips twisted into a sad smile and he reached over to push my hair out of my face. "Because if you were happy about it, Lex, you'd have showed up in my classroom to tell me in front of twenty other people. You didn't."

"I'm too scared to be happy," I admitted.

"What are you afraid of?"

"Honestly? I'm afraid of screwing her up."

I'm afraid she's going to be like me.

In an instant, he shook his head. "Never gonna happen."

"Oh yeah? How do you figure?"

"Because I'll be there to stop you," he said with a wide grin.

"Nathan, I..."

"Can't ask me for that? I know. This is me volunteering to take care of your shit. Again. Deal with it. Besides, it's not like I'm the only person involved. My mom is more than onboard and your parents will get over wanting to kill you sooner than you think."

At once, my face paled. "Oh, shit. How do I tell my parents?"

Chapter Sixteen

FATHER AND DAUGHTER

It was more than a little nerve-wracking as I waited for the plane to land. My stomach was doing little flips and I sipped again at the ginger ale the flight attendant had brought me. When the seatbelt light came on, my hands were shaking. Ironically, it wasn't fear that had me on edge, but adrenaline. The kind I had coursing through me when I was expecting a confrontation. At that point, I was wound so tight, I pitied my parents if their reaction was as explosive as I was expecting. Mine would be worse.

Once the plane had landed and we were finally able to disembark, I was missing the snail's pace of my fellow passengers. Moving through the terminal, I gave into almost every ounce of procrastination I could find. Using the bathroom. Buying another ginger ale. Stopping to check the maps of the airport. Anything that reasonably delayed having to see my parents.

It would have worked better if I hadn't missed them so much. While I loved Anne and Josh like family, they weren't replacements for my mom and dad. After all that we had suffered as a family, I'd underestimated how strong our new bonds were. I was eager to have them feel less taut.

Following the signs for baggage claim, I wondered if it was going to be one or both to pick me up. I'd called my mom two nights before to let them know I was coming to report for duty. She promised she'd pick me up at the airport, but my dad hadn't said if he would be coming or not. On the one hand, I understood if he chose not to. I was far from forgiven, and I knew that. Yet, I also hoped I didn't have to be alone with my mother. It would be almost impossible keeping the baby a secret from her.

When I made it to baggage claim, I began to laugh. Mom was standing right by my exiting point, holding a piece of cardboard with 'Ryder

Pride' written on it in construction chalk. It was cast aside as soon as we were able to wrap our arms around each other. For the longest time, neither of us would let go.

"Oh, Lex. You've no idea how happy I am to see you," she sighed as she eased up on her grip.

"I'm happy to see you, too."

"Well, I guess we better grab your things and get going. I left your father in charge of cleaning up. I'm sure you can imagine how well that's going."

"You've taken possession already? That was fast." Normally it took a month just to close on a house.

"It was a foreclosure. We drew up a line of credit with the bank, closed on the house, and took possession the next day. We're actually really impressed with the state of it, for being abandoned."

"It was abandoned? How's the plumbing?"

"That was the first thing we started on."

The entire way to the car we talked about the new house. It was a ranch style with two bedrooms and one bathroom. Perfect for empty-nesters.

As we pulled away from the airport, however, the conversation turned. She started to ask me about Cedar Creek, Anne, and Nathan. I gave her every last detail of prom and she asked how Nathan had managed to live in our old house. When I explained about Oak Grove Investments, her jaw almost fell into her lap. We spent the rest of the ride going over details of the company I owned half of.

When we pulled into the dirt driveway, I had to take a breath. Somehow, I'd managed to make it all the way there without letting it slip. Now I just had to get through the reunion with my dad.

"He won't bite, Lex," Mom said with a small, encouraging smile.

"Not literally, just figuratively," I sighed as I pushed open the car door.

She didn't answer as she popped the trunk and grabbed my duffel bag. As soon as we walked through the door, we grinned at one another as we heard the saw going in the other room. A fine layer of dust drifted through the air, causing me to sneeze.

At once, the saw shut off and my dad appeared in the doorway of one of the bedrooms. In the same second, in the exact same way, we stood there and appraised one another. My eyes traveled over the middle-aged man with the jarhead haircut, flannel shirt, and paint-stained jeans. While I could pick out a few minimal similarities between us, the only real way to tell we were father and daughter was in our bearing. Ryder Pride abounded between the two of us, and it filled the room in that moment as we each debated how best to proceed.

"What do you think so far?" Dad asked, indicating the house.

"It'll be a good starter home. But you'll put some of this land to better use if you add a garage. Make it big enough for a workshop in back and fence in part of the yard and it'll be perfect. Great for young kids and pets."

"Is that all?"

"All that's in the budget, until I get a better idea of what I have left."

Dad looked at Mom. "She's got a point."

"Thought you didn't want to do something big after the last one?" she teased.

He shrugged. "Other than opening it up between the kitchen and living room, there's not a lot to be done here. We could afford it."

"I'll crunch some numbers," she said. Dad and I grinned at each other, knowing it was a yes.

Reaching back into the room, he pulled out the string line. He tossed it to me and said, "Go mark it out and get the measurements for your mom."

"Yes, sir," I said with a grin. "Let me just change real quick."

As I fished my overalls out of the duffel bag, I couldn't help but remember the day Nathan and I were reunited. It seemed they had all kinds of new memories becoming attached to them.

Once I was changed and out in the open air, I breathed a sigh of relief. While I knew my dad hadn't quite forgiven me for my disappearing act, it wasn't hurting him as much as I expected. At least, not that he was letting me see.

"Oh wow. This place is fantastic. How did you find it, Lex?" Mom asked as we followed the hostess to the table I'd reserved.

Survival lesson number one: always spring dangerous news on someone in a public setting. It almost guaranteed that they would subdue their reaction. And with their temperaments, there was no way I was going to tell my parents I was pregnant in a location where they had home field advantage. A fancy restaurant was as close as I could get to neutral territory and I was going to use it.

I smiled at my mom's reaction. "Nathan's been letting me use his computer. I figured that since I'd be out here, I'd treat you guys one night."

After we were seated and given our menus, my dad asked, "Nathan is that one kid that always hung around with you and Matt, right?"

Well, that was one way to remember him. "Yup, he's my best friend."

"I thought that was Matt?"

My mouth fell open. It was surreal to realize that he didn't understand the relationship I had with Nathan. It felt like the whole world knew how close we were. For my dad not to realize it completely baffled me.

At the same time, he only saw what was in front of him. Nathan and I had been friends for years, and he met my parents only a couple of times before I turned thirteen. After my Ascension, Matt was with me as often as Nathan was. And when we left, it was Matt I got phone calls and video chats from. With all of the silence layered around our friendship, I supposed it could look like indifference instead of comfort from an outside perspective.

Shaking my head, I let him have this truth that had somehow been overlooked. "He is, but he's not the one I'd turn to first. Nathan's held that position since we were nine. That'll never change."

My dad nodded, but before he could say more, we were interrupted by the arrival of our waitress. It was just enough of a break that for the rest of dinner we kept the topics light and conversational. It was a pleasant evening right up until we were asked about dessert and all three of us declined.

As we were waiting on the bill, Mom smiled at me and said, "This was a wonderful gesture, Lex. Thank you." I could hear the 'but' hiding on the edge of her sentence.

"You're welcome," I said in the same tone.

"Now are you going to tell us what this is all about?" Dad demanded. Subtlety was definitely not a Ryder family trait.

It's time for the heavy, I thought to myself. Taking a deep breath, I said, "First of all, I want to apologize for how I left. It was disrespectful and I'm sorry for worrying you."

"So why did you do it?"

I debated on how to answer that. Explain about the dream? Or rip off the bandage? One look at my father and I knew he no longer had the patience for this.

"Because I'm pregnant."

When the silence fell between us, it was oppressive. Yet, I monitored every sound. Silverware scraping against plates; wine being sloshed around glasses; the low murmurs of conversation. Despite all of the noise, I knew I could hear a pin drop. I was prepared for anything.

Except what came next.

"We know."

Chapter Seventeen

ALONE

My eyes flew wide open and they shot up to my mother's. "What?" I gasped.

"We know," my dad said in a hard voice.

I was shocked. This was not at all how I expected this conversation to go. Some low volume, meaningful lectures building up to a full explosion back at the house ... I was prepared for that. But for them to know...

"How?" There was only one person who could have told them, and he knew better.

"You wouldn't leave without a reason, Lex. We know you better than that. Something had to have happened for you to take off before we came home," my mom said in a soothing voice.

"And your mind automatically jumped to

that?" I scoffed.

"Not automatically," she hedged. "I was ready to believe that it was the dream that called you home."

"But?"

"But then I gave Grey your letter, and I watched him cry. He disappeared before I could get a reason out of him. We haven't seen him since."

Deductive reasoning. Now that was a Ryder family trait. Lovely.

I took a deep breath and released it nice and slow. "Nor will you."

"What's that supposed to mean?" I barely refrained from rolling my eyes at my dad's accusatory tone. "He is not leaving you to deal with this on your own!"

Just like that, the adrenaline was back. "Don't," I warned him. "Just don't."

"What do you mean? What are you and Grey going to do?" Mom asked, easing into the conversation while my father calmed himself.

"Grey and I are not going to do anything. This is my child and he won't contest that. He can't."

"Of course he can," my father hissed. "He has responsibilities to that child, Alexandria. Hell, he has rights, too!"

"No, Dad, he doesn't." He opened his mouth to argue but I held up a hand to forestall him. "Grey won't contest my decision because he knows it is the right decision. He has sacrificed any rights he has to her in order to give her and me a chance at freedom."

"And I'm sure he's very selfless about it," my dad sneered.

"He is!" I snarled back. "Do you think he wants to wait eighteen years before he's allowed to see his daughter? Or even acknowledge her as his own? Grey did this for the same reason I did: to protect her. She deserves to have a nice, quiet childhood. Something he could never provide for her, but I can. And I will."

Together, my father and I seethed in silence. A volatile aura hovered around us, and our poor waitress stepped into it to leave the bill. I took care of it quickly and the woman darted out of the line of fire.

It was with that simple distraction that my mother casually asked, "It's a girl?"

With my best possible effort, it would have been impossible not to smile at that. I did not give it my best effort. As soon as the words left her lips, I cracked.

"Yes, Mom, it's a girl."

At once, she was beaming. Reaching out, she took my hand in hers before repeating the gesture with my father. "Looks like our family is going to get bigger. Congratulations, Baby Girl."

I squeezed her hand before I reached out for my dad's. He hesitated only a second before taking it. "Thank you. And congrats on being grandparents."

Two days passed by too quickly. Mom had approved of the garage and a fenced-in portion of the yard. Until my dad had it built, my services weren't needed again. In about a month, we'd be able to put the finishing touches on everything else. For that, I'd come to stay for about the last two weeks.

It was just Mom and I again on the ride to the airport. I think my dad opted out because he couldn't stand the idea of there being any semblance of a permanent goodbye between us. And almost as soon as we were alone, she started fretting.

"I know you want to come back in a month, Lex, but are you sure all this traveling is good for the baby?"

"Well, considering my flight attendant was four months pregnant and still flying, I'd say that I've got some time, at least. Besides, you think a Ryder baby can't handle it?"

"So, she is going to have our last name?"

It was kind of funny how accepting she was of this now. After dinner, they'd wanted more details, and then balked at the idea of me knowing the day after I conceived. Add in the fact that I knew it was a girl already and they'd been a little overwhelmed. Somehow, I wasn't surprised that my mom was the first to adjust to reality.

"What kind of question is that?" I scoffed. "She's going to need it when it becomes apparent that she has as much Ryder Pride as her mother."

A wide smile pulled at her lips as we stopped at a red light. For a second, she closed her eyes and shook her head. Then she sighed, "You know, I'm too young to be a grandmother, but I'm really excited about this."

"I wasn't," I admitted. "Honestly, I don't think I am going to get to the point of excited. But the hardest part is over, so I think I can learn to be happy about it."

"What was the hardest part?"

"Admitting it was real. I mean, part of me knew as soon as it happened. It's the reason I left Grant like I did. At the same time, when I got home, it felt like maybe it wasn't true. Like I could just go on living this life and being happy as this person. Then the morning sickness started and I couldn't pretend anymore that this wasn't real. Once I took the test, that was it."

"Will it be hard for you to be happy about this?" she asked with concern.

"I don't know. I suppose it just feels surreal. It might for a while. And I think the biggest issue I have with this is ... this is Grey's baby."

For a second, my mom seemed stunned. "That's the bigger issue?"

"Yeah, I think it is," I murmured. "I don't know why. I just... It's weird, but I feel like this shouldn't have happened. We're only eighteen and we went and created another living being.

At the same time, I feel like maybe that was the whole reason we were together. The second I felt her, Mom, I stopped feeling the way I used to about Grey. I mean, our feelings were dying out a little at a time, anyway. But right then, he almost seemed like a stranger to me. I can't explain it."

It took her a while to respond, but I was surprised when she asked, "Would you rather someone else was the father?"

"No," I groaned. "No, it's not like that. I just... I guess I wish the situation wasn't how it is. I guess I just wish that he could be more involved.

"I don't know, Mom. I never thought I would have kids. But when I hoped for it, I wanted a relationship like yours and Dad's. I wanted a partner like that and I wanted to be able to give my child the kind of life you guys gave to me."

"You never thought you'd have kids? Why?"

A sarcastic smile pulled at my lips. "I'm the Witch of Old Grove Road. That doesn't entice many people into a romantic relationship."

"Matt didn't mind that you were a witch. And you had Grey. Who's to say someone else won't come along who thinks you're amazing?"

Now I remembered why I'd had the 'puppy

love' conversation with my dad. Closing my eyes, I sighed, "I don't want someone who thinks I'm amazing, Mom. I just want something real. Anyway, it's not like I'm on the lookout for anyone. I was just saying that, before all this, I couldn't imagine having kids."

She nodded as if she understood, but I knew she didn't. Which was fine, all things considered. I just wanted her to change the topic.

Then she murmured, "I hate the idea of you doing this alone."

Once more, my mouth dropped. "I'm not alone," I said as if it should be obvious. "I've got Nathan and his parents. I have you and Dad. Matt, eventually, will be upgraded to uncle status. I'm not alone, Mom. The only person I don't have is Grey, and that's because we can't risk it."

"Why is that? Because of his sister?"

"For starters," I said. "More or less, we're not giving Crone's Crescent a chance at her. If they find out about her, they will try to claim her. And if that happens, I will burn all of Grant to the ground before I let them take her."

A tiny smile pulled at her lips as she glanced askance at me. "Talking like a mother already," she teased.

At once, Anne's words to Nathan reverberated in my skull. *Lex has already accepted that she is a mother. Not that she will be; she already is.*

Chapter Eighteen

FRESH WOUND

It was a black night when I returned to Cedar Creek. No moon shone through the thick clouds and rain poured down in a torrent. Mud splashed onto the hem of my dress with each step I took. As I continued down the lane, the oak trees William's father had planted those many years ago towered over the road. Each one felt like a sentry standing guard over me and mine.

Just me, now.

My family was all beyond my reach, and I was finally ready to face the woman who stole them from me. It had been a long time brewing, but the time had come for Margarite and I to settle the cost and pay the balance.

The thoughts continued to churn in my mind as I approached my old home. With the rain washing over *my cloak, I stood at the half-rotted fence and stared at the cottage that had been abandoned for a year. In a flash of lightning, I could see that the thatch roof had a gaping hole above where we used to sit for supper. The chimney stones looked close to crumbling near the top where the sun had done the most damage to the mortar. And ivy leaves had begun their domination of the rest of the house.*

Everything my home had been was gone now.

It was still mine.

Margarite could claim the land now that William was dead and I was gone, but she couldn't deny that it still belonged to me. Each flower in the garden trembled with delight at my presence. The trees hummed in greeting. Even the stones emanated a feeling of joy once I returned to my domain. And far off in the distance, a great stone circle sent out a single, powerful pulse, recognizing me as kin.

I was home, and there was naught Margarite could do about it.

My eyes flew wide right before we pulled into the driveway. Jerking upright, my eyes darted around, taking stock of the rainy evening and

Nathan behind the wheel. Then the brick house loomed above me and I relaxed in an instant.

"Hey, Sleeping Beauty. Glad to be home?"

A yawn ruined my nod as I climbed out of the truck. When I went to retrieve my bag from the narrow backseat, Nathan already had it in hand and was heading for the front door. I rolled my eyes as I followed him inside.

It wasn't the same house that Mary had come home to, but I recognized the feeling the second I crossed the threshold. Every wood beam and brick that made up this house held a part of me, and it recognized that. That was something I really appreciated in that moment.

"Lex? You okay?" Nathan asked as he hung his coat up in the closet beneath the stairs.

"Fine," I remarked, kicking off my shoes and joining him.

"Come on, what is it?"

I let the smile spread. "I'm not allowed to discuss it with you until after graduation. So, until such time, the answer is: I'm fine, Nathan. Don't worry about it."

"That's not fair," he pouted.

"You're the one that made the rules," I countered.

Ignoring that remark, he asked, "So you had another vision?"

I rolled my eyes. "Nothing big. Just a snippet on the way home. I was coming home to the cottage, but it'd been abandoned for a year. I kept thinking about how I was the last one in my family and that Margarite would pay for that. There was also something about her being able to claim the land now that I was gone and..." My mouth fell open.

"And what?"

My eyes raised to his and I murmured, "William was dead. When I came back after a year, William was dead. Which would explain the disarray and the need for vengeance. I think I blamed Margarite for William's death."

"Is there a reason to blame her?"

I shook my head. "I don't know. Memory for another time, I guess."

Nathan mimicked my head shake. "I hate this. I hate not being able to get into this with you yet."

"Don't. This isn't much different from my Alyssa Rice experience. I'll remember what I need to whenever it gets triggered. I'm just really curious why it's all coming to the surface now when it hasn't before."

"Well, maybe it took different triggers before. You said the first memory was at the circle, so the location was the trigger then. What else set them off? The avens flower on prom night..."

"Coming home, tonight. But that's about it," I said.

For some reason, I didn't want to tell him that the anniversary of us saying goodbye was the catalyst for the day Mary met William. Somehow, it seemed bad enough that I had to spoil such a good memory with such a painful one. Nathan didn't need that, too.

Nathan appeared thoughtful for a moment before he turned and headed for the office. "What're you doing?" I asked as I followed him.

"Adding questions to the list."

"Such as?"

"Was Margarite responsible for William's death? And why is this all being triggered now? Also, I'm making a note to look into William's life a little more. You know one thing about record keeping in olden times? They keep track of the money and the land and they don't give a crap about anything else unless it's a gossip pit. If a rich trader dies and his wife vanishes, I'm pretty sure that counts as inciting gossip. Also, you said they had a daughter? What was her name?"

"Mercy. But you won't find any records of her. At least, not in relation to Mary or William."

"Why not?"

With a sigh, I sat on the edge of his desk and asked, "Do you know anything about the spell Freyja used to change your mom and Sarah's identities?"

Nathan shook his head. "I didn't know there was a spell."

I gave him a half-smile. "There is. It was her eighteenth birthday present to the twins. It's why no one in Cedar Creek recognizes them as Fiona and Faylin, despite the fact that they've been here forever. That same spell also changed their birth certificates and identification. With that one spell, Freyja made them into whole new people.

"Well, when I was burning, I performed a similar spell to erase Mercy. No one who had ever met my child could remember me as her mother.

So, you won't find a birth certificate for her."

"Could you please stop that?" he grumbled.

"Stop what?"

"Saying 'I' when you mean Mary."

"Oh. Sorry. It's just, this isn't like being in Victoria's head or Freyja's or Azure's or Alyssa's. It's not like reliving someone else's memories, Nathan. I can't separate myself from her because I was her. So it's more natural for me to say 'I' than 'Mary.'"

"In some ways, I get it Lex. But who you were in another life isn't who you are now. For me, it's confusing."

"Fine. Point taken. I'll try to make the distinction."

"Thank you." Then his head tilted to the side and he asked, "Who's Azure?"

Before I could stop myself, my hand went to my stomach. With a sigh, I said, "A story for another time."

Nathan's gaze rested on my hand and I slowly moved it away. When his eyes raised to mine, there was a distance in them that I didn't like. "Lex, can I ask you something?"

"When have I ever said no to that?"

"It's kinda personal," he amended.

"You can ask me anything, Nathan. I just may choose to delay answering."

He nodded as if that was the kind of answer he was expecting. Then he asked, "How are you dealing with all of this?"

"All of what?"

"Being a single mom."

I wasn't sure what I'd been expecting him to ask, but that wasn't it. Pushing off the desk, I took a seat in the leather office chair. For a second, I chose my wording. Then I said, "When I told my parents about this, they had pretty much the same reaction you did. About the father, anyway. My dad wanted him to be responsible, but my mom was more worried about me doing this by myself.

"You know what I told her? That I wasn't alone. I had them, you, your parents, and Matt, once I tell him. I've got an army of people ready to step in and take any part of this load from me that I need them to. That's family.

"The only person I don't have is her father, and that's in her own best interest. So, to answer your question, I am perfectly fine being a single mother. Now tell me why you're asking."

"Because you don't say his name."

I tried to retain a stoic expression as he continued, "I know I'm not his biggest fan, but I thought you would have mentioned him at least once. Instead, it's like you've taken a vow of silence about him. I don't know. Maybe I would understand it better if he wasn't her father."

It took me a few seconds to gather the words, but at last I said, "Do you remember when I said I would tell you all of the details that you or I could handle? There are some things I just can't handle right now, Nathan. Especially because he is her father. One day I will make good on my promise. I will tell you the whole story. Right now, it's still–"

"A fresh wound?"

"Not in the way you think, but yes, it is. Nathan, I'm carrying the child of a man I never, ever considered spending my life with. He and I weren't even in love with each other when we created this baby. Worse is knowing that I took his child away from him. He knows about her, but he's not allowed to have anything to do with her. That is heartbreaking. It is downright devastating.

"Nathan, I just let the pregnancy become real to me. I'm not ready to relive the details that led to this. And I'm not ready to admit how much of an asshole I am right now. So, yeah, it's a fresh wound."

"I'm sorry, Lex. I shouldn't have asked."

"It's okay that you did," I assured him. "You're my best friend. If I can't talk to you about this, who would I have?"

Nathan forced a smile. "My mom. Your mom. Matt."

"Shut up," I groaned. "Why do you always do that?"

"Do what?"

"Every time I try to show a little appreciation for having you in my life, you add in everyone else."

A grin crept across his face that didn't touch his eyes. "Maybe I don't like being singled out for attention."

"Maybe you should have thought of that before becoming friends with the Witch of Old Grove Road."

"In my defense, I didn't know you'd become

famous when we were nine."

I chuckled to myself at that. "No. No, we did not see that coming."

Leaning against the desk, Nathan wasn't looking at me when he asked, "Would you change any of it?"

"How is that a fair question?" I asked. Rubbing my hands over my face, I eventually sighed, "No, Nathan, I wouldn't."

"Not even Morgan or the trial?"

"Or the baby?" I interjected, remembering what he'd told his mom. He still refused to look at me. "No, I wouldn't change even those things. They are the most difficult and scary things I've had to face in my life, and I can't imagine not having gone through them. Even this. Before, I couldn't imagine being a mother. Now, I can't imagine not having her. This is my life, Nathan."

For better or worse.

Chapter Nineteen

PILLARS AND INCENSE

Now that Anne and Nathan were aware of my current physical state, I found my routine taking on new adventures that I couldn't remember agreeing to. While I still tried to catch up on some of the research on the town and Margarite, I often found myself answering Anne's phone calls around noon. Meeting Nathan at the café had died with the pregnancy reveal, so the three of us often had lunch together either in town somewhere or back at Anne's. And every single time that woman slipped a new article from the internet or a magazine into my purse. Something I would've been more grateful for if it didn't feel so bloody overwhelming.

It was rare when I got a day to myself where

I could focus on other things. The Tuesday after I returned from Colorado, however, I took the morning off and Nathan's afternoon was taken up with Oak Grove Investment business. It was the perfect time to immerse myself in some good, old-fashioned witchcraft.

My energy workings were exceptional, considering how often I flexed that particular muscle. Yet, my general knowledge had suffered over the years. Grey's cousin, Faye, had been right when she told my parents that runes and chakras were forced onto young witches prior to their Ascensions because energy workings would be all they wanted to do afterward. I had been no different, and it was time to fill in some gaps.

Given my extensive knowledge of plants, I skipped that subject and thought about trying my hand at runes. It took one memory of Grey for me to shut that one down. After a while, I found myself immersed in a book about chakras. And the more I read, the more I thought of Caroline Rook.

Around lunchtime, I decided to set the book aside and head to town. Though I'd never admit it, Nathan wasn't wrong to encourage me to get to know the other witches. They would always stay at a distance if I pushed them there, but if I kept pushing them, I would never feel like Cedar Creek was a safe place to raise the baby. I did not take her from her father to put her in a place with the same dilemma.

When I entered *Rook Candle Company* it wasn't totally without merit. In my absence, the stockpile of witchy necessities had drained down to bare essentials. Between Caroline's store and the occult supply shop down the street, I was fairly certain I could gather a regular hoard once more. So as soon as I walked in, I retrieved an old-fashioned wicker basket from a stack by the door and started shopping.

As soon as I entered, Caroline emerged from her curtained-off backroom. A smile spread across her face once she spotted me, but it grew when I immediately turned to the shelves of pillar candles. In seconds, she was at my elbow.

"Do you often perform candle magick?"

"In itself, no. What rituals I do perform, however, I often use candles as intention markers."

"Are you in it for the color or do scents play

a role?"

"Strictly color. Are all of your pillars scented?" I asked, pausing in the act of reaching for another.

"Most of them are, but the tallest ones aren't. As most people are more likely to show them off than burn them, the scents of the smaller ones are apt to please. For those of us that burn through candles in obscene quantities, it's easiest to purchase candles tall enough to last us some time."

As she'd predicted, my basket was full of only the tallest pillars. I shot her a wry smile before I glanced over to her specialty section. My lips pursed as I scanned the available wax figures, though I had no idea what I was looking for.

"Is there a special ritual you have in mind?" Caroline inquired as her gaze followed mine.

"I'm not sure. It was just a thought."

"Oh? Perhaps I can be of some assistance," she offered.

At first, I thought about dismissing her. Then I realized that she might actually know her stuff, and probably better than I did. But I wouldn't know if I didn't give her a shot.

"Okay. What would you recommend for a birthing ceremony?"

"Interesting. Is this ceremony to take place during labor, the actual birth, or over the baby shortly after it emerges?"

"I'm not sure. What are your recommendations for any of those circumstances?"

"Well, during labor would be the hardest to pin down. Is it for the sake of the child, the mother, or both? If it is for the child, I would try a white pillar with probably some silver angel script markings in it. In a general sense, I would say the markings would be an angelic prayer for prosperity, health, patience, endurance, and innocence. The colors, of course, would mean much the same thing as the script.

"Now, if the candle is more for the mother, we go with a lavender or violet candle. Childbirth has to be one of the most spiritual and emotional times of a woman's life, and the candle would acknowledge that. For that, I also wouldn't recommend any script, but I would add a scent. It'll be hard enough on her as is, so it would be helpful to give her something to focus on. With a scent and the color, it engages her senses of sight and smell. Also, I would make the scent something edible to engage her memories so that her sense of taste becomes involved. Anything at all that helps her focus on anything but the pain. And it would have to be a pillar candle so that it can withstand her squeezing it if she has the urge.

"And for both I would recommend a white candle with purple angelic script with the same kind of distractions available."

At once, I shook my head. "I'd have lighted a white candle and called it good," I admitted.

Caroline chuckled. "We all have what we love. If I asked you which plants to grow in my garden to best promote fertility and union, I'm sure you'd have an answer on the tip of your tongue, yes?"

I grinned. "I'd give you a bouquet based on if you wanted a physiological response or a magickal enhancement."

"I have no doubt of it. Just as I can go down to the bakery and ask Basil her best recipe that will eliminate the common cold."

"Careful now, even a kitchen witch will have competition for the best chicken soup recipe," I warned.

"Just you wait until you get that cold. I'll have Basil send over some of hers and you'll never question it again," she promised with a knowing smile.

"I will remember that," I assured her.

"Good. Now, what else are you in need of? Is it pillars alone you were after?"

"Pillars and incense."

Though I didn't much like incense, sometimes it did wonders for a witch's focus during complicated rituals. It was also one of the easiest ways to pay respects for a witch on the move. If any were in a hurry, placing the correct incense upon an altar was almost as good as a full ritual.

Once I'd picked out the sticks that I wanted, I paid Caroline for my merchandise and turned toward the door. That was when she asked me, "Have you met Basil, yet?"

"No, I haven't. I stopped in there a couple days after I came home, but we weren't introduced."

"Is that because she couldn't feel you?" As she said it, Caroline waved a hand in my direction, indicating the mask I'd forgotten was held over my magick.

A tight smile pulled at my lips. "Yes. I learned a few new tricks and was trying them out in a setting I knew would test them. After a while, it just became a habit."

She nodded. "I can understand the usage behind this trick, but I think you should consider having a more formal meeting with the others. So far, they're more than a little jealous of you honoring me with your presence."

"I'll keep it in mind." I had just reached the door when another thought occurred to me. Turning back to face her, I asked, "How do you stay in touch with Nathan? Why?"

"According to him, all formal requests need to be in writing. So, we send him text messages," she remarked with a grin. "As for why ... you're not ready to accept us yet. He has done so. Until you know us or we know you, he is the one trusted on all sides."

"Thank you, Caroline. And I will give that formal introduction some thought."

In fact, I gave it plenty of thought as I meandered up the street to *Blue Moon* which was the standard supply shop for anything that wasn't candles or books. Of course, the way they really drew customers in was the athame display in their window. Even boys would be unable to resist the allure of so many knives.

For a moment, I debated going in and checking it out. There were a few things I could use from there, but I had most of the tools and stones at home to perform any necessary ritual. I also didn't want to give myself away as a witch just yet. After a few moments of debate, I returned to the bike Nathan had let me borrow and headed for the cottage.

I spent the rest of the early afternoon working on a new spell. Before my encounters with Faye and Azure, it hadn't occurred much to me to create my own spells. What I did was more instinct than intention, most days. But the rebounding shield that Faye had created had saved my sanity. Azure's spell to strip witches of their magick had taken years of trial and error for her to master. All of which served to inspire me. If I had the power of a Titan, what could I use it for? What *should* I use it for?

Chapter Twenty

SEE TO BELIEVE

Over the next few weeks, Nathan threw his own rules out of the window and became more than a little invested in the Mary Sullivan mystery. So invested that his finals were suffering. When his final grades came in, he was riding a steady C average in most of his classes. Anne wasn't pleased, but she also couldn't complain since he wasn't headed off to college like Tyler.

The day of his graduation ceremony, it felt like a weight had been lifted from both our shoulders. The last impediment to us spending time together was finally gone. Which added to our codependency in unhealthy ways, I had to admit. To give us time to ease into it, I did the only thing I could, and at eight weeks pregnant, I returned to Colorado to help my parents finish off the house.

As soon as I arrived, I wanted to turn around and go right back home.

Instead of greeting me with a sign made of cardboard and chalk, my mom pulled a book out from behind her back when she saw me. It was the number one bestseller for women in my condition, and I loathed it on sight. A fact she took note of as I approached, causing her to grin like a fox.

"You can't expect me not to have fun with this," she remarked when we'd finished hugging.

"No, I get it," I said with a sigh.

"Yet, you're not amused."

I shook my head. "Sorry, Mom."

She rolled her eyes as we headed toward the parking garage. "What's wrong?"

"Nothing."

"Lex." It was her no-nonsense voice and I sighed in response.

"Sorry, it's just... You're the only one excited about this."

Her eyebrows lifted and I hurried to look away. "Really? No one else?"

"Not really."

"Okay, are they genuinely not excited or are they hiding it from you because you're not?"

I had to think about that for a minute. Was it likely? I doubted it. But was it possible? Absolutely. That is exactly the kind of thing Anne would do if she thought I needed just the bare minimum. Which I did.

"Okay, that might be it," I conceded.

"You're not excited about this at all, are you?" she asked in a lower tone.

"Mom, I don't even want to be having this conversation right now."

"Fine. Fine. But just so you know, I am. So you might have more to take home with you than you anticipated."

My eyes widened as they shot to my mother. "What did you do?"

"You'll see." Then she flashed me an unrepentant smile.

When we arrived at the house, I found out what she meant the moment I opened the door to the guest room. All across the foot of the bed, she had arranged swaddling blankets, onesies, outfits, and even shoes that the child wouldn't be able to fit until she was three months old.

"Mom," I groaned, hiding my face in my hands.

"You were duly warned."

"It's a good thing I pack light."

With a sigh, I began clearing the bed of the baby items. When I got to the little foil balloon she'd left on the nightstand that said 'Congratulations! It's A Girl!' I shot her a disgusted look. She didn't think it was so funny when I threatened to pop it. When all of the stuff had been relocated to the dresser, I flopped down on the bed, leaving just my feet hanging off the edge. A minute later, my mom joined me.

"Okay, now I really need to know what's going on. It's one thing not to be thrilled, Lex, but you seem miserable."

"Only when people bring it up," I mumbled into the pillow.

"Honey, you're having a baby. It's not exactly a subject you can avoid forever."

Turning my head to face her, I gave it my best effort to shrug. "It's been working so far."

Her eyes narrowed as she studied me. "How many people know you're pregnant?"

I held up a hand and started ticking off

names. "Besides you and Dad, there's Grey, Nathan, Anne, and Josh."

"Six people? Lex, you're already two months. By the time I was that sure about you, my whole family had received a card in the mail to announce it."

"I haven't seen Matt, yet. I'm not telling anyone until I can tell the last musketeer, okay?"

"That's the lamest excuse you've got? You video chat every week."

"I'm not telling him this over video chat."

"Why not?"

"You know why not."

"No, I don't. Now tell me why you're stalling."

"Because," I snapped, "the second I tell everyone, they're all going to start looking at me different. They're going to stop seeing Lex and start seeing an incubator. Mom, I just got home. I'm finally getting my life back. I'm not ready to trade in *my* life for *our* life yet. I thought I could resign myself to it after I took the test, but if it feels like resignation, then maybe I'm not ready to have a kid."

My mother was silent for a moment before she murmured, "There's always adoption."

"Don't be ridiculous, I'm not giving my kid away. I'm just frustrated because she's taking over my life and I am not prepared for that."

"You know, I thought I pretty much had this mom thing down ... for about ten minutes after you were born. Thank you, once again, for proving to me that I have no clue how to make you feel better."

I took the pillow next to me and hit her in the face with it. Before she could grab it, I did it again. The third time, she just let me.

"Was that helpful?" she asked when I set it aside.

"A little bit, yeah."

"So, what do you want to do, Lex? Never talk about it?"

"No. Of course not. I'm just so used to not talking about it, that you being this excited is a bit of a shock. You know, I thought you and Dad were going to skin me alive for this."

"We considered it, but that's too much work. Messy, too. Easier to stand back and laugh as you struggle through everything you put us through."

"Oh Gods, I hope not!"

"You'll be okay, Lex. Motherhood is a challenge, no doubt. But when have you ever backed down from one of those?"

"I'm not backing down. I'm just whining," I clarified.

"Yes, you are. And on that note, maybe you should sleep it off. Emerge when you're hungry. The yard can wait until tomorrow."

My mom didn't wait for a reply as she scooted off the bed. Before she could leave, however, I had to ask, "Mom? Will I be happy?"

"Baby Girl, I don't think you can even imagine how happy you'll be until the second she's in your arms. There's nothing more sacred in this world than that bond."

What she didn't say was that there were many women who didn't feel that way. What I didn't say was that I was afraid that I was one of them.

After my nap, I headed to the kitchen. Mom was in the middle of chopping vegetables and I decided to get started on the salad. For a while, we worked in silence with only a little commentary on my nap and the improvements made to the floor plan. Even then, I could feel an unspoken question hanging in the air.

"Lex, I'm going to ask you something out of pure curiosity, so don't take it the wrong way."

I couldn't even pretend to be surprised. With a wave of my hand, I motioned for her to go ahead.

"Tell me the truth, now. If you didn't have responsibilities in Cedar Creek, would you and Grey still be together?"

My first instinctive reaction to that was to laugh. Hard enough to cause my mother to roll her eyes at me and go back to her roast. Really, it was answer enough, but it also got me thinking.

If I had nothing waiting for me in Cedar Creek, what would be different? If I wasn't leaving and I told Grey that I was pregnant, would we have stayed together? No. We no longer felt the same for one another and we'd tallied up our own baggage that interfered with our ability to trust one another.

But it would have affected how we raised our daughter. Even were we not together, we would have a detailed custody arrangement with alternate holidays in place. At this point in time, he'd have already started on the nursery. We'd be fighting over names. I would have to talk him out of purchasing every stupid thing they peddle to overprotective parents. And he would be a thousand times more excited than I was. For this baby.

There had been another he wasn't as excited about. When he was only fifteen, he learned he was going to have a son, and he'd resigned himself to marrying his baby's mother. What had begun as a sense of duty and moral obligation had transformed into love, devotion, and hope for him. He was reluctant to have a child at such a young age, but Grey was absolutely in love with his son when his sister murdered the child.

If anyone knew what I was going through, it was Grey. And I couldn't call him to discuss it. I couldn't rub salt in his wounds. This was something I would have to overcome on my own.

Shaking my head, I asked my mother, "Did you like Grey that much?"

She shrugged. "You were happy with him, Lex. After what we'd been through and all the pain, it was like watching a miracle occur before our eyes. You weren't on the sidelines anymore, and you were enjoying your life. I will be grateful to Grey for the rest of my life for giving you that joy."

A smile pulled at my lips as I remembered every instant that she was talking about. And she was right. Grey had made me happy. He'd taught me to live in the moment and reminded me that my magick could be enjoyed. I'd also learned that it was okay to rely on someone else, even if they were only temporary additions.

"Honestly, Mom, there would have to be a lot more missing factors for Grey and I to make a life together. As happy as I was with him, it's nothing compared to being home."

"I hope that's true, Baby Girl. But it's something I'll have to see to believe."

"You will," I assured her.

Chapter Twenty One

CRAZY

A week flew by faster than I thought possible. My dad had the garage and fence finished—chain link since white picket was too expensive—and had even added a covered walkway between the back door and the garage. What I had left in my landscaping budget was going straight to paving stones. Concrete may have been cheaper, but to pour it and brush it right to prevent cracking would have cost us more in time and effort than we wanted to deal with. After we were finished laying the pavers, I had just enough left to ease a few flowering bushes into place and added an elevated flower bed between the gate and garage. Long before my two weeks deadline, the house was officially finished.

"I say we enjoy it for a few days, and then throw her on the market," Mom said, raising her wine glass to me and my dad that night.

"Sounds good to me," I said with a grin, raising my own glass of lemonade.

Dad valiantly tapped his beer bottle against Mom's glass, took a swig, and announced, "I'm getting pictures tomorrow and taking them to an agent."

While Mom and I laughed in the moment, we knew he was serious. No later than eight thirty the next morning, he knocked on my door and told me to clean up the room so he could get a photo. I did as he asked before marching over to the couch and passing out there for another few hours. It was almost noon by the time I woke up.

"Ah, pregnancy fatigue. What's that like again?" my mom teased as she sipped her tea at the kitchen island.

"I've slept probably twelve hours, cumulatively, and I'm still tired," I groaned.

"See, I don't remember having that with you. Lots of kicking. Having to pee every five minutes. And you were adamant about being fed often. But tired? Not really. I had to sleep in new and interesting positions or else you wouldn't settle down, though."

"She has to be taking after her father then, because I am tired all the time."

Before she could respond, my phone began to ring. Pulling it out of my pocket, I smiled as I saw the name on the screen. For a second, I held it up so she could see before I flipped it open.

"Hey, Nathan. What's up?"

"Lex, I think I did something … crazy."

I snapped the phone closed and let it drop onto the counter. My mom watched with wide, alarmed eyes as I turned on my heel and headed for the front door. She moved into the doorway of the kitchen, making sure to keep an eye on me, as I reached the front door and yanked it out of the way.

"You brat," I pretended to scold as Nathan pocketed his cell.

Without pause, I took a step forward and threw my arms around his neck. In that instant, I was overwhelmed with a feeling of security. A contented sigh escaped me and I hugged him a little tighter. It felt like being home just having his arms around me.

Nathan chuckled at my reaction, but didn't let go. When I finally took a step back, I kept my hands on his forearms to prove to myself that this was real. "What are you doing here?"

His smirk was conniving as he said, "I know something you don't know."

At once, my eyes dropped to the computer bag hanging at his side. "That good or that bad?"

"I'll let you be the judge. But it's big."

"Big enough for you to fly across the country to show me?"

"Told you it was crazy."

"Just a bit," I assured him. "Well, come on in. Mom is boring holes in my back trying to get a good look at you." I shot a glance over my shoulder to watch my mom stick her tongue out at me. Chuckling to myself, I took his hand and dragged him to the kitchen.

As soon as we walked in, my mom surprised us both when she hugged him. "Nathan, how are you?"

"I'm good, Mrs. Ryder."

"Don't even," she reprimanded him. "If Lex

can call Anne by her name, you can most certainly call me Mel."

He grinned. "Yes, ma'am."

"Would you like something to drink? Are you hungry? I just finished making lunch," she said, already moving toward the refrigerator.

"He'll have a water," I told my mom while I headed to the cupboard. Nathan knew better than to protest while I fixed him a plate. When I set it down on the island, I shot him a grin. "We don't set the table in this house."

Before he could respond, my mom asked, "So, Nathan, what brings you all the way out here? Lex didn't tell us to expect you."

"Well, it was kind of a spur-of-the-moment decision. I actually didn't tell Lex I was coming. Sorry for the intrusion. I just thought it'd be fun to surprise her."

"It's fine. We welcome the surprise," she insisted.

"And she's still rabidly curious. So go ahead and tell her about it."

Nathan shot a glance at me before he told her, "Well, when Lex got home I was able to show her Morgan's family tree and it led back to a name she recognized. Which started us on a mystery."

"Do I want to know what this mystery is?" she hedged.

"Something a bit similar to Alyssa Rice." For now, that's all she needed to know.

"Ah," she said, seeming to agree with my decision.

We were both saved from awkward follow-up questions by the sound of my dad's truck pulling into the garage. Mom looked between Nathan and I for a moment before she announced that she was going to tell him we had a visitor. We had just enough time to nod before she was gone.

"Is it really okay that I'm here? I'm sorry. I wasn't thinking when I made the trip."

"Nathan, it's fine. You're not intruding. And I was coming home in a couple of days anyway. Now, show me what you've found."

Shaking his head, he tried to hide the grin as he turned on his computer and started opening documents. "Now, I'm going to warn you, it's not a lot. Record keeping back then was pretty much nonexistent unless you were important. But what I did find were several journal entries preserved from the time period."

My chest tightened. "Why?"

"Cedar Creek had more than one witch trial in its history. Nothing like the carnage in Salem, but enough that a local preacher kept a diary of incidents. Because of their relationship to witches, they were preserved and copies of the pages made it onto the internet. There's one thing in particular I thought you'd like to see."

When I pulled up the document he described, the first thing I saw was Margarite's name. The next thing I saw was the date she was hanged.

Chapter Twenty Two

LOVE LIKE THAT

It was the middle of the night and all through the train people were sleeping. Including Nathan. When he had suggested the train ride, it had been a cool idea. It was something neither of us had ever done, so it was an adventure. The only issue being that it would take almost two days to get home, instead of a few hours. It'd also taken quite a bit of planning, considering the train lines didn't run straight across the country, and instead several would have to be taken to get us home. All the same, it was an experience I was glad to have.

Leaning my head against the window, I watched shadow after shadow flicker by on the other side of the glass. The dim lights of the cabin reflected my face back at me. After a few minutes,

I couldn't take staring at myself any longer and looked away.

My eyes landed on Nathan and I smiled. Like most people, he looked different as he slept. His face was more relaxed and took on a younger quality. For the first time since I'd known him, he looked truly at peace. Nothing was weighing on his mind, and his anxieties had been put to bed. In that moment, he was vulnerable.

While I watched him, I couldn't help but remember the past few days with my parents. The day he arrived, he'd explained that he planned on getting a hotel room. An idea that was shot down by every member of my family. Even my dad. While he wasn't allowed to share the guest room with me, my dad made it plain that Nathan could at least take the couch. When I offered to take the couch in his stead, both men refused outright. Apparently being pregnant also made me fragile in their eyes.

Not that it worked out in their favor. On the second night of his stay, we'd all stayed up watching movies. Halfway through one, my eyes started drifting closed. After jolting awake for the third time in ten minutes, Nathan had chuckled and suggested I go to bed. I'd tried to be stubborn about it for a while, but I knew I couldn't fight it any longer. Instead of listening to him, I grabbed a pillow from the end of the couch and tossed it in his lap before lying down. Through a yawn, I informed him that he could carry me to bed like he always did. Nathan had laughed and called me a brat. Then he began running a hand over my hair and I was asleep within seconds.

When I woke up the next morning, it was to find that no one had tried to move me. Instead, someone had given him a pillow of his own and had thrown a blanket over me. I was starting to lose track of how many times we fell asleep on the couch together.

I hadn't realized how much I wanted to have that experience with Nathan and my parents. The fact that it seemed so easy and natural made me feel almost giddy. It had been one thing when Anne welcomed me into her family, but to have my parents return the sentiment with Nathan was more than I'd ever hoped for.

With a contented smile, I stood up from my chair and climbed into the bed beside him.

As soon as I got comfortable, I felt him move. A moment later, Nathan's arm wrapped around me and his chest came to rest against my back. In seconds, I was out.

My fingers shook as I once again adjusted the vase my mother had given to us upon our wedding day. The avens flowers almost didn't have stems long enough to put them in a vase, but as they were sentimental to me, I required them always to be in my home. Today was certainly one for sentiment.

With Mercy away at my mother's, it would provide the opportunity to deliver the good news to my husband. Then we would have even more time to celebrate without interruption. As I thought it, a hand strayed to my womb, desperate to feel the pulse of life within me.

All of a sudden, a piercing sensation shot through my chest. I collapsed against the table with a cry, knocking over the vase. Glass shattered, the water pooling across the wood and carrying the flowers over the edge. Trembling, I sank to the floor of our house. Heat smothered me so that I could not breathe, yet ice filled my veins and caused my heart to seize.

Closing my eyes, I reached for the magic. I begged for it to examine my body and reveal what ailed me. When it had done so, I was shocked to know that it found nothing. Before I could urge it into a second inspection, it whispered a name in my ear and a cry erupted from my soul.

"No," I whimpered. "Not him. No."

In my desperation, I no longer cared to control the magic. As it gathered around me, I gave it one command. So long as the magic brought me to my husband, I had no care for what else it chose to do.

In the blink of an eye, I had gone from kneeling on my cottage floor to sitting in a dry riverbed. Scrambling to my feet, I whirled in place. The breath was knocked out of me the moment I saw him. Having fallen from above, William had landed in such a way that his thigh was caught between the iron jaws of the bear trap the men had set earlier in the season. From the amount of blood pooling around him, I knew I did not have much longer with my husband.

I rushed to his side. Kneeling beside him, I pulled William's head into my lap.

"Mary? You are here? How?"

"Hush, my love. I am here. I am here," I said through my tears. Leaning over him, I placed my lips

to his cheek.

"Should not be," he said before a cough silenced him.

"Let me help you, my love. Let me—"

"No," he growled.

"William, I can—"

"No. Too dangerous."

"I cannot lose you!"

For a moment, I almost did not see him beckoning me closer. When I did, I lowered my head so that my ear was next to his lips. In a rasp, he confided one word. "Pushed."

My entire body stiffened. "Who?"

William shook his head and I could feel the beginning of a cold, hollow rage pushing through my body. If he refused to tell me, it said all I needed.

"Margarite." It wasn't a question. But when William gave the barest nod, the magic knew what I intended to do.

"Keep safe," William urged through another bout of coughing.

It was a promise I dared not make him. What was to come could claim my life, but I knew before its end that I would take hers. If it took every ounce of power I possessed, Margarite would pay for this.

"Mary?"

"Yes, my love?"

"This is not our end. We shall meet again, my beloved."

It was the most he dared to say and I knew why. I had gotten to him much too late. His skin was already growing cold and clammy. Too much blood had been lost, and he was losing more as each second passed. Even if the magic allowed me to heal his wounds, it was still possible that he could not recover his strength enough to survive such loss. And if the magic did allow it, there was still Margarite to contend with. Now that I had two young ones amidst this life, there were some risks I could not yet take.

Thus, I sat there and shared declarations of love with my husband as he bled into the earth. I was with him when his last breath was taken, and it was I who closed his eyes. At last, the pain made way for the magic and I found myself sobbing on my cottage floor.

William did not know that I was carrying his son.

My eyes snapped open and I launched off the bed in the same instant. Throwing myself into the bathroom compartment, I began vomiting into the toilet. When my stomach was empty, I sat back against the wall and let myself cry.

A few minutes passed before I heard Nathan's timid voice ask, "Lex? You okay?"

It took a minute to force words out through my raw throat. "Yeah. Be out in a minute."

Pushing myself up onto my shaky legs, I leaned over the vanity and turned on the water. After rinsing out my mouth, I took a shot of mouthwash and swished it around until all I could taste was mint. Then I wiped the tear stains off my face, blew my nose, and exited the bathroom.

In the bed, Nathan was holding himself up on one arm, staring at me. As soon as he saw my face, he pulled back the covers and patted the mattress. I crawled into the bed and let him wrap his arms around me.

I tried to focus on him. How his arms felt. That feeling of home whenever he was close. His scent. Anything and everything about him that would help distract me from the memory. At the same time, I kept one hand pressed against the spot where I knew my child was. She was safe, and that was another life. It was a mantra I kept repeating as I fought the sobs.

In a way, I still grieved for that loss. Not in the same way I grieved for Morgan, but in a way similar to how I had grieved the separation from Nathan. It was a more acute, less final kind of pain, and that was what made it so poisonous in its delivery. At the same time, I was inclined to agree with William. A love like that didn't have an ending; only several new beginnings. And nothing would be allowed to stand in its way.

Nathan had far more patience than I could ever possess. Instead of waiting until I was calmed down to wheedle answers out of me, he didn't say a word about it for the rest of the trip. He didn't ask between trains or on the cab ride home. Even when we reached the house, he didn't bombard me with questions as soon as the door closed. When he suggested that I rest a while and take a nap, I almost exploded with the information.

"Margarite killed William."

He didn't ask me the obvious question, 'How do you know?' Instead, he said, "That explains why Mary betrayed her. How did he die?"

"A bear trap. Margarite pushed him off an embankment right into the trap the men had laid earlier that season. The trap snapped on his thigh and shredded his femoral artery. He bled out right before my eyes."

Nathan's eyes snapped to mine. "You were there?"

A humorless smile spread across my face. "First time I ever teleported. Turns out it's a talent that follows me into every life."

"Did you see Margarite push him?"

I shook my head. "No. Now that's the really messed up part. I was in the cottage, trying to make everything perfect so that I could tell him I was pregnant."

Nathan's jaw dropped. "Mercy?"

I shook my head. "She was at her grandmother's. This one was a boy."

"So, Mary had two children. But she was only concerned for her daughter when she died?"

I nodded.

"Which means her son didn't survive or she left him somewhere he'd be safe. This also explains why she vanished the day after William's funeral."

Leaning against the wall, I took a breath and let it out slowly as my mind picked through the less painful details of the memory. "You know what's funny? I knew it was Margarite the second it happened. There was no question in my mind that she did it. Which means she did something prior to William's murder that made me certain she was capable of it."

"You think she killed before?"

"Yeah, I think so."

"Lex, I can try to find something, but..."

"I know. Record keeping back then was not a priority. I'm just glad you found what you did. Thank you, Nathan."

"Thank me when it's over."

I snorted. "And when do you think that'll be? This isn't like Alyssa. I can't just remember everything by touching something of Mary's."

Nathan's head tilted to the side a little. "Have you tried it?"

"I've been in the cottage for years and never once got a glimpse of Mary's life," I reminded him.

"But you weren't trying to remember any-thing back then. You had one mystery at a time, right? This is the next one. So why not try to solve this one how you solved the others?"

"You're making too much sense, you know that right?" I pretended to grumble.

"And you're ready to fall asleep standing up. Go take a nap. I've got things to follow up on anyway."

I grinned at him and headed for the couch.

"Seriously? You have a bed upstairs."

"But the couch is closer. Go do your thing. I'll be here when you're done."

Nathan rolled his eyes and headed for the office.

Chapter Twenty Three

BETTER

By the beginning of July, I was coming in at eleven weeks pregnant and the thickening around my middle was more felt than seen. It also heralded the end of my nausea; something Nathan and I would have celebrated if we didn't feel like it would jinx us. That, alone, would have made it the best week of my pregnancy. Yet, there was one more thing to make it even better.

Matt was on his way.

For the past few weeks, we'd been video chatting on Nathan's computer, and I'd urged him to come for a visit. Well, after much prodding and pleading, he was finally coming home for the holiday. Which meant the last musketeer was about to get the big news.

Nathan and I were waiting at the airport and I was practically bouncing with anticipation. I was trading off between pacing and rocking back on my heels. The whole time, Nathan watched me with an amused smirk.

"You weren't this excited to see me," he pretended to pout.

I rolled my eyes. "I was scared shitless to see you. Pregnant, remember?" Unconsciously, I began to rub the scars on my left arm. Lowering my voice, I murmured, "And the last time I saw Matt, I tried to kill him."

Without a word, Nathan reached over and took my left hand in his. I let my other hand drop away from the ravaged skin. As they both often tried to remind me, that was all in the past now. With the three of us back together, I might actually be able to keep it there.

A few minutes later, I spotted Matt heading toward us. In an instant, I was back up on the balls of my feet and waving my arm above my head. Matt grinned and began to mimic me. As soon as he was close enough, he dropped his bag and opened his arms to me. Letting go of Nathan's hand, I stepped into the embrace.

"It is so good to finally see you," Matt said a second before he lifted me up.

I laughed but Nathan's anxiety spiked. Taking pity on him, I told Matt, "Okay, you can put me down now."

Setting me back on my feet, Matt held me at arm's length and made a show of examining me. "Well, your hair is back to normal. You still have a hole in your nose. And let's see," he said, raising my hand above my head and pushing me into a twirl. "Yup, the tattoo is still there. Perfect. Just how I pictured you."

"As opposed to what? The video chat two days ago?" I chuckled as he pulled me into another hug.

"Exactly," he said, letting go of me. Grinning at Nathan, he asked, "How've you been?"

A knowing smile pulled at his lips as he answered, "Better."

The same smile appeared on Matt's face and I knew this was something between the two of them when he answered, "I bet. And how are you handling the lightning bug over here?"

It was our turn to share a smile. "We're doing okay."

Looking at them both, the nostalgia filled me. It had been far too long since the last time we were together, and I could feel my hormones responding to that. Tears filled my eyes and I turned quickly to hide them.

"Alright, let's get going. It's a long drive home."

"Lead the way," Matt said, picking up his bag and falling into step behind us.

As it turned out, the ride home wasn't as long as I could have wished. Too soon we were pulling into Cedar Creek, and Matt grew quiet. He hadn't been gone as long as me, but it had still been a while since his family moved.

We headed to the house first to drop off Matt's stuff. Then we started walking. For the rest of the day, Nathan and I dragged Matt around town to check out everything he'd been missing. I even took him to Basil's and bought us a giant cinnamon roll to share. Later, we headed back to the house so that Nathan and I could start cooking.

It was a full family dinner that night. Even Nathan's brother, Tyler, and his girlfriend showed up. I was soon surprised by how friendly

Tyler and Matt were with one another. When Nathan noticed, he explained in a low voice that Matt had created a bridge between the brothers while I was away. While it hadn't made Nathan and Tyler the best of friends, they both felt like Matt was part of the family.

After dinner, Matt and Tyler even made plans to hang out for a while. I pouted. Nathan told him to meet us at the lake. There wouldn't be any kids there this time of night, and I could chase off any lingering teens.

As Nathan and I were walking through the woods, I said, "I don't think I like sharing Matt with your brother. I don't even like your brother."

Nathan shoved his shoulder against mine. "You've been getting along with him since the summer started."

"Because he's too afraid to talk to me," I snickered.

It had been funny the first night Tyler walked into our kitchen and found me chopping vegetables at the island. I'd glanced over my shoulder, said hello, and gone back to what I was doing. He'd repeated the greeting and hadn't said a word for the rest of the evening. After that, it'd been easier because he brought Kelsi along. She and I actually got along pretty well.

"True," he conceded. "But Matt and Tyler hit it off, so what can you do?"

"Tell Tyler he can have him tomorrow," I muttered.

"Are you really that upset?"

"No. Yes. I just ... today felt like old times. Better, even, because we're not dealing with a murder investigation hanging over our heads. I miss the three of us being together. You guys are the people I've chosen in my life, and it feels better when I get to be with both of you."

Nathan nodded. "I get it, but you're not his only friend. Matt is popular around here. You'll get to see him the most, but that doesn't mean you'll get to see him all the time," he warned.

"I'm okay with that. Just as long as I get him tonight."

"And you will. As soon as they finish their beer run."

My mouth fell open. "That's where they went?"

Nathan laughed. "Tyler just turned twenty-one. What did you expect?"

I was dumbfounded by my own stupidity. "How did that not occur to me?"

"Because you can be so focused on some things that others fly straight over your head."

"Shut up," I grumbled as we hit the sandy edge of the lake.

Not too long after Nathan and I lit a fire, a truck pulled up. We heard talking and laughing as the passenger side door opened. Then it slammed shut and the truck pulled away as Matt made his way toward us. Sure enough, there were two six-packs in his hands.

Reaching the fire, he held up his cache like it was a prize. "Now, I know this is a little late, but I did promise that we would celebrate your birthday how we should have celebrated your Sweet Sixteen. That being said, this is cheap beer because it's all a broke college kid can afford. And this is nothing like we would have done for your sixteenth. Sorry."

He dropped into the sand and separated two cans. Matt passed one to Nathan before he turned and tried to hand me the other. I had to fight the grin.

Shaking my head, I said, "No thanks, I can't."

"Come on, Lex. I'm just trying to make up for lost time here."

"And I appreciate that, but I can't drink that crap."

His eyes narrowed. "Are you a wine person?"

"Don't know. Never tried it," I laughed.

"Have you tried anything?"

"Nope."

"Well then, try some of this and see if you like it."

Nathan and I glanced at one another before he hid his grin in a drink of his beer. Smiling wide at Matt, I repeated, "Sorry, I *can't*."

It took him a second to catch on, but when he did, his eyes shot to my stomach. Slowly, I moved a hand to cover my womb and had the pleasure of watching his jaw drop. "Holy shit. Are you kidding me right now?"

I couldn't hold back the laugh any longer. "It's a girl."

Matt let loose a long whistle as his eyes darted to Nathan and back to me. "Hot damn. I guess congratulations are in order. Good luck on all of your parenting endeavors," he said, raising his beer in a toast to me. Noticing my empty hands, he cursed again. "We don't have anything for you to drink."

"It's fine. I can drink from the lake if I get thirsty."

"The hell you will," Nathan growled.

"Why not?" I scoffed.

"Uh, let's see, two decaying bodies mean anything to you?"

"Whoa, what?" Matt asked, sitting up straighter.

"Magick, Nathan. Their bodies didn't harm anything."

Nathan pushed himself to his feet. "I'm running up to the cottage. Do not let her drink from the lake just to spite me."

Matt raised his hands in the air. "Do I look like I'm about to get in the middle of this? You can continue this lovers' spat on your own."

Rolling his eyes, Nathan ignored me calling his name as he headed up Old Grove Road. Once he was out of sight, I released a sigh and looked at Matt. All of a sudden, he wasn't in the mood to joke.

"Okay, before he comes back, I've got a few questions."

"And he can't be here for those?"

Ignoring me, he asked, "Who is the father?"

My body stiffened. "You did not just ask me that."

"Don't get offended. I was just wondering if it was your ex."

"Of course it was my ex, you idiot. I've only been with one man."

"Okay. So, does he know? What's going on there?"

"Yes, he knows. And there's nothing going on there. I left him. That's all there is to it."

"Good."

"Good?"

"It would just complicate things more. How did Nathan take it?"

"A lot worse than you just did."

"But he's okay with it now, right?"

"Yeah, I guess. I don't know. We haven't talked about it much."

"Lex, you're pregnant. How have you not talked about this?"

"Matt, I'm going to have the rest of my life to devote to this child. I can take these last few months for myself."

Matt tilted his head back and stared at the sky. I could read his lips when he mouthed, 'What am I going to do with you?' Taking a breath, he looked back at me. "So, your ex knows and he's not in the picture. Nathan is in the picture, but you don't talk about it. What kind of sense does that make, Lex?"

I would never admit to him how hard that hit me.

Beside me, Matt shook his head. "You may want to think that these last few months are about you, Lex, but you know you're the only one who sees that. Nathan's a planner. Do you really think it's just about you now? You are adding one more person to his family. Nathan takes care of his family."

Matt waited until I would meet his gaze before he finished, "Just answer one question for me. I'm the uncle, right? But what is Nathan?"

I didn't answer.

Chapter Twenty Four

CRUSH

As Nathan predicted, I didn't get to keep hold of Matt for long. For the rest of the week there were long stretches of time where he was hanging out with the other friends he had left behind. While it bothered me a little, it also had a nice sense of normalcy to it. Almost as if this was what our future held, once he was out of school and he could come back home. It would take years, and I doubted he'd settle back in Cedar Creek for some time. Yet, in a way, we all knew that this was where he'd land when he finally decided to settle down.

Also, in an attempt to establish some normalcy in our lives, Nathan and I ended up at the cottage that Saturday. While I kept the house tidy every day, Saturday was the day that I did a full clean on it. Afterward, I always spent some time in the garden. It was around then that Nathan appeared. While he had no interest in gardening, he was happy to hang around and keep me company while I worked.

I was already immersed in the weeding when he arrived with a book in hand. Turning, I smiled at him over my shoulder before returning to my work. Silently, he stretched out on the bench and began reading in the sunshine. For almost an hour, we continued on our tasks without a word.

At last, I took off the gloves and pushed to my feet. Stretching my arms above my head, I glanced over my shoulder at him. "What're you reading?"

"A really boring book," he grumbled, turning the page.

"Then why are you reading it?"

"To learn things."

"Learn what things?" I asked, turning around to fully face him. Then my jaw dropped. "Is that the book my mom gave me?"

The title of the book jumped out at me—not that the image of the heavily pregnant woman on the cover didn't give me a clue. Of course, the most surprising part was realizing that Nathan was over halfway through it.

"Why are you reading that?" I demanded, drawing closer.

"We've got a kid on the way. At least one of us should read it."

My first thought was that Matt was right. My second was...

"I should have known," I murmured to myself.

Nathan's eyes raised to mine. "What?"

I was so stunned that the words fell from my lips. "I'm in love with you."

It took all of two seconds for my brain to catch up with my mouth. In the meantime, I watched as Nathan's lips parted and his eyes grew wide. And as soon as reality fully slammed into me, my face turned red and I darted toward the cottage.

I didn't make it far before Nathan's hand encircled my upper arm and he spun me around to face him. He brought his other hand up to caress my cheek. There was only a second for me to notice it before I felt him pull my face toward his. Then Nathan kissed me.

That kiss could have gone on forever and it still would not have been long enough. Nothing in my life had felt as right as that moment when his lips met mine. After everything we'd endured together, I now knew it was for this. For the first time in my life I knew exactly what perfect felt like.

The second time came after we paused for breath and he leaned his forehead against mine. "I love you, Lex. Always have."

"Why didn't you tell me?"

Nathan smiled and he stared over my head as he chose his words. Then he met my gaze with a knowing expression. "I was scared shitless. Best friend, remember?"

Shaking my head, I couldn't help but laugh at that. Of course, I would have laughed just to laugh. In that moment, I couldn't imagine being any happier.

"How long have you known?"

He shrugged. "I had a crush on you when we were nine. Realized I loved you when we were thirteen."

"And you never told me," I pretended to admonish.

"You didn't feel the same."

On the one hand, I couldn't deny that. While I'd formed an attachment to Nathan at a young age, it was never a crush. Yet, after my Ascension, I also couldn't remember when it didn't feel like love. Back then, I had chalked it up to him being my best friend. Even when his ex implied it, all I could think was that she was confusing loyalty for love. Instead, I really was as blind as they all believed. But so was he.

"Nathan, I've been in love with you for years. It just took me until now to realize it."

As I said it, his head tilted to the side a little. "Why now?"

I chuckled a little before I met his gaze and declared, "You said 'we've got a kid on the way' and I realized I'd been waiting for it. Expecting it. You and me ... we aren't something I thought of as a maybe, but as an eventuality. You're my family, Nathan, and I always knew I would have you forever. Now I know what I want that forever to look like."

The next morning, Nathan had to run to the grocery store, leaving Matt and I alone at the table. I waited just long enough to hear his truck leave the driveway before I asked, "How long have you known?"

Matt glanced askance at me, a small smirk pulling up his lips. He didn't even ask what I was talking about. Instead, he responded with, "About him or you?"

"You have to ask?"

He shrugged. "Nathan I knew about before you and I started dating." He paused a moment to give me time to absorb that. "And yes, I still went after you. Both of you admitted that you barely spoke to one another, and I never saw you two together except that one time at the store. I'm also a bit of an ass and it made me feel good to know that, of the two of us, you liked me."

I rolled my eyes at that.

"You were harder to figure out. Obviously. Even you couldn't do that much until now." Matt chuckled a little as I pretended to throw something at him. Then he said, "I didn't understand what was between you two until the day that Morgan died. When I showed up at your house to comfort you, the only person you wanted was him. It was right about then that I realized you were meant for each other."

I lowered my head and began to push the eggs around my plate. Out of the corner of my eye, I could see his expectant expression.

"Lex? Is it something I said?"

"Nah. Well, yeah. Kinda. I just find that phrasing awkward. That we were meant for each other."

"Are you serious?" he asked in a perfectly deadpan voice.

"What?"

"Lex, you're a witch. Aren't soulmates and fated destinies kind of in your existence description? And you don't believe in them?"

"I do. A little bit," I admitted.

"I'm going to need more than that," he insisted, folding his hands and resting his chin atop them.

"I don't know. Maybe it's because there's such a stereotype about witches believing in soulmates and destiny that I kinda pull back from that side of things. Because of the things I can do, I try not to get caught up in the cultural aspects of it. Things like astrology, tarot cards, and palm readings I don't get near. It's just that—"

"You're a snob," he said matter-of-factly.

"What? I am not!"

"Dude, you are. You've got all this power and you can do all this amazing shit, no doubt. But because of that you look down on other practitioners."

"I do not look down on them," I growled.

"Really? Look, you may not touch tarot cards and palm reading, but for some people that may be the only time their magick manifests. So should they back away from it just because it's expected of them?"

"That's not what I'm saying..."

"No, but that's how you're reacting. How many of the new witches in town have you actually talked to?"

"Excuse me, when did this become an interrogation?"

"When you lost the ability to suck it up and admit you're prejudiced against witches without magick."

"I'm not prejudiced, Matt. I just can't relate to them."

"You won't know until you try. So far, you haven't."

"Why are you pushing this so hard?"

"Because Nathan wasn't the only one who let them settle here, and he's not the only one they keep in touch with."

Well, that felt like a sucker punch. Then I got angry. "Seriously? They're so afraid to approach me that they keep whining to you and Nathan behind my back? And those are the people you want me to be friends with?"

"Get off your damn high horse. You know that's not what it's like."

"Isn't it? Then why else am I getting the lecture?"

"Because you scare people and no one deserves to live in a constant state of fear."

"How am I scaring them? I haven't been anywhere near them!"

"That's how you're scaring them! They're afraid you already hate them and that you will kick them out at any given moment."

"Okay, but did you tell them that I wouldn't do that?"

"Of course I told them. I'm not a total dick.

That doesn't mean they're not still worried about upsetting you."

"I'll talk to them. Is that what you want me to say?"

"Yes. Call a meeting or something if you have to. Just make some friends that you haven't kissed, okay?"

"Low blow. Nathan and I literally just got together."

It was in that moment that Nathan walked through the backdoor. He took one look at both of our faces, shook his head, and went to put the milk away. His back was still to us when he asked, "Do I even want to know?"

"Matt's kicking my ass into going to play with the witches."

"Is it working?"

I didn't answer that. Instead, I sat back in my chair and seethed quietly. Yet, a stupid grin pulled at my lips when Nathan sat beside me and grabbed my hand under the table. I could tell already that our desire to touch one another all the time was going to become a problem. For other people.

As I sat there, assaulted by all of the same

giddy feelings as the day before, I realized that Matt may have had a point. In the absence of female friends to confide to, I was missing my mom. I wanted someone I could talk to about my feelings for Nathan without hearing a sarcastic reply every ten seconds. It would have been nice to have someone sit there and listen to me be a mushy teenager for a bit. Which was why I was also missing Delaire, Catori, and Faye. When I first got together with Grey, I had them to discuss things with. Now, they were no longer an option. And that was my fault.

Taking a deep breath, I looked between them both for a long minute. Then I said, "I wish you could understand it. Why I avoid them. Why they're afraid of me. I've tried explaining it before but maybe you guys need a refresher course. I was both murderer and victim in the saga of Alyssa and Victoria. I burned alive as Mary Sullivan when I was only nine years old. And they're not the only memories I have of dark deeds done by covens. When you see the witches, you see companions for me. When I look at them, I sense a threat to myself and the baby. Is it fair to them? Probably not. But it's going to take a lot more than dumping us in a room together and telling us to get along."

"Not all witches are bad, Lex. When you had Morgan—"

"Morgan set me up to be prosecuted for her suicide. Love her as I do, that's another memory to add to the ever-growing list."

"Well then, you need new memories. Better ones. In the end, you're going to be the one to decide whether these people stay or go. Wouldn't you rather you had that figured out before you give birth to my niece?"

All I could think was, *Damn him.*

Chapter Twenty Five

FIRST STEP

I'm doing this on my terms.

No matter how many times I thought it, it didn't change the feeling of having Matt at my back with a pitchfork to herd me forward. All the same, the boys had promised not to interfere. And Nathan wasn't the only one with a flair for the dramatic.

There was a total of sixteen new witches in Cedar Creek. Most were adults, but there were a few teenagers in the mix. Of them, there were a handful able to perform energy workings. By noon, every one of them found a scroll sealed by an emerald ribbon, inviting them to tea with Witch of Old Grove Road.

Before three o'clock, I sat at the head of one of the long tables I'd borrowed from the community center. White tablecloths made them look more appealing, and there were a few flower arrangements resting in central locations, helping to break up the hodgepodge of a tea set. It all looked just quaint enough to fit the fairytale setting the cottage and garden fueled.

The practitioners were the first to appear, each ranging between ten to fifteen minutes early. They'd gathered together at the end of the road and proceeded to walk the mile and a half in a large group. Frightened creatures preferred the safety of a herd, and my summons had certainly spooked them.

I closed my eyes and felt the cloud of tension hanging thick in the air. It grew more ominous the closer they came. A fact that did not bode well for our relations. Honestly, one would have thought I made it a habit to chop up children and serve them in a stew.

The tension eased when Basil, Caroline, and the other three energy workers appeared. It was this handful of truly aware individuals that they allowed to lead them the rest of the way to my house. Then, one jolt of familiar energy strode to the fore and made it her task to open the gate and cross over the salt line.

My eyes snapped open and I slowly rose to my feet. "Rebecca. I suppose I should have known," I said with a small smile.

She smiled back as she slowly approached the table. "Yeah, well, there are a few recent converts."

As she said it, I began to recognize other young faces in the crowd. I'd danced beside many of them at prom. Which was probably why they were of a more easy nature as they approached the tables. Around me, the cloud of tension began to ease as more people filed through the gate.

"Welcome. Please sit," I instructed.

I kept Rebecca in the seat to my right, since I'd known her the longest and appreciated the new ideals she was trying to uphold. Caroline got the seat to my left, as she seemed the unspoken leader of this new community. In the strange atmosphere that came without words but with a flurry of movement, the witches took their seats. At last, I joined them.

Holding my head high, I suggested to Caroline, "Would you please introduce everyone?"

All eyes were trained on either Caroline or

myself as she began to go around the table and announce everyone's names. My eyes followed her words, meeting every gaze as their names were said. I also paid attention to the order the names were said in. While Caroline made a point of going down one side first, it was soon apparent that those similar to myself sat to my left nearest one another, and then the ranking lowered as it circled the table. While there was no official coven in Cedar Creek, there had certainly been an evaluation of worth and a ranking system was now in play.

To allow them this, or to break it? That was the question.

When Caroline ended on Rebecca, I let my gaze perform another sweep over the habitants of the tables. "My name is Alexandria Ryder. I am the Witch of Old Grove Road. Cedar Creek is my domain."

At once, the tensions that had begun to ease spiked in every mind. As was the point. No, I was not an evil monster intent on throwing them out of their homes. Nor was I the witch they could cajole, control, or contend with. That was something they needed to be aware of from the start.

"I am glad that you all have accepted my invitation. Please, help yourselves to some tea and cookies."

As a point, I reached out and grabbed the nearest pot. Then I turned to Caroline and poured for her before I did the same for Rebecca. Afterward, I served myself.

For several moments, the clatter of china was all that could be heard. Timid, soft voices slipped through when they thought the noise enough to cover whispers, and I smiled. It was a rather different scenario than the first time I met Morgan.

"This is lovely, Alexandria. Thank you," Caroline said after taking a sip.

Beside her, Basil took a bite of one of the cookies and gave a noncommittal shrug. I took that as my cookies weren't bad, but hers were better. Nothing more could I expect from a kitchen witch.

"Thank you for inviting us," Rebecca added, trying to cover the quiet.

"It was past time," I assured her.

A sly smile pulled at her lips. "Nathan got to you," she guessed.

"Matt." It wasn't the first time he'd hit me with stark reality, and I was glad it wouldn't be the last.

She chuckled. "He told us to expect something from you. Didn't think it'd be a garden party."

"Well, there were alternatives. But I didn't have a gothic mansion handy." In an effort to be more inclusive, my eyes traveled over the gathering. "Did Matt warn you all about me?"

"Alex, I didn't mean it like that," Rebecca muttered hastily as the fear spiked again.

"I know. I was just teasing. But if you would prefer to hear now why I've asked you here today, I'm willing to tell you."

There were quite a few nods and a murmured, "Yes, please," from one of the younger crowd.

"Okay," I said. "The truth of the matter is that my best friends vetted each and every one of you before it was determined you could stay in Cedar Creek. I trust their judgment like I will trust no other. I have kept my distance from many of you out of respect for that judgment. The time has come, however, for me to make up my own opinions about each of you.

"I would like to tell each of you that this isn't some test that determines if you stay or go, but that would be a lie. This is a test. And you will remain or leave by my will. It sounds harsh to say it, and I know that it is unfair that you should be uprooted based upon the opinion of a stranger. That being said, I hope that you understand that this is my home. This will always be my home. And I will protect and defend all of Cedar Creek with every drop of magick I possess. If I find that I cannot trust someone inhabiting this town, they will be removed."

"That's tyranny," announced a middle-aged woman that Caroline had called Terry. She was on the left side of the table and appeared to rank right below the energy wielders.

"It is an absolute. While I would prefer not to hand anyone an eviction notice, I have no qualms about doing it if I feel it is necessary."

"So, what can we do to assure you that we mean no harm?" Basil asked.

I offered them all a smile. "Talk to me. Allow me to get to know you. And stop emailing the boys every time you don't wish to disturb me. I'm home now. If you have questions, concerns, or just want to talk, then you are able to come to me. I'm sorry if you ever felt that wasn't possible."

"You were really busy right after you came home," Rebecca said in a breezy tone.

"I was. You see this garden? It about broke my heart to see it once I came home. Many of the plants had to be replaced and I have to fight with the weeds on a weekly basis to keep them from encroaching."

"Nathan's not a gardener, I take it?"

"No, he is not."

"He has a good head for design, though," said Basil's husband, George.

"And repair work," Terry added. "Came out and fixed my dishwasher yesterday morning not five minutes after I called him. Good kid."

That seemed to be the general consensus and I reveled in it. If no one else believed that I had gotten damn lucky with Nathan, at least the other Cedar Creek witches did. It was almost as if someone had told them that if they talked up Nathan, they'd appeal to my good side. Honestly, I wouldn't have been surprised if Matt emailed them with pointers.

Besides Nathan, the conversation took several twists and turns. First into the garden, then into essential oils, then it drifted into the stores they operated. Somehow, we all landed on *Basil's Sweet Retreat*. Apparently, there wasn't one of us not addicted to her bakery. At last, however, the afternoon had begun to wane and a more tranquil mood settled over us.

When it seemed the last of the conversation had died and we were all enjoying our surroundings, one timid voice asked, "Alex, can I ask why you left?"

In a way, I'd known it was coming. I still didn't have an answer prepared. Looking around the table, I found all eyes on me.

"In a word? Oleander," I said with a forced smile. "For a more condensed version, the reason that we left was because my father saw his child embroiled in a witch trial and thus learned how deeply feared and ostracized his teenage daughter was. Cedar Creek broke his heart."

I didn't tell them that I had poured salt in that wound for two straight years. I was sure the scars in my arm implied it well enough.

After an awkward silence, I told them, "You can ask other questions. I won't get offended."

"How old are you, child?"

"Eighteen."

"So young to have endured so much," Clara continued.

I wanted to say that my age had nothing to do with it, but when I thought back on those moments of my life, I knew it had everything to do with it. At nine I was young and impressionable and curious. It was the perfect recipe of naivety coupled with confidence that drove me after Alyssa's story in the first place. When I was thirteen, I had more arrogance than any being had a right to, and that confidence blinded me to everything I didn't want to acknowledge. In the end, it cost me. And the time between fourteen and eighteen I could blame entirely on teenage angst and hormones. There was no way I was living any of that down.

"We are what life makes of us. No more; no less."

"Well, we are glad that your trials have created triumph," Caroline said, raising her teacup in a kind of toast.

I smiled as I watched the others also raise theirs in the same kind of salute. It would have been more amusing had her words not been re-peating in my ear.

For triumph to truly be forged from my trials, there was one mystery left that I had to solve.

Chapter Twenty Six

FAMILY HEIRLOOMS

Two days after the garden party, my parents arrived. They'd found a house that had seen much better days an hour north of us. Depending on what other issues they found, it would be a project that could last them almost six months. I was happy. They were close enough that a phone call could bring them in a hurry, but far enough away that I could still feel like an adult.

When they flew in, I insisted I would meet them there instead of them going out of their way to stop in Cedar Creek first. After a long day of travel, they deserved a nice meal out on the town and to go home and get a feel for their new live-in renovation. Besides, it would be the perfect opportunity to drop the Nathan bomb before they all had to be in the same room together again. Granted, they'd gotten along well enough before, but I wasn't willing to push my dad's civility further than I was sure it would go.

When I appeared at the new house, I knew that it would easily take a full five months of constant renovation. New flooring had to be put in it, the roof needed to be fixed, and the ceilings in the kitchen and downstairs bathroom were torn down. Someone had also done a number on an old fireplace. It looked like someone tried to burn the place down for insurance and had failed.

"Why take on such a heavy project?" I asked as we loaded into the car to head out for dinner.

My mom snorted. "You want the truth? You've got months left on that pregnancy and we want to be close by. If we finish this sooner, we'll probably move closer."

I nodded but didn't respond. For the rest of the ride to the restaurant, I tried to figure out how to slip it into the conversation that Nathan and I were a couple. Unfortunately, that wasn't the kind of thing that fit into any topic category. As it happened, we were about halfway through dinner when my mom finally gave me an opening.

"So, Lex, where's Nathan tonight? I thought he might have joined us."

"He's at home. With Matt," I said, keeping my eyes on my plate.

"Matt is in Cedar Creek?" she demanded.

I nodded. "He's been there for about a week."

"And we couldn't head straight there from the airport?"

"Miss him that much, did ya? He'll be pleased," I said with a grin.

"Is he staying with you and Nathan?"

I almost answered without catching what she said. Then my eyes shot to her face and I saw the sly smirk teasing her lips. It was my turn to have some fun.

With a shrug, I remarked, "Yeah, he's been staying at our house. Except for when he couch-hops every couple of days."

My mother looked mildly disappointed at my response. Probably because it didn't give her a clue where to go from there. Which was how I knew that she was in the same position I'd been in all night. She was trying to figure out every subtle way to find out if Nathan and I were a couple.

Too bad Ryders couldn't do subtle.

"You know, it was always easy to think of Matt as the cool uncle that sends money for birthdays and drops by for the holidays. Turns out, he's taken to the role with his usual excitement. He's trying to come up with nicknames now and they're getting worse by the day."

My dad snorted. "Nicknames don't come until after the sonogram. And then it's usually whatever the technician compares you to."

"By the time I got my first sonogram with you, you were a peach," my mother informed me.

"And I called you 'Peach' for the entire rest of the pregnancy," Dad admitted.

I laughed. "Well, that's obnoxious."

"What does Nathan have to say about it?" Mom asked.

"Or is he trying his own hand at being an uncle?"

For a moment, I considered stringing them along a bit longer. In the end, I said, "Nathan calls him an idiot. And no, he is not going to be her uncle."

My dad's features became perplexed. "So, what? You're going to claim Matt but not Nathan?"

"I did claim him, Dad. But he has a more important role to play than an uncle."

"Which is?" Mom was quite literally on the edge of her seat. If I delayed any longer, she would tear the words from my throat.

"Matt is her uncle, but Nathan is her dad."

My mom positively beamed. "We can talk about this now?"

I chuckled. "When did you figure it out?"

They exchanged a glance. "I knew when you opened that door and found him standing there," my mother said. "That's the happiest I have ever seen you, Lex."

"Do you get it now?" I asked in a low voice.

She nodded and I released a relieved sigh.

"This is what you want, Lexi Girl?" my dad interjected.

I nodded. "I love him. I always have."

"Then I'm happy for you. But I have to ask... You're carrying another man's child, Lex. How does Nathan feel about that?"

More than anything, I think my laugh reassured him. "I asked him the same thing the day we got together. You know those two days I came to visit in Colorado to tell you I was pregnant? Nathan used that time apart to start on the nursery. She's his daughter, Dad. And he'll take a bite out of anyone who suggests otherwise."

"Just like that?"

"Just like that."

"And what about Grey?"

"Grey is her father, and I will never tell her different. But her dad is Nathan. That is the man who will raise her and be there for her for the rest of our lives. And he's more excited for her than I am."

It still stung to admit it, but the nursery was proof. Two days after he learned I was pregnant, he was making a home for my child. Two months after I learned of her, I still hadn't read the book my mom gave me.

My dad looked skeptical, but my mom had had this conversation with me enough to know it was true. Reaching across the table, she took my hand in hers and squeezed tight. On my other side, my dad did the same.

"Looks like our family just got a whole lot bigger."

It was the first time in my life that I considered our dinner table packed. Even excluding Tyler and Kelsi, we still had my parents, Nathan's parents, and Matt to feed. The room was nothing short of chaotic.

For one quick breath, Nathan managed to lean in close and ask, "What's it going to be like for Thanksgiving?"

"And Yule?" I shot back.

In point of fact, it seemed like we were making enough food to feed an army. My mom had designated herself in charge of the salad. Anne was working on the dessert. We entrusted the dinner rolls to Matt. Since I was on a rosemary kick—no food aversions, but plenty of cravings—I was making rosemary chicken. Beside me, Nathan was working on the three sides: rice, potatoes, and asparagus. Our dads were left in charge of setting the table.

When we were finally all seated, there were about three conversations going at once. Nathan and my dad discussed nothing but the company and its dealings. Mom and Matt had a sidebar conversation going on that bounced between his schooling and her plans for the new house. Anne, Josh, and I talked about how Sarah's family was getting on. They were due for a visit sometime in the next few weeks and I was glad to have an opportunity to see Nathan's aunt again. While I would never get over her helping hand that got me put on trial, it was her clever defense of me that kept me from being convicted of a crime that was never committed.

It was while we were in the middle of that conversation that my mother finally broke up hers and Matt's to say to Nathan, "I'd love to see the nursery after dinner, if that's all right?"

At once, Nathan's eyes shot to mine. I responded with an apologetic shrug. Before he could answer, Anne asked, "You guys already started on the nursery? Why didn't you tell me?"

Nathan looked at his mom. "I didn't think anyone would be that interested."

"How much have you gotten done so far?" his dad asked.

"Not a lot. Removed the wallpaper, primed it, and got the furniture set up."

"I regret mentioning it to you, now," I said with a mock glare for my mother.

"What did I do?"

"It's what you're going to do. I can see the wheels turning in your head right now, trying to figure out how to design it."

"I am ... not going to deny that. But you'll thank me for it when you get into the nesting phase."

"Can I help?" Anne asked her.

"Of course!"

Nathan and I shared another worried glance. "Do we get any say in this at all?" I asked.

"Don't be ridiculous. We'll run everything by you and Nathan before we make any decisions," she sighed. It was like I was a client.

"Fine. Then I will show you the nursery after dinner. But before you see it, I want to lay some ground rules."

"Oh?" Anne asked.

I nodded before I looked directly at my mother and said, "Keep the pink to a minimum."

"How minimum? Like an accent wall?"

"Like a throw pillow," I remarked in a dry voice. "It's bad enough that most of the clothes on the market for girls are either pink or white. I can't escape that. But I can make damn sure not to drown in it."

"Fine. How about green?"

"I like blue better."

"You would pick blue," she sighed.

"What furniture do you have so far?" Anne asked her son.

"The crib, cradle, and a day bed that was already in the room."

"Your crib and cradle?" The question seemed innocuous, but I could sense there was a deeper meaning.

Nathan stared at his mother for a minute before he nodded. "Family heirlooms belong in the family, right?"

"That they do," she answered.

A few minutes later, the conversation shifted to other matters, but my mom was still looking at me with a reassuring smile. Leaning close to me, she lowered her voice as she asked, "You're still not used to talking about it, are you?"

I shook my head.

"It's okay, Lex. There's still time to get yourself used to it. And I'm here now. Which means you'll have plenty of opportunity to hear about it from me and everyone else in your life. We'll acclimate you in no time."

"Well, someone needs to," I said with a forced smile.

The sooner they managed it, the better. I didn't know how much longer I would let myself go before I tried to be happy about her. But it was so hard to be happy when I felt like I was carrying someone else's child.

Chapter Twenty Seven

REGRET AND
JEALOUSY

I looked about my house with a feeling of dismay. Yet again, I had chosen to rest when much work needed to be done. My chores were but half complete when I had decided three hours might be spent in repose. Shame coated my skin, but I could not find the will to throw myself into my daily tasks.

The shame burst into panic as a pounding sounded upon my door. Seconds passed remarkably slow as I hurried to make myself presentable. At last, I was able to throw myself at the door and open it.

Waiting for me on the other side was Margarite. One hand was clasped around her cloak as she fought the bitter winter wind to keep it, while a gloved hand clutched her customary basket. With one look at her, I wrenched the door aside and almost pulled her into the safety of the cottage. Together, we pushed the door closed behind us.

"You should not have ventured out in weather such as this," I admonished as I helped her to remove her cloak.

"Have you not learned by now that weather bows to me?" she teased.

It was her greatest gift, the manipulation of forces unwilling to be manipulated. The weather, especially, was stubborn against the slightest attempt at coercion. Yet, Margarite whispered to the wind and it often shifted course. That did not mean it would not exact a price at a later date.

"Your tricks with the wind have sought their vengeance. Another minute and you would have flown away into the wilderness."

"Twas a mild disagreement. No more. Why did it take you so long to come to my rescue?"

A blush burned my face and I tried not to glance at my unmade bedding. I attempted to hide my face as I added more wood to the fireplace, stirring the flames higher. It did not stop her from noticing.

"Mary? Are you unwell?"

"I am not ill."

"That is not what I asked."

"I am weary of late. Before you arrived, I was attempting to rally myself from my bed, where I have wasted half of the day," I sighed as I stirred the fire once more.

"I see no waste," she quipped. "Your house is often impeccable and your garden remains the most extraordinary in the village. One day of rest cannot mean the degradation of all that you accomplish."

My eyes lowered to the floor and I admitted with great shame, "Not a day, Margarite. A week has passed."

When I turned to look at my friend, I found her beaming at me. "I wondered as much," she said more to herself than to me.

"What is it?"

"You know what it is, Mary. When was the last time you bled?"

It was an instinctive reaction that caused my eyes to seek out the moon, despite being inside. "The waxing crescent," I announced.

"The waxing crescent was two days ago, my friend."

My blood was not coming.

"Margarite..."

She nodded. "You are with child, Mary."

Tears filled my eyes and my hands lowered to my stomach. After a year of marriage, I was pregnant at last.

"I have to tell William!"

I was almost to the door before she took my arms and pulled me to a halt. Laughing, she said, "Mary, it is nigh a blizzard out there. You will have to wait to tell him until his return."

There was no stopping the disgruntled expression that crossed my face. Margarite laughed all the more for it. "Be patient. He will be home soon enough. When he does arrive, however, let him relax. Let him enjoy being home and warm and having his wife's attention. Then, when he is at his most content, tell him. Be sure to watch his face as you do, for this is his first time hearing that he will be a father. That is a moment you will savor for a lifetime."

Before I woke up, I was treated to one more memory. The one where Mary told William. As predicted, he'd all but leapt for joy. They'd laughed and danced and made love, and I got to experience all of it. And when my eyelids opened to take in the cottage bedroom, my entire chest was aching with regret.

Regret and jealousy.

Mary had been waiting to fall pregnant. She'd wanted nothing more, because she already had everything else to make her happy. A little one was all she was missing from her family. Their eras determined that it was their destiny to have as many children as they could, and hope that most of them survived to adulthood. While I understood it, that yearning she felt for life inside of her was something I couldn't imagine feeling for myself. At least not for Grey's daughter.

"I'm sorry," I murmured into the night. For her and me.

I wanted to be happy. I wanted to be as excited and thrilled as Mary and William. I wanted to dive headfirst into planning the nursery with my mom and Anne. I wanted to fight with Nathan about names. I wanted to be curious about her and imagine her future. I wanted to want her ... and I didn't.

Unable to be alone with my thoughts any longer, I climbed out of the bed and teleported to our house. Pushing open our bedroom door, I watched Nathan stir in the bed. His eyes opened a fraction as I stepped into the room and closed the door behind me.

"Lex?"

I couldn't speak as I crawled into bed with him. Instead, I curled up against him and began to cry. At once, his arms wrapped around me and he pulled me closer. For some reason, that only made me cry harder.

Given that it was the middle of the night, I wasn't surprised to find that I cried myself to sleep in his arms. More surprising was the fact that he also managed to sleep for a while. When I finally woke up in the morning, it was because he was waking up at the same time.

For a while, we reveled in the feel of each other. Then he asked in a low voice, "Want to tell me what that was about last night?"

Releasing a breath, I propped a pillow against the headboard and sat up slowly. "Grey Walker."

"What?"

"That's the name of the baby's father. Grey Walker."

His body tensed a little. "Why are you telling

me this now?"

"Because I'm about to tell you the rest of what happened in Grant. I'm going to tell you what I've never told anyone else. And I'm going to tell you so that you understand why I don't know how to love my daughter."

Without giving him the chance to respond, I dove into the story. I told him about the bond that existed between Grey and I from the moment our eyes met. I told him how potent it was and what it heralded. Then I told him about giving in and allowing myself to fall for Grey.

I left nothing out. Not Grey's secrets. Nor Azure's and Spring's. Every detail that I could remember, I gave to Nathan. He needed to know those things in order to understand what I would say next. And when I finished the tale with Grey urging me to run, I knew that Nathan understood why.

"I have no idea what caused the bond between Grey and I, but I knew it had to be something powerful and with a purpose. Now I know. *She* is the reason. And that's why she doesn't feel like mine."

The entire time I spoke, Nathan had been

silent. Listening and absorbing everything I said. At that, however, his eyebrows rose and he cocked his head to the side to look at me.

"Last night, I experienced another memory. I relived finding out that I was pregnant with Mercy. Then I relived telling William. And two happier people could not exist." As I spoke, I could feel a few tears escaping from my eyes. Then I took a breath and admitted, "I don't feel like that with her. I'm not happy about her, Nathan. I'm not excited and I don't feel blessed. And I know that it's because she doesn't feel like my child."

"Lex..."

"Don't. Don't try to say anything. You've heard the whole story now. Something in this universe created that bond between Grey and I just so we could have this baby. Something else created this child, Nathan. And as much as I want her to be mine, I know she'll never be. I can't explain it better than that."

For a long moment, he didn't say a word. Then a challenging expression settled over his face and he looked at me and said, "So what?"

"Excuse me?"

"So what if she feels like someone else's. Lex, you're the one carrying her. You're going to be the one to give birth to her. You are going to raise her to be an awesome, powerful woman just like *you*. Yeah, something else may have intervened on her behalf, but it did so with you in mind as her mother. Because something out there knew that no one could do better.

"I get it. You can't connect with her and that sucks. But it's not because you don't want her, Lex. And it's not that you don't know how to love her. It's because you've decided that someone else has more rights to her than you do, and that's bullshit.

"Right now, there are only two people on this whole planet that are on equal footing with you. Her father and me. Because she's my daughter, too. I don't care who her parents are or why or how she was brought into my life. But she's here and she's mine, and I don't give a shit who says otherwise. So, do us all a favor and love her in spite of whether or not you think you deserve her."

Chapter Twenty Eight

CLUE

Over the next few weeks, the other witches of Cedar Creek and I had been making strides to get to know one another better. As it happened, a weekly garden party was just the thing to keep us all in touch and welcoming of one another. Enough so that Cameron—a carpenter—decided to make us our own table. It took up permanent residence out back of the cottage, and we all added our own hodgepodge collection of chairs. It was a nice setup.

"Hey, Alex, can I ask you something? I know you don't talk about it ... at all ... but I wondered..."

I looked at Karrie for a minute and smiled. "You want to know about Alyssa Rice."

The entire table grew quiet and I watched

Rebecca shoot her friend a quelling look. "It's alright," I told her. Then my eyes traveled over the table, meeting every gaze that I could. "But the thing about Alyssa Rice is that she's finally at rest. The reason I haven't talked about it isn't because it's something traumatic or because I think no one will believe me. I don't talk about it because it's part of a story that has ended, and there's no need to bring it up again."

"Sorry," Karrie muttered.

"Don't be. I won't give you details, but I can tell you the gist of it. Alyssa Rice was a prodigy in magick just as much as she was in music. When she was around six or seven, she and her best friend, Victoria, were inducted into Cedar Creek Coven. They were both powerful in their own way, but Alyssa's ambition outstripped her sense. When she made to cross a line, Victoria stopped her. It was an event that crippled a coven that had lasted centuries. It disbanded the year Victoria was served justice for her crime."

For a time, they all remained silent. Then Rebecca said, "I never knew there was a coven. All I knew about was the Witch of Old Grove Road."

I nodded. "Not surprising. They were very good at covering their tracks and keeping their magick secret. Had to be, or they never would have made it out of the witch trials alive."

Basil carefully set her teacup down on its saucer before she asked, "It goes back that far?"

"Went," I corrected. "And yes. It was born sometime in the 1600s. What I was told was that, in order to protect sacred spaces, the Native Americans began enlisting the help of the only beings that could guard against white men: white women."

"How do you know this? Is there some secret library you're not sharing with us?"

My eyes darted to the cottage. "There's history gathered in every tree and stone for miles around. You just have to know how to look for it."

"What else did you find?"

"How big was the coven?"

"Were they all like you?"

I smiled as the questions kept rolling in. "I can't speak for every age of the coven, but I have seen it in its beginning stages, and I have seen its final days. There were far more in the beginning, and most of them were like me."

"Why so many in the beginning and so few in the end?"

For a moment, I was about to say that I didn't know. Then another memory crashed into my brain, courtesy of a red poison ring. At once, I sat up straighter and pulled out my cell phone.

"What're you doing?" Rebecca asked.

"Calling Nathan. You guys just gave me a clue," I said so everyone else could hear me.

"Hey," he said after the third ring.

"Hey, there's one more thing I forgot to tell you," I said by way of greeting.

"Okay, what's that?"

"I know what happened to Margarite's second daughter." He would kill me for finding out like this, but I needed someone already wrapped up in the story to think this through with me.

"Tell me."

"Her sister rose to power over the Cedar Creek Coven when Francesca was in her late teens or early twenties. To escape her sister—who was trying to banish the *infamy* surrounding their family name—Francesca and twelve other witches traveled deep into unknown wilderness where they created their own settlement.

"Thirteen witches, Nathan. How large would Cedar Creek Coven had to have been to have thirteen witches to spare and still thrive for centuries? And what infamy was Margie trying to dispel?"

"What kind of magick in them?"

"Energy workers. All thirteen."

"And it still passed down in Cedar Creek for so long... Knowing the population size of it around the time it was disbanded, it's almost impossible not to say that about half the town was made of witches back then."

"Exactly."

"What are you getting at?"

"Remember that preacher's journal entry about Margarite's hanging? If about half the town were witches and Margarite was their High Priestess, then how is it she and two others alone were hung for it? Why were they allowed to hang in the first place? There was enough cumulative power in Cedar Creek Coven to make the whole thing a figment of everyone's imagination. So why did they let it happen?"

There was a thoughtful silence for a minute

before he asked, "When Mary was executed, was the whole coven there, or just part of it?"

"I'm not sure. Mary considered twelve of them to be close enough that Mercy knew them as aunts. I'm thinking they must have limited the coven to thirteen in the beginning. If that's the case, then yes the whole coven burned her."

"Well, maybe they considered it justice. Margarite forced them to kill their friend; maybe they decided it was best just to let her hang."

"And she suddenly lost all her powers too?"

As soon as the words were out of my mouth, I knew what must have happened.

"Mary," Nathan and I said together.

"She wanted revenge."

"And she wouldn't come back without a way to get it," I added.

"So now we just have to figure out why Margarite killed William in the first place."

"Yup. I'll let you know when the next vision hits."

"Okay. I'll be home in an hour."

"See you then."

When I hung up with him, I found everyone still staring at me. Rebecca was the first to break the silence with a simple, "What the hell?"

I shrugged. "Alyssa Rice isn't the only mystery in Cedar Creek. Nathan's helping me to figure out one that's a little closer to home."

"How close?" Caroline asked.

My eyes went to the cottage. "That close."

"Okay, now we're curious. You have to tell us."

There was a general consensus to that fact and I shrugged it off as best I could. Honestly, it didn't seem like a compulsion to keep Mary's story to myself. Probably because Mary's story was mine. With Alyssa, Victoria, and the others it was always someone else's story. Someone else's life. Someone else's thoughts and secrets and betrayals. But everything that had happened to Mary had happened to me. I owned that. So, I could share it if I wanted to.

But not yet.

"You can have the same deal Morgan got. When I have all the answers, you will. Until then, we all have to practice patience."

Nathan was waiting for me in the living room

when I got home. As soon as I saw him, I kicked off my shoes and dropped onto the couch beside him. Leaning my head on his shoulder, I closed my eyes and let myself enjoy the few moments of peace.

Then he asked, "How do you know about Francesca Vaile?"

I groaned a little before sitting up and meeting his gaze. His expression was perfectly blank as he waited for the answer. There was no avoiding it forever.

"You remember what I told you about what happened to Azure?" He nodded. "And I told you about the ring that I took visions off of. Well, the first vision I got from the ring was of a blonde woman who'd ridden with twelve witches into the wilderness. They were in search of a new home, and they were running from her sister. Because of the infamy surrounding their family names, each member of this new coven chose new names. When it came to Francesca, she announced that she was a Vaile no longer. From that moment forth, she was a Walker. And so all of her descendants shall be."

Nathan closed his eyes and leaned his head

back. For a while, he said nothing. At last, he took a deep breath and released it slowly. Only then did he look at me.

"When did you figure it out?"

"When you first showed me your family tree."

"So before I knew about the baby."

"Yeah."

"And after..."

"Would you believe me if I said I forgot?" His eyebrows rose in a questioning expression and I hurried to add, "I'm serious, Nathan. We were busy with so many other things and there was never a moment where I thought I needed to blurt out that you and the baby have common ancestry."

When Nathan wrapped his arm around my shoulders, I knew I was forgiven. For a minute. "Is there anything else I should know about?"

"Well, runaway Vaile ancestor, homicidal aunt, ambitious father... No, I don't think there's anything I'm missing."

"A name for her."

My eyes snapped up to his. "You really want to discuss this?"

"Lex, how far along are you?"

"I'll be sixteen weeks tomorrow."

"Exactly. Most people are at least dismissing names by now."

"Most people won't know they're having a daughter for another month, either. But I'm special so I get to make my own rules."

"My kid, too. I get to help with the rules."

"I know that. But talking about names right now... I'm still trying to wrap my head around the nursery situation."

All of a sudden, his demeanor became cautious. "Speaking of the nursery..."

"Oh what now?" I groaned.

"Your mom has a few bedding options for the crib. They're waiting for your perusal upstairs."

"How long ago did she leave?"

"She hasn't. She's still up there. Probably looking up matching curtains on the internet."

"Oh shit," I said, leaping to my feet and darting for the stairs.

As soon as I reached the nursery, I flung the door wide and my eyes landed on the daybed where my mother was sitting. The second she raised her head to look at me, white mist began to gather over my eyes.

Chapter Twenty Nine

HOPE

I stepped into the room to find Elizabeth bent over her darning. Her husband, Thomas, had gone to a meeting with the other local men. As she had since I arrived, Elizabeth had declined the offer of socializing—claiming that pregnancy proved too cumbersome for her to leave her house. Of course, it wasn't her pregnancy she referred to.

"Mary! I thought you were to bed. Is the little one asleep then?"

"Yes. Mercy has driven herself to exhaustion." As I eased down onto the chair beside the fire, I remarked, "Your son, however, is fitful."

At once, her eyes flashed with the same greedy pride that had come to define her during this pregnancy. I knew it helped us both to refer to the boy as hers. Since *she was unable to bear children, this child of mine was as close to motherhood as she would get. And it would provide him with the blessed anonymity that I desperately needed him to have.*

A few moments passed before Elizabeth set aside her chore and moved her chair nearer mine. When she was close enough, her hands closed the gap between us and she rested them on my swollen stomach. As he sensed her presence, the child shifted in her direction. It was this reaction more than any other that assured me I had made the right choice.

"Have you and Thomas discussed a name yet?"

For a moment, she appeared uncomfortable. "We have talked of it a bit, but no decision has been made."

It was too easy to take the thoughts from her face. "No. Do not name him for his father. None must ever know there is a link between your son and my husband. For his own well-being, Elizabeth, you must promise me this!" I had her wrist in a steely grip and forced her eyes to meet mine.

"I promise, Mary. I swear it on my life. We shall not name him after William." Only then did my grip relax.

"I am grateful," I whispered.

Rising to her feet, Elizabeth took up a comb and

began to run it through the lengths of my hair. My eyes closed and I leaned into the familiar ministrations. As she did so, she hummed so that the baby could hear her voice and know that it was she that gave me pleasure.

When she had finished, she replaced the comb and sighed, "I do not know how it is that you can do this, Mary. But I am grateful to you for it."

"I could choose no other, Beth. You alone could I trust with such a precious part of myself."

Her back was to me so that I could not see her tears, but she made an effort to nod. "And Mercy? What is to become of her?"

"Mercy will have to remain with my mother until I find other means to protect her."

"We would gladly take her, Mary."

"I know you would, my friend. It would be the greatest wish fulfilled if I could leave her also in your care. Yet, I dare not leave her so near to her brother. The chance of harm befalling both is too great. For the sake of themselves, they must be kept apart."

"Then know that I have faith in you. If this is what you are willing to do for the sake of your son, I know that you will do all that is needed for your daughter. You will protect her, Mary."

I could only wish that I knew how.

"Whoa," I said, reaching out a hand to steady myself against the door.

"Lex? You okay?" my mom demanded. Before I had time to calm her, she was at my side and guiding me to the daybed.

"I'm fine, Mom. It was just a vision."

"You're sure?"

"I'm sure. Now, what are you doing here?"

"Can't I pop in for a visit while I'm in town?"

"You could ... but you don't. Now what is it you have to show me this time?"

Despite the state of their current renovation project, my mom seemed to take every opportunity to stop in and make decisions about the nursery. In the first week, she ambushed me with six different colors for the walls. When I chose a light blue, she'd all but scoffed at me. Now she was on a mission to make the room as unique as possible.

"Okay, so we decided the daybed is staying right here. I like where Nathan has the crib and dresser. Obviously the cradle will move into your room for about the first month. So that leaves us with the rest of the space to work with. I'm thinking that a changing table would be a waste of space. You'll end up changing her diaper on the floor more times than you'd care to think, so I think a dresser-top changing station is the way to go. On this wall, however, I'm thinking a bookcase with baskets in it for storage. What do you think?"

I thought this was just going to be about bedding.

"I like it. Just like I liked it last week when you suggested it. Now let's dig into specifics. What do you have in mind?"

"Theme."

"Theme?"

"Yes. I need to know what theme you'll be going with. Princess? Animals? Mermaids and magick? Before I go buying anything with character faces on it, I need to know what we're shooting for here."

"Mom. Remember who you're talking to, please."

"Oh, get over it, Lex. You wanted in on the decision making, and you're here for it. But you don't get to drag out the process because you want to coddle yourself. Now pick a theme."

"Fine. Victorian."

"Really?" she asked, seeming a little excited.

I shrugged. "This house is at least that old. Plus, Nathan and I were looking up ideas last night. I'll have him send you some of the pics."

She took my hand in hers. "Did you really?"

"Yes, Mom. I really did."

"Does that mean it's getting easier?"

"Well, I'm starting to get a bump, so it's a lot harder to ignore. I guess at this point I'm just glad I haven't gotten sucked into the baby frenzy that the rest of you have. Nathan just asked me about names."

"One: the baby frenzy is fun. Which you would realize if you stopped pretending to be too cool to get involved. Two: most of the fun is in deciding the name. Almost all of us would love to have that discussion with you. Three: you are a buzzkill."

I opened my mouth to deny it ... and no words came out. After a quick second of thought, I replied, "I'm doing the best I can, but let's not expect miracles, okay?"

Instead of answering, she gave me this strange look and asked, "Lex, do you ever acknowledge her?"

"What do you mean?"

"Do you ever talk to her? Sing or read to her? Do you include her in anything at all?"

"Mom, she's kinda attached to me. I include her for the stuff she doesn't even want to know about."

"You know what I mean, Alexandria."

Ouch. I got the full name out of that.

"Fine. No, I don't read, sing, or talk to her."

"Maybe that's what you should try. How about for an hour every night, you just come in here, stretch out on the daybed, and tell her about your day. Or read her a book. Or just listen to music. You'd be surprised how responsive babies are to their surroundings. Especially their mother's voice."

Which was why Elizabeth had been trying to imprint her voice into Mary's son's memories. She probably sang to him all the time. And who knew how often she talked to him. I could almost hear her voice crooning—

Shaking my head, I took another glance around the nursery. "Fine. I'll give it a try. Turn my unborn child into a diary, why don't I?"

"Or instill some hope into her." As she said

it, my mother pulled a familiar notebook out of her bag.

Taking the book labeled *Ryder Pride* from her, I said, "I thought that was in my room."

"Now it's in hers."

I rolled my eyes. "Thanks, Mom."

"You're welcome, Lex."

A few minutes later, she had to go. We said our goodbyes in the nursery and she saw herself out. Nathan found me about ten minutes after she'd gone. I was sitting on the daybed, reading my parents' love story to the baby.

The whole time, I wondered how I would tell her about her father and our bond. I didn't even know how I would describe mine and Nathan's history. At least with that one, I knew we were nowhere close to 'the end.'

When I finished, Nathan sat on the daybed and I stretched out, laying my head in his lap. "You feeling okay?" he asked as he started playing with my hair.

"Yeah. Just thinking about what my mom said."

"What's that?"

"That I should start talking to the baby and

acknowledging her as another person instead of an entity stuck inside my body."

He chuckled. "Well, that might help."

"How do you talk to something that can't talk back?"

"*Someone*," he corrected. "And you do it with cats all the time. Why is your daughter so different?"

"I told you why."

He took a deep breath and let it out slowly. For a moment, he seemed lost in thought. Then he hit home. "Lex, how did you know you were pregnant with her?"

It was my turn to sigh. "I had a dream. I was standing in the middle of Old Grove Road. I saw Faye, only she was older. When I went to follow her, a hand held me back."

I was seeing it all again. Faye fading into the trees and that quick step forward. Then the pull. When I looked back, there she was.

"I noticed her eyes, first," I murmured. "They're silver, like Grey's. She has his dimples, too. But she mostly looks like me."

"What else?"

Shaking my head, I said, "I don't know.

She was only there for a minute. I couldn't stop staring at her. She seemed so ... perfect. Then all I wanted was to hold her, but when I did, she vanished. Well, not vanished. That was when she melted into me, so-to-speak. Then there was you."

Nathan waited almost a whole minute before he said, "Can you hear yourself when you talk about her?"

"Don't..." I warned.

"Why not? Come on, Lex. You love that little girl in your dream. But you still have her, and you can't deal. What is going on up here that you can't realize that they're the same person?" he asked, flicking my forehead.

"It's different for me, okay. It just is. Right now, she's foreign and strange. In my dream ... she was familiar. More than that, she was this miracle. Fulfillment of a life I never thought I could have. In my dream, I knew who she belonged to. I knew she was mine and Grey's. But there is no me and Grey and I feel adrift because of it. As shitty as it sounds, I don't think I would feel this way if it wasn't Grey's baby."

"Why is he so important?" He didn't say it like he was jealous. He said it like he was trying to understand.

That made one of us.

"I wish I knew."

"Come on, Lex. What's the truth?"

"The truth? The truth of it is that I did exactly what Azure did. I took away his child and left him with nothing." I covered my face with my hands and released a heavy sigh.

"You didn't know him, Nathan. You didn't get to see what it cost him when his son died. Even though he wasn't in love with Spring and they were just kids, he was building his world around that little boy. That was his reason for living. But then he lost him and Spring told him the truth. Those are wounds that have never healed right for him, and I get it.

"What I don't get is how I could do that to him all over again. The second I realized I was pregnant, I knew without a shadow of a doubt that Crone's Crescent would have nothing to do with my baby. I would burn all of Grant to the ground if they so much as looked her way. And I think Grey knew that, and that's why he told me to go. It wasn't that he was letting me have this. He was choosing to save his coven by letting us go. I hate myself for doing that to him."

"Don't do that, Lex. You don't know what he was thinking when he told you to go."

"He knew what I was thinking. That's enough to know."

Shaking his head, Nathan tried a different angle. "So, she's yours when you talk about his family, but when you talk to us, she's his."

"That's not–"

"That is exactly it. If there's conflict, no one can protect her like you can. But when it comes to making a family for her, you don't know how to do it. And you think he would."

"I know he would."

"He wouldn't be able to do it alone, Lex. And neither can you. The only way we do this is together."

I raised my eyes to his and held his gaze for a moment. Then I held out my hand and smiled when he took it. "Together, then."

Chapter Thirty

KINSHIP

I stared at the list for several seconds, trying to figure out what was left to answer. We knew how William died, why Mary went after Margarite, how Margarite's family came to own the cottage, what happened to Mary's son, how Margarite died, and how Mary protected Mercy. What I still needed to figure out was why Margarite killed William, what revenge Mary unleashed, and what happened to Mercy.

In at least one instance, I knew it was in Nathan's hands. My memories were of Mary. Unless Mercy returned and left an imprint on anything in the area, I wouldn't know what happened to her. Ruling out that possibility, he was searching everything that could have gone into print. So far, there was zero luck on our side.

When it came to Mary's vengeance, I had a feeling that was still some way off. Knowing myself as I did, I would want to savor my own genius. It would be one of the last things I saw before this story found its end.

Margarite's decision to murder William was taking both of our skills to pinpoint. Whenever Nathan had time, he went through all of the documentation pertaining to the fur trading business that Henry and William were partners in. If modern murder taught us anything, it was that money was always a powerful motive.

Unable to stare at nothing any longer, I got to my feet and decided to take a walk down to the cottage. It was about due for some cleaning, and the cats would be whining to get fed. One of the females had dropped six new fluffs into the mix. She was almost done nursing, so I could go and get her fixed soon. Thankfully most of them were gray or striped. They were always easier to relocate than the black ones.

I was about halfway there when my feet suddenly redirected themselves. Wading into the shadows cast by the trees, I stepped around the ferns and avoided crushing the white wild blossoms. Around five minutes passed from the time I left the path before I arrived at the edge of the circle.

Taking a deep breath, I took one step over the outer ring and sank into a memory.

I awoke with a thrumming in my chest. Powerful energy flowed through me and I knew that it was due to much more than the rise of the full moon. For a moment, I basked in it as it settled into me. Then it began to pull.

Beside me, William was sound asleep. All the better that he did not sleep as lightly as he thought. He was fond of warning me about what unpleasant situations I could find myself in should I wander too far from the cottage. While he had known of my talents for some time, he had not seen the extent of them. As the night was my mistress, I crawled out of the bed and slipped into her welcome embrace.

Beneath the trees, it was easy to lose track of time. Yet I never foundered in my direction. The pull was stronger beneath the moon, and I felt myself drawn onward upon invisible ties. As I grew nearer my des-

tination, I was caught unprepared as the silence of the night gradually lessened into the soft chants of wild women.

Witches.

I almost turned back. Were I to appear in their space, they would know me for what I was. A fact which could ruin us all. Yet, to walk away was to deny the only community I could hope to have. To know them was to ensure that I kept their own secrets as they must now keep mine. Releasing a shaky breath, I turned once more and let the power lead me onward.

It pulsed long before I reached it. Large, heavy waves beat out in the steady rhythm of a heartbeat. I was forced to catch my breath each time they crashed over me, and I knew that it was not the call of witches that drew me on. It was the summons of the most sacred kind, and it had caught me in a snare I was not fool enough to escape.

A few moments more brought me to the end of my journey, and what I found caused me to stand still. A large stone circle encompassed the clearing, bearing within it a smaller circle large enough for one person to lay within. As one did now. She was a young woman no older than thirteen, and she was shed of her clothing. At the edges of the large circle, nine women were arranged, chanting over the fate of the woman. There was a tenth witch circling the smaller circle, brushing strands of ribbon over her body. Yet, what caused me the most surprise was the sight of children sitting outside the edge of the clearing. Behind each of the witches present, two young beings sat on their heels. They watched with such intensity that none seemed to notice my trespass upon their ritual.

When the thought of disappearing into the trees seemed ideal, the power clamped down upon us all and I felt my legs quake. The pulses came faster then, as if they were in tune with the youngling's heart. All of a sudden, it caved in on itself. The magic folded into the center circle. Into the girl.

Before that moment, I had known with absolute certainty that the girl was no more than plain. She had no gifts of her own, and no need to look for them. Yet, with the collapse, the magic seemed to delve into her and not only opened a hidden door, but carved it from nothing in that same instant. Now, it would be impossible not to call her a witch. A sister.

I fell to my knees.

Never in my life would I have believed such a place could exist. That a force was placed upon this planet that might allow us access to the gifts of Gods. When I *had begun to show an inclination for magic, my mother had told me that I was descended from Gods. At times she claimed I was bred of the great nephilim. No matter the tale, I knew that my power was an inheritance. Not so with these women. Their power was not born into them; it was taken from this place.*

"Mary?"

My mind was still reeling over the implications so that I did not immediately recognize the voice. Only when she knelt before me in the ferns and her face was of a level with mine did I recognize Margarite Vaile. I could feel my chest constrict as I recognized the wife of my husband's business partner. The fact that her presence here was as damning as my own was little comfort.

"Margarite?"

"I thought that must be you." Her expression was enthusiastic. Mine was horrified. "Is this your first visit?"

Years of practical lies layered themselves over my tongue before I could open my mouth. Yet, to lie to them was to cut myself out of this sordid community. For much of my life, I had lived in fear and trepidation. Perhaps, this once, I did not need to give in to my baser instincts.

"I was called," I answered, nodding my head to the young woman being helped to her feet.

"Ah, yes. Awakenings tend to send out as much as they intend to give. Josephine is fortunate that the circle sought to bestow so much into herself."

"That was no awakening. It was a gifting. This sacred space gave unto her that which it holds because she could hold none of her own."

My fierce reaction did not seem to upset her. "For many, it is a gifting. There are few that experience a true awakening. I count myself fortunate to be such a being. Is the same true of you?"

Astonishment clung to me as I stammered, "I have never had it suppressed. Do you mean to say that you carry magic within but were unable to access it before..." I waved my hand at the expanse of the circle.

"Precisely," Margarite remarked with a wry smile.

"How is that possible?"

"I might ask the same of a witch born with magic who had no need of awakening it."

Once more, I cast my eyes over the circle with its collection of witches and audience of children. It was foreign and frightening. I was intrigued and excited by what it might mean. More than anything else, howev-

er, when I looked upon the center circle, I felt a strange kinship with the magic living between the stones.

"What is all of this?"

"This, Mary, is Cedar Creek Coven. We are the protectors of the circle and guardians of each other. Would you like to join us?"

When the mist faded, I was standing in the center of the circle. Around me, the magick pressed in. Like Mary, I found comfort in it. It was familiar. Like Nathan or Morgan, it was a part of me. At last, I knew why.

As was the case with Mary, I believed my magick to be an inheritance. Similar to Margarite, it was a smothered gift. Until my Wiccaning in this place, my magick had never felt the need to expose itself. I was Awakened in this place. Just like countless witches before me.

Taking a deep breath, I let myself take a seat on the blackened scar where my past had died and tried to wrap my mind around the fact that the circle could *make* witches. It was one thing to acknowledge that it had the power to awaken buried magick. There was something altogether

frightening knowing that it could take a prac-
titioner like Rebecca and give her the ability to
perform energy workings at my level.

Part of me knew that it must have been for
the protection of this place, why it kept creating
witches out of women. The Natives left the land to
their successors because they knew they couldn't
guard it forever. For the sake of the power em-
bedded in this land, the more protectors it had,
the better. The more powerful those protectors,
the less likely it was to be sullied.

Until the witches tarnished it themselves.

There was a reason I never knew what the
circle was capable of. Why not one person could
remove the stain before me. The barrier built
around it was more than a network of layering
spells put in place by the previous generations of
Cedar Creek Coven; it was also the containment
wrought by the magick being taken for granted.
While the witches had been trying to protect
it from others, it'd been trying to protect itself
from them.

Then I showed up and we felt kinship all
over again.

As I stood there, a new awareness seeped

into my skin and caused the hair on the back of my neck to stand on end. Because I wasn't the only one the magick felt attached to.

Chapter Thirty One

WEAPON

It was a secret I hadn't intended to keep, but even a week later, I hadn't divulged it to anyone. Not even Nathan. There was just something about the implications of it that seemed too great.

If I told Nathan, it would end there. I knew that much. But if I told Matt or Anne or my parents or anyone else, it felt like it would implode. It almost seemed like if the more people knew, the more eager the circle would be to share its power. And though I shook my head over it a thousand times, the suspicion never went away.

New questions arose, however.

Assuming Nathan and I were right about the witch population in Cedar Creek back in the late 1600s, then there was still the question of what happened to the descendants. During that vision, each witch had two children sitting on the edge. They were witches in training.

If I thought about it too long, it looked like a setup. It looked like they brought two children each to the circle so that half of them could stay in Cedar Creek and continue guarding the circle ... and the other half could go out into the world and spread their magick. Considering the first half to leave all went with Francesca to Grant, it seemed less likely that I was wrong. Which, if it was true, then there were several more generations that could have raised their kids in the same way and shipped them off in the same way.

All five of the major covens could have started in Cedar Creek.

There were supposed to be six.

Cedar Creek had grown and the circle had intended that the coven grow with it. Had it not been for the saga of Victoria and Alyssa, it might have. But that begged the question in itself: where were the descendants of Victoria's peers? There were others trained as Alyssa and Victoria were. So, where were they? Did they stay in Cedar Creek when the coven disbanded, or did they seek new lives elsewhere? And of those that stayed, was it right of me to find out who they were? Was that my responsibility?

How was it not?

My purpose was to protect the circle. I was the Witch of Old Grove Road. That was the destiny I had signed up for long before I knew what it meant. Long before I knew what I was protecting.

If any one of the covens tried to take it, I couldn't defend it on my own.

It was a hard pill to swallow, but it was also reality.

Witches were coming back to Cedar Creek. It wasn't just me anymore. Of the residents drawn to the craft by the arrival of the others, was there the potential for more in them? Could I make Gods out of mortals? Were some of them Titans like Azure and I?

The problem with all of this was that I didn't want to recreate a coven. I didn't agree with covens. In my limited experience, no two people thought the same about everything, and it shouldn't be mandatory to practice the craft the way someone else proclaimed. That was not my cup of tea and I wasn't about to do that to anyone else.

But I had to admit that it had its advantages. During Summer's Ascension, I saw the teamwork and community that was built by Crone's Crescent. Everyone had their role to play and they did it with a sense of duty and conviction. While it seemed somewhat like a cult at times, I could tell that they really thought of each other as family.

Maybe I could use that. A community instead of a coven. Matt would be thrilled. The garden parties were a step toward that. If I dropped the hint at the next one and suggested we create a network through all of New England, I doubted they would balk at the prospect. For solitaries or covens alike, they would have the support of the Witch of Old Grove Road. And everyone else connected through the web.

It was a solid plan. All I needed was to run it by Nathan. And admit what I hadn't told him about the circle.

I knew telling him was going to be a challenge, just because I knew for so long and didn't include him. Yet, the more I spoke, the more withdrawn he seemed. Then the tension began to build until every muscle in his body was taut. I didn't understand why until his eyes bored into mine and he asked, "And you're going to have her there?"

"That's where I always intended to have her."

"Just like Morgan."

"And Victoria. Nathan, what's the issue?"

For a minute, he didn't say anything. But it worried me most when he stepped away and turned his back to me. Shaking his head, he sighed, "You said in your vision that the circle either creates witches or wakes them up. What will it do to me?"

That was one of many things I'd thought over in the past week, and I was eager to set his mind at ease. "Nathan, your magick is awake. You're not smothering it or hiding from it, you're just also not interested in it. And it's taking the hint to keep its distance. You have nothing to worry about from the circle."

"You sure about that? And what will it do to our child?"

The way he said it caused my spine to straighten. His tone wasn't just defensive, it was accusatory. As if he thought...

"Nathan, the magick won't hurt her. It wouldn't dare. It created her."

He shook his head. "You created her, Lex. You and Grey. Magick may want a piece of her life, but it can only go so far."

"Grey and I would never have been a thing without it," I reminded him.

"And I believe you. But the fact remains that you have the power to set the boundaries here. Even in regards to how magick affects our child. The question is: what boundaries will you impose?"

Taking his hands in mine, I sighed. "I wish I could tell you that it wouldn't do a thing. That because she's my daughter, her magick is already guaranteed to be badass. And while that's part of it, I'm not sure that's the whole. But if the circle decides she didn't get enough from me or Grey, I won't be upset if it gives her more."

"Why?" There was genuine fear fraying his voice. "Lex, you have enough power to move mountains and you don't know what to do with it most days. Freyja committed suicide because she couldn't find a way to cope. So how is it better if our daughter has more power than you and Grey combined?"

Straightening my spine, I made a point to hold his gaze with mine. "Because Gods and Titans walk amongst us, Nathan. It will take a Nyx to keep them all in line."

His features grew cold. "I thought you believed no witch should have to bow to another."

"I don't."

"That's not what that just sounded like. It sounds like you want to use our kid as a police force on the entire magickal community," he snapped.

"No! Gods, no! I don't want to use her for anything. All I want is to raise a child the whole damn world can be proud of. And if someone does try to preach to her or induct her, I hope she's strong enough to make them eat their words. I want to raise a woman who does not bow to the world."

She was my child, not my tool. All I had to do was teach her everything I could about being a decent human being and hope she improved on the base model. Then I would have to step back and watch her create her own life. While it didn't seem so difficult while she was in the womb, I was starting to feel some of the same panic I was sure I'd given my parents. And all I could pray for was that she wasn't too much like me.

Nathan's jaw strained a little before he asked, "What if I didn't want you to have her there? What would you say?"

"I'm sorry. That's not something I can compromise on."

A look of disgust crossed his face as he turned away from me. Unable to leave it like that, I reached out and grabbed his sleeve. "Nathan, wait. I want to explain."

"Go ahead. It's not like I can stop you, right?"

"Why are you acting like this? The circle is sacred ground and I finally understand why I have this child in my life. Why does the idea of her having power scare you so much?"

"Because I saw what it did to you!"

It felt like he slapped me.

"For crying out loud, Lex, you depend on it. There's so much of it ingrained into your system that you can't imagine a life without it. Yeah, you went a year without using, but you always knew you'd pick it back up again. It's like a drug. And now, instead of just accepting things as they are, you want it to be more ingrained in her than anyone else. After the backlash and the coma, I can't see how you of all people would want that near our child."

And the blows just kept coming. After so many in such quick succession, I went from stunned to pissed in the space of a heartbeat.

"You ignorant jackass," I sneered. "Magick isn't a drug to me, it's part of my DNA. From the moment I Ascended, it was written into the cells of my body. To take it from me now would literally drive me insane and I would have no reason to live. You know how I know that? *Because Azure killed seventeen people by taking away their magick.* It's not a dependency issue. It's a survival mechanism. And I'm sorry that you're too afraid of yours to see it as a gift instead of a curse. That's a personal problem. But you are not about to make me feel guilty for being talented and proficient, and you damn well will not make our daughter feel ashamed for having those same incredible abilities."

"You think I shouldn't be afraid of something that almost killed you?"

"Magick rebounds! It happens! It's not like it was an intentional attack on my person. In point of fact, it was holding back when I was trying to kill our best friend. I did that. The fact that I used magick instead of a knife or gun or a bloody length of rope doesn't change reality. It was a weapon in the wrong hands, and I freely admit that. But it is a weapon I will never be without, and it is a weapon your daughter will carry with her every second of her life. The question isn't whether or not she should have it. The question is how are we going to teach her to use it. Will it be in the right hands when she holds it ... or not?"

As I said it, Nathan's face fell. That was when I realized he had the same fears for her that I did. We were terrified of screwing her up. And he was even more afraid because he knew about Azure and how dark she could go.

"This is about Alyssa, isn't it? Alyssa and Victoria and Azure and Freyja. You're afraid that she'll lose her balance."

Nathan shook his head. "This isn't about them. It's about my mom and Aunt Sarah. You want to say that magick is a sentient being, but then claim that it follows commands, while you can't deny that it reprimands witches that don't follow its rules. I don't know those rules, Lex. I doubt even you do. So how are we supposed to expect a child to adhere to them? What happens the one time she doesn't?"

I wanted to comfort him, but I didn't know how. What he said was true. Magick had rules that it demanded be followed. What he didn't want to know was that witches made rules, too. For him, it was all one giant stretch of blackness, and there was no light. To soothe his wounds, I would have to make him see it.

Chapter Thirty Two

COMPROMISE

Anne poured another glass of lemonade and pushed it toward me. A command more than a hint, and I obediently took a sip. I was still staring off into space, unable to meet her gaze after my admission.

"I remember my first fight with Josh. It was stupid, really. About Valentine's Day, of all things. You see, I told him I was a pagan. He knew I didn't hold with holidays created by the church. Especially ones that honored supposed saints. Mind you, he knew all of this when we first started dating. So, when he left a bouquet of roses in my locker with candy and a teddy bear, I threw a fit. Right there in the middle of school.

"I tracked him down in gym class and threw

all of it at him. Not just shoving it in his arms or any of that. No, I baseball pitched it. The bear went first and he caught it. Which really irritated me, so I chucked the candy at his head. He didn't catch that. And while he was still stunned, I whacked him upside the head with the roses. Not my finest moment, but still one of our favorite memories to laugh at."

She paused there, waiting to see if I would ask. Instead, I took a sip of my lemonade and continued to stare at my feet. Nodding to herself, she continued, "Want to know why I did it? To humiliate him. I wanted to make him feel how I felt when I opened that locker and at least five other girls stopped to admire the lovely crap that my boyfriend got me for a stupid Hallmark holiday. It's not a day that means anything and there was nothing romantic in the gesture. He did it out of blind loyalty to the idea of what couples should do on Valentine's Day.

"I had to make him regret it. Not just for being someone who followed the crowd, but also for not respecting my wishes. I told him that if he wanted some other girl that cared about stupid, useless trinkets that there was a whole school for him to comb through. And I told him that his disregard for my opinion was a personal affront and that if he could not respect me enough to believe what I said, then we had no business being together."

Apparently, Anne was as opinionated over Valentine's Day as I was about stupid *Romeo & Juliet*. Not that there was any other correlation between her story and my circumstances.

"I know. You're wondering what this could possibly have to do with you and Nathan. The point is, Lex, he's not going to understand right away. You're going to have to explain your reasons over and over, and even then, there's no guarantee he'll see it in the same way. But he will learn to respect your position, and he'll honor your wishes."

Shaking my head, I sighed, "It's not my position that's up for compromise, and I think that's his problem."

For a moment, her shoulders sagged in relief that I responded at all. Then she asked, "Why isn't it? What is it?"

Leaning back in the chair, I let my head fall back so I could stare at the ceiling. "I'm having the baby at the circle. Considering what we just discovered about its enhancement abilities, it worries him. But this isn't something I can budge on. Magick is the reason she exists. There is no other explanation. If this is all it's asking of me, I will do it."

"Is this all it's asking for? Are you sure it won't ask for more?"

I nodded. "It wouldn't dare."

"How do you know, Lex?"

"Because it has meddled in my life enough. If it asks me to birth her in a place where it can be part of that, fine. Easy choice. But it will not ask anything else from me or I will call in that debt, and it won't like my terms."

"I understand that, honey, but she's not just your baby. Nathan deserves a say, too. And frankly, so do I."

"I know what he deserves and I know that you both have earned it, Anne. But of all the decisions to be made, this one I have made myself and I am not going to compromise."

"Why is it so important to you? Why won't you hear him out?"

"Oh, I heard him loud and clear," I said, my

voice slipping into a snap. "He thinks magick is inherently dangerous and that I am a puppet on a string where it's concerned. He thinks because it's built into me more than anyone else, that I'm at a higher risk of self-destructing."

Shaking my head, I let my tone grow sharper. "You know what the worst part is? He acts like I'm doing this just because I want her to be like me. I am the *very last* person I want my daughter to be like. I don't want her to go through an ounce of what I went through. There are things I have seen and done that I pray she will never need to learn. Because she deserves the chance to be a better person than her mother." Tears filled my eyes and I quickly scrubbed them away with the back of my hand.

"He acts like I just want her to be powerful. All I want is for her to be *safe*. He sees destruction because that's all I've ever shown him. And all I can see is what can keep her safe. Magick protected me even from myself. For her, it will do so much more. It will be so much more. And it means that once she's born, I won't have to worry about someone hurting her unless she lets them. There will be no thrown drinks or slaps to shut her up. No scars. No threats. She will be Nyx. She will be what everyone else fears, and I am perfectly content with that, because that means she will have no one to fear.

"One day, Anne, she will return to Crone's Crescent. I know that. I'm not an idiot. Someday far into the future, she will meet her father and she will be surrounded by his people. That's two hundred magick users at any given time. A thousand during holidays. Do you think I would let my child walk into that without every possible advantage she could get?

"Nathan can bitch and complain all he wants to, but if the choice is between relenting to his fears or keeping my child safe, he won't win. Which is why I took the choice off the table."

Reaching across the table, Anne ran her fingers through my hair. "Fair enough," she murmured. "Now tell that to him."

For the first time since I sat down, my eyes drifted to the doorway of the kitchen. Nathan wasn't there in person, but I knew he had heard every word. As he had done to me when he found out about the baby, I kept him with me for this conversation. In some ways, it was a lot easier this way. At least with Anne, there was someone willing to listen.

"Go to him, Lex. I think there's more to this conversation than I know about. Go on."

I did as she asked, melting from my chair in her kitchen to the couch in our family room. A few minutes later, Nathan slipped into the room and took a seat at the other end. We couldn't bring ourselves to look at one another.

"I almost died, Nathan," I murmured at last. "If Azure had her way, you'd never see me again. I would go from a padded room to a sheet being wrapped around my neck. Without learning Faye's shield, I would not be here today and our child would not exist. This is the exact future she was trying to erase.

"So believe me when I say that I will do absolutely anything and everything in my power to make sure our baby will not have to experience that. If the circle is willing to give her more power, I will let it. Because Azure is proof that there are witches out there just as strong as I am. I need her to be stronger, Nathan. I need to know that there isn't another being on this planet that can stand against her. If anything happens to her, I won't survive it."

"Neither will I." Shaking his head, he let his head fall into his hands. "Damn it, Lex. I'm just as scared as you are. Everything about magick and other witches and covens terrifies me. And I guess I'm just hoping that she'll be more like me and not give a damn about her magick. Because if that happens, then at least the target on her back won't be as large. But if she has the kind of power that the circle can give..."

Moving toward him, I reached out and took one of his hands. "Nathan, I didn't have a target on my back because of my magick. I had a target on my back because of who I am as a person. I'm prideful and arrogant and rude. And I don't concede and I don't compromise. When I'm angry, I like making enemies. If I'm hurting, I like hurting others too. I am an asshole and I don't blame people for reacting to that. But you can't confuse the two. If you're worried about me, be worried about how I provoke people. Don't blame my magick because I'm a terrible person."

"Lex, you're not—"

"I am. We both know it. Just give credit where credit is due. And don't try to turn something utterly neutral into something evil. Magick is an entity without prejudice or morality. People are the only creatures that live by those. As long as we raise our kids not to be the asshole their mother is, we'll be fine. Okay?"

He shook his head and ran a hand through his hair. "I'm sorry for what I said. I just..."

"You meant it." Every single word that had hit me over and over again, he had meant. Because he was afraid and he didn't understand magick. "It's okay, Nathan. I forgive you. And I'm sorry for what I said, too. You hurt me so I felt like I had to hurt you back."

Leaning back against the couch, he wrapped an arm around my side and pulled me closer to him. "You're forgiven."

I took a deep breath and snuggled closer to him. "Does this mean our first fight is officially over?"

"I think so. We still have a lot of issues to work through, but we'll manage."

After a minute, I shifted to look up at him. "So, is now a good time to discuss community expansion?"

"What?"

I grinned.

Chapter Thirty Three

COMMUNITY

Everyone was more than a little surprised when they arrived for the garden party and Nathan was sitting beside me. It was still a bit of a surprise to me. But there were things we were working on, and this was the role he'd asked for. I was more than willing to let him have it.

"Fancy meeting you here," Rebecca said as she sat on his other side.

"It was time," was all he said.

As usual, a sort of potluck had begun to occur, with Basil making the largest contributions. When we were all settling into our little feast, questions were being thrown Nathan's way and he dodged as best he could. They were so determined, however, that I eventually had to step in.

"He's here because I had an idea and he's going to help me sell it to you all."

"Oh, this I gotta see," Rebecca quipped, shooting him an expectant smirk.

"What idea is this?" Caroline asked.

I shared a glance with Nathan, wondering just how I was going to word this. Then I took a deep breath and said, "I like you guys. Didn't think I would, but I do. What I like most is that we're not so wrapped up in each other that we don't have our own lives, but if there's something any of us needs, we can go to each other. No questions asked. To me, that's a community. I really appreciate that."

"So do we," Caroline said with a smile.

"Hell yeah," Karrie remarked.

There were a few other words of agreement before Nathan nudged my shoulder. Basil noticed in an instant and her eyes narrowed in on us. She wasn't the only one.

"What else?" Rebecca demanded.

"I want to do more." My eyes moved around the table to study their confused expressions. "I don't want this sense of community to be limited to the witches of Cedar Creek. Having spent time with a large coven, the most admirable thing is how supportive everyone is of everyone else. They help the younger kids learn runes and tarot decks while the adults share healing remedies and spells. It's the closest I've been to other witches, and that's the only thing I was envious of. If we can, I want every witch in New England to feel like they're a part of the same thing."

"Why this sudden desire when you ignored us for weeks?" Terry asked.

Nathan opened his mouth in an instant but I put a hand on his to keep him silent. Then I smiled at Terry and told her some piece of the truth. "I'm afraid. As I'm sure most of you noticed, I'm pregnant. This winter, I will have a daughter and I will have to decide what kind of world I am bringing her into. The reason I avoided all of you was because you frightened me. The reason we are here now is because I refuse to be afraid in my own home. And the reason I want a community in place all over New England is so that I don't have to worry so much.

"We are building a community here. It's one I want my daughter to feel comfortable being a part of. And it's one I think other witches could benefit from. I'm willing to take that step. The question is: are you?"

There was a long period of silence before Rebecca whipped her head around and exclaimed, "You're pregnant?"

All at once, we began to laugh. Half of us were laughing because we thought it was obvious. The rest were laughing at her accusatory expression as she glared between me and Nathan.

"Does Mark know?" she demanded.

"Why would I go out of my way to tell Mark?" Nathan replied.

"How many people know?"

"Before I started to show? Six."

"What? You're not show—"

Rebecca's words cut off as I stood up out of my chair and pulled the sundress tighter around my stomach. Her mouth dropped and we all started laughing again.

"When did that happen?"

Karrie rolled her eyes. "She means: how far along are you?"

"Oh, there's a lot of questions. I'm just getting started," Rebecca promised.

"She'll be eighteen weeks tomorrow," Nathan

said, smiling wide as he took my hand under the table.

"How come you didn't tell us?"

"Rebecca, hush. They're telling us now."

"Yeah, now that she's almost halfway through her pregnancy."

"Hey, at least you knew before Mark," Nathan said with a shrug.

"So not helpful," she growled. "Why was it such a secret, anyway?"

"Rebecca, you almost didn't learn today. There was never going to be an announcement made and I wasn't going to 'tell anyone' until I started showing and they asked."

"Seriously? No announcement?"

"What about a baby shower?"

"Arrival cards?"

"Have you been doing any belly blessings?"

In the middle of the cacophony of accusations, Caroline leaned close and murmured, "I already started on the candles for the birthing ritual. Hope you like a lot of color. I couldn't help myself."

Nathan and I both chuckled. "You've known since then, haven't you?"

"Well I knew you weren't asking for a friend."

"Have you picked out a name yet?" Rebecca sighed.

This time when I exchanged looks with Nathan, my expression was chagrined. "We haven't discussed names yet."

"Oh my Goddess, you guys are useless. That's it. I am your official Maid of Honor and I will get this shit sorted."

"Excuse me? We're having a baby, not getting married."

"Yet. And since you're doing everything else ass-backwards, I can at least make this decision for you. Now, whose last name is she going to have? Did you at least get a sonogram?" As she spoke, Rebecca pulled a pen and notebook from her purse and opened it to a new page.

Just as I opened my mouth to protest, Nathan squeezed my hand and said, "Ryder. We're taking Lex's last name."

Everything stopped as we all stared openmouthed at him. Rebecca was the first to recover as she leaned closer to him and asked, "*We?*"

"Yes."

"Why?" At least five of us asked the question

in unison.

When Nathan looked at me, there was a sexy, devilish smirk on his face that I knew was going to get me in trouble. Then he asked, "Lex, are we going to have more kids?"

Deer. In. Headlights. The question had me sitting there with my mouth agape as the idea of having more kids while I was only about halfway through my first pregnancy derailed any cognitive response. But the idea of having Nathan's kids... Babies with his green eyes and heart of gold. Well, maybe it was the hormones from carrying kid number one, but a number two didn't sound bad at all.

My face burned as I tried to force my voice to sound casual. "I don't know. Probably."

The tone I was going for didn't seem to work because there was no disguising the self-satisfied smirk spreading across that man's face. "And whose last name will they have?" It was a rhetorical question and my lips pursed in answer. "Exactly. So, what's the point in keeping mine?"

I had no witty remark for that. In all honesty, I was flattered and more than a little possessive. This was something he couldn't take back. I wanted it now. I wanted to slap my name on him and proclaim loud and proud that he was mine and no one else could ever hope to have him. If this was how men felt about their wives taking their last name, I totally understood the appeal.

In a way, it defined us. Both of us. It said we were the same. That we were a team and we were unconquerable. More than anything, it marked us as a family.

Chapter Thirty Four

TRUE NATURE

Every time the moon was full, I found myself drifting between the trees to reach the sacred circle. When I had become accustomed to the pulse of the space, it was the laughter I listened for in order to guide me. While most of the witches chosen by the circle were women, there were sons sitting on the edge of the clearing with their sisters. Magick did not prefer one sex over the other, thus it was intended that, upon the age of thirteen years, the young ones would each have the opportunity to be gifted or experience an Awakening of their own. Thus, before the beginning of every ritual, it was not uncommon for the young ones to leap over the stones and run around in pure childish joy. Their mothers would long ago have put a stop to it if the circle did not seem to thrive from the experience.

"Jo!" screeched one piercing voice as I drew closer.

When I reached the edge of the clearing, I found Gertrude, a girl of ten years, standing with her hands fisted on her hips as she scowled at her older sister. While still new to her powers, Josephine had made quite the practice of it, for she held her sister's bonnet aloft with her thoughts alone.

"Josephine! Gertrude! Take your places," snapped their grandmother, Edith Cross. When her eyes traveled over to me, she gave a quick harrumph before taking her place in the center circle. That was as far as the courtesy extended between Edith and myself.

The truth of the matter was that Edith was the first to be gifted magic by the circle. She was also the eldest, which made it undeniable to those present who should lead them as High Priestess. Once it had become known to the others that I had been grown with use of my magic, however, an enmity had grown between us. She was resentful of my knowledge and experience, while taking it as a personal attack if I offered the others what little wisdom and advice I could. We were not destined to be friends, she and I.

"Why must you always be the last to arrive?" Margarite pretended to admonish.

"In your first year of marriage, how often did

your husband take you to bed and keep you there?" The smile upon my face was nothing short of satisfied.

"Such a vulgar thing to say in front of a fair woman," she giggled.

"You knew well the audacious things I would say. Do not pretend you did not invite them."

"I shall not. They are what keeps a smile upon my face."

Edith issued another command for us to take our places and I dipped my head to Margarite as we went our separate ways. Had it not been for the growing camaraderie I felt with her, it is unknown how long I would have endured Edith's withered tongue and pretended ceremonies. Alas, Margarite and I were never more free than when we were at the circle with one another. Besides my husband, she was the dearest friend I had.

The vision had caught me by surprise and I was quick to steady myself against one of Caroline's display tables. At once, the other woman was at my side. One hand went to my arm while the other immediately sought my forehead.

"I'm fine," I said, waving off her attention.

"Just a memory."

"That was a memory?"

"Yes. Of a past life. Though I don't under-stand what could have triggered it." As I spoke, my eyes grazed over the table, looking for some-thing that may have set off the vision.

"Does it normally require a trigger?"

"Not always, but most of the time."

Once more, I wished this was like Alyssa or George or Benjamin. I wanted a simple puzzle with easy-to-find pieces. After nine years of wondering about Mary Sullivan, all I wanted now was to be able to set aside a block of time and track down every last answer.

Unconsciously, I ran a hand over my grow-ing stomach. As we'd entered September, I was officially at twenty weeks, and I looked it. While Anne insisted on me seeing a doctor, she hadn't been lax in my care. She'd measured my stomach and kept a close watch on my weight gain. Every house I went to was well-stocked with foods she approved of—as well as a few she didn't. So far, everything was right on track.

Until it felt like an insect crawled up one side of my stomach.

At once, I threw my hand over the spot, slapping down the fabric in case there was a spider or something. Then it happened again and I got a clue. My mouth dropped as I placed both hands over the spot and waited. The third time it happened, I laughed aloud.

"Alex? What is it?"

My eyes were watering a little as I looked up at Caroline and explained, "I think I'm feeling her move."

Her smile widened and she took an automatic step toward me. Then she stopped and said, "I think you should go see Nathan, now."

If he wasn't out at one of the rental properties, I would have agreed with her. As it was, I knew one other person who would be just as excited. In a moment, I thanked Caroline and teleported to my parents' new project house.

"Mom," I called as I appeared in the living room.

When no immediate answer came, I pinpointed her location and headed to the back of the house where she had transformed part of it into a sunroom. Looking through the glass-paned door, I found her dozing on a wicker sofa.

Had I been there for any other reason, I would have let her sleep. After feeling another flutter, however, I was quick to open the door.

"Mom?"

She jerked awake in an instant, flying up in one swift motion. As soon as she saw me, she threw a hand over her chest and leaned back. "Alexandria Marie, don't you ever scare me like that again."

"Sorry, Mom, but I didn't think you'd want to miss this."

"Miss what?" she demanded as I came to sit beside her. Without answering, I took her hand and placed it on my stomach. We only had to wait a few moments before that same sensation crawled across my skin.

"Can you feel that?"

"Hold on," she murmured, leaning closer. Another flutter occurred and I held my breath. It wasn't until the third that a wide smile broke across her face and I almost sagged in relief.

"So, it is what I think it is," I sighed. "I wasn't sure, because it felt so weird. But if you can feel it too, that means it's real."

"How do you feel?" she asked as she leaned

back.

"Weird, honestly. But it's a good weird. It's one thing to know she's in there, but having her move and kick makes it all the more real. It helps."

My mom took one of my hands in hers. "Is it getting better?"

"I think so. A little at a time. Having proof that she's another person helps ease the disconnect."

"If it helps so much, why haven't you gone for an ultrasound yet? If you think feeling her move is life-changing, wait until you hear that heartbeat for the first time. And that sonogram picture..."

"You've been talking to Anne," I accused.

"About so many things." She was entirely unrepentant. "I've also been in contact with a young woman named Rebecca who claims she is your Maid of Honor. Care to tell me what that's all about?"

I groaned a little before I began to explain the garden party conversation. My mom listened with a smirk. When I got to the point where Nathan announced that he would take my last name, she laughed outright.

"Nothing will make me happier than seeing your father's face when he finds out about that."

"I don't care. I want this, Mom. More than just wanting to marry him or have a family with him, I want him to take my last name. I want the feeling of us being one unified force."

"You'll have it, Lex. I have no doubt of that."

"Neither do I."

When it came to Nathan and I, I didn't doubt a damn thing.

For the next few hours, my mom and I discussed everything Rebecca had been digging for. Apparently, I was getting a baby shower where my only job requirement was to show up. Fine by me. It sounded like she was going to take care of everything. Which, honestly, made her excellent Maid of Honor material.

When it began to grow dark, I released a sigh and said goodbye to my mom. I arrived in our bedroom with the idea being that I would take a nice, long bath. Thanks to a little magick, the tub was full by the time I was able to undress and I sank gratefully into the water. As I leaned back and began to run through the events of the day, one question nagged at me. What was the purpose of the vision from earlier?

Then the white mist traveled over my eyes.

Never before had Edith called for me. Were it not a gathering of the Coven, we had little use to see one another. For her to request my presence now meant that it was urgent.

To accentuate the thought, my pulse quickened as I felt drawn to the circle. It was broad daylight. Our spells to hide the circle were still weak. What could she hope to achieve by having us meet there at an hour where any could follow me?

That spark of paranoia caused me to weave a spell to silence my steps and erase signs of my passing as I all but ran to our sacred place. It was that spell which may have saved my own life. For once I reached the edge of the clearing, I was met with a sight that caused me to drop to my knees.

Peeking through the foliage hiding me from the two women, I tried to make sense of what I saw, but could not. Margarite—my dearest friend of the past four years—stood over our High Priestess with an athame to her throat. In an effort to form an excuse, I thought it must be some kind of trust ritual. It was well known that, after Edith, Margarite had the ambition and drive to become High Priestess. Given the animosity Edith oft showed to me, I was eager to see my friend step into the role.

Not like this.

"Your true nature emerges at last, Margarite. Tell me, do even your bosom friends know you for the serpent you are?"

"An apt description, it is. For you know, before Kisusq left the circle in your care, she performed a naming ceremony for me. It is too complicated to say in Mohegan, but in our tongue, I am known as Snake Between the Shadows."

For a moment, I refused to believe it was my friend's voice speaking in such a lofty tone. She spoke with a freedom of thought that allowed me to see for the first time just how constrained she was around me. Everything about her seemed lighter somehow. As if she had broken the masks that bound her and was at last appearing as she truly was.

"Kisusq always did know which of us had the darker hearts. It is why she warned me against you."

"Did she now? Clever woman. Alas, I think you will see her far sooner than I. The time has come,

Edith. It is time that I take my place as High Priestess of Cedar Creek Coven."

"I will not make it easy for you, Margarite. The deed will need to be done by your hand. I dare not condemn myself in such a manner."

Margarite's laughter rang throughout the clearing, causing a shiver to run up my spine. With amusement still in her voice, she remarked, "A woman openly practicing witchcraft dares not take her own life for fear of condemning her soul. My, my how our childhood beliefs still bind us."

"Is that what you think I fear? Nay. My soul is on the same circle as yours. Yet, I will not have the coven believe me to be such a coward."

"Have you not heard? History is written by the victors. Of which you are not."

Before Edith or I could respond, Margarite shifted her grip on the athame before slicing a quick, clean path across Edith's throat. My hands shot up to my mouth as I muffled any sound—my spell forgotten. I squeezed my eyes shut and looked away in an attempt to save myself that sight. Too late. Already it was a moment I knew would continue to repeat in every waking hour.

I paid no more mind to the things Margarite was doing in the clearing. It was now well past time for me to be gone from this place. Sinking more power into my spell, I slipped away as quietly as I could. Upon my walk home, but one thought intruded.

Edith's gifts were prophetic. She knew this was going to happen. And she had called upon me to witness, not interfere.

Chapter Thirty Five

LEGACY

I felt cold and the bath wasn't helping. My hands gripped the sides of the clawfoot tub and I focused on taking deep breaths. My earlier vision hadn't been meant to torment me with the fact that Mary and Margarite had been close. It had been to show me that Edith was the High Priestess, and Margarite wasn't. Then she was. All because she'd killed her predecessor and made a play for the role.

No matter which life I was living, it wasn't something I would be able to stand for. If Margarite's plan was to make a play for the coven, Mary would have tried to stand against it. Unless she had a reason not to. A reason like her husband dying and having the need to get her kids out of town.

That bitch.

It may have been centuries gone, but I could taste the bloodlust on my tongue. In this day and age, it was more than what she'd done to Edith, more than William's murder, and even more than driving Mary out of Cedar Creek. What infuriated me so much was the fact that she got everything she wanted. The coven. Her wealthy life. Two brilliant, powerful daughters ready to step up and face their destinies.

All I could do to hurt her was to expose what she was and take from her that which she'd stolen from me: the opportunity to watch her children grow.

To do that, there had to be a very particular spell, and it would have taken about a year to perfect it. Much like the one I was working on.

And it took Mary dying at Margarite's hands to trigger it.

I wasn't sure how I knew, but it clicked into place as soon as my thoughts ran across it. To trigger a spell to take a life, one had to be offered. There was always a balance to pay. A son in exchange for a husband. A witch in exchange for a witch.

A daughter in exchange for a son.

Releasing a heavy breath, I closed my eyes and leaned my head back against the tub. This was it. This was always it. The balance had to be paid. For Grey as well as for me. It was magick that robbed him of a son. Magick owed him a child, and it gave him one. It just had a terrible idea of how to get it done. Instead of giving him a child to love and cherish, it gave him one more person he could only love from afar.

I practically leapt out of the tub. After getting dressed, I was quick to write Nathan a note, letting him know that I would be at the cottage. Then I changed locations and got back to work.

For the sake of my family, and to pay my own balance, this spell had to be done before my daughter arrived.

There was also one more thing I wanted from Grey, and I knew exactly how to get it.

The self-addressed envelope felt heavy in my hand, though I knew a slip of paper with a single word and a lock of hair were all that resided within it. Ever since I'd sent it four days ago, it was all I could do not to break down in tears now that it was back in my hands.

When I felt him coming, I lifted my head and stared toward the back of the garden. He was taking his sweet time in traversing the trail and I couldn't decide if I was relieved or annoyed. The longer he took, the more time I had to stare at my own handwriting and contemplate what else it might contain.

As soon as I saw Nathan appear between the trees, it felt like a fist loosened around my heart. Between the dread and anticipation, I was running on raw nerves. One look at him soothed everything. Especially when he smiled at me like that.

By the Gods, how did I not notice it before? I really was that blind, because there was no denying how much that man loved me. If I could be sure of nothing else, I would always be sure of that.

Once he was close enough, I stood up and wrapped my arms around his neck and pulled him into a deep and lasting kiss. After a few minutes of holding Nathan hostage, I released him with a self-satisfied smirk. That didn't mean he let me go.

"Hi," he said, leaning his forehead against mine.

"Hi."

Several seconds passed with us lingering in that position. Then he murmured, "You said you had something to show me."

Releasing a breath, I stepped back. Taking hold of his hand, I led him back to the bench. Then I smoothed the wrinkled envelope over my thigh and watched as his gaze zeroed in on it.

"You asked me for a name. I couldn't have that conversation with you, and I finally figured out why. One: she's not just my kid. She's also his. And she's yours. Two: I already gave her a name. Mine. And it wasn't fair of me to try to give her two more. Not when she has two other parents that deserve a say.

"So, I wrote to Grey asking him for a name. This is his reply. And when we've read it, I would like for you to choose your name for her. What do you think?"

Instead of answering me, Nathan placed a hand on the back of my neck and dragged my face to his. Placing his lips against my forehead, I could feel his smile when he said, "You always have to make sure things are fair."

I shook my head. "I do not require fairness. Only justice."

And this was just. As her father, it was Grey's right to name her. As her dad, it was Nathan's right to have a say. In this way, we all got what we wanted, and what we deserved. She was my legacy, she was Grey's buried treasure, and she was Nathan's baby girl. We deserved this. As a family.

"Open the envelope, Lex."

Taking a deep breath, I ran a fingernail beneath the sealed portion. As I pulled the dark lock of hair free, a flutter traveled across my stomach as the baby seemed to recognize the gift her father had sent. Holding tight to his hair, I removed the small, folded note and held my breath. With Nathan's help, we opened it and got our first look at our daughter's name.

It was perfect.

Rowan Rosemary Ryder

I kept staring at the words, repeating them over and over in my mind. It fit. Every single piece of it fell into place and I couldn't imagine my child having a better name.

When I opened that envelope and saw 'Rowan' written in Grey's hand, all I could picture was our first unofficial date. Standing at the glass door of his basement and examining the fairy village at the base of the rowan tree... It was the start of us, that day. The real start.

Nathan had chosen Rosemary. In his words: it was simple, clean, and didn't have the weight of the world on its syllables. I'd laughed, but he was right. Rosemary was hers alone. It was the one part of her name that didn't come with history, and she didn't have to share it with anyone else.

We had finally named our baby girl. All three of us.

Which had been the hardest secret I had ever kept. Yet, with all of the nagging that was still being done during the Sunday garden parties, I wanted it to be a distinct pleasure to hit them all at once.

In the past week, what no one knew was that

I went and got a sonogram done. And my mom was right. Nothing made her more real than seeing her on the screen or hearing her heartbeat. But she was also wrong. Because I couldn't think of her as something other than 'the baby' until she had her own name. Now, she was Rowan.

"They're going to want to kill us," Nathan chuckled, looking over the little announcement cards.

"Maybe they'll learn to stop nagging." As soon as I said it, I rolled my eyes at him.

"So how do you want to do this? Drop them off and not even mention it, or send everyone a singing telegram?"

"Oh, tough choice. Classic you and me or annoy the shit out of them in petty revenge?"

"We do like petty revenge."

"Yeah, but I think it would piss them off more if we go the classic route."

Nathan began to chuckle. "Can you imagine Rebecca's face?"

All at once, I was laughing with him. "Oh, we have to now!"

"Okay, after the reveal with the parents tonight, we'll just start throwing cards in mailboxes."

"Deal."

Gathering together the many copies of the announcements we made, I stashed them in the piano bench with all of the sheet music. Just in time, too. Not ten minutes later, Anne and Josh knocked on the front door. Then they walked right in.

"Mmm, is that rosemary chicken I smell?" Anne asked as I stepped out of the parlor.

"Yep. Cravings strike again. Nathan's cooking tonight."

"Fantastic. I have had one hell of a day," she sighed.

Josh pointedly walked away, unwilling to hear another story about labor and delivery. All things considered, I let her tell me all the stories so I could take mental notes on how not to act or which warning signs to look for. So far, so good. Until she launched into the lecture about me not going to a doctor's appointment, because she didn't have all the equipment that hospitals did. While I smiled through it all, she thought it was me being my regular self. Which made this big reveal all the sweeter.

My mom and dad arrived about twenty minutes later. Punctual as usual. As it happened, my dad was also in the mood to complain, since they hadn't yet had a decent offer on the house. It was a conversation that took up most of dinner, but we knew it wouldn't last.

Right on cue, as dessert was winding down, our moms started talking about the nursery. Nathan and I exchanged a quick look before I set my glass down and remarked, "We actually added something to it today."

There was a deer-in-the-headlights moment as my mother stared at me. Then, in a slow, cautious voice she asked, "What did you add?"

"Nothing major. Just something small ... and meaningful."

"Like...?"

"Do you want to see?" Nathan asked.

"Yes, we do," Anne announced, standing up from the table.

I barely halted the grin. "Does everyone want to come?"

Our dads exchanged a disinterested look, but weren't given a chance to answer as Nathan pointedly motioned to the stairs. With a resigned sigh, the two men followed me and the moms from the room.

To be fair, when we opened the door into the nursery, there wasn't a moment of instantaneous recognition. The walls were still the same light blue with spongy clouds going across the ceiling. Same lace curtains and silky, ivory bedding for both the daybed and the crib. They'd even attacked the old cradle and put a fresh layer of lacquer over it so that it shined in the light. Yet, when their eyes landed on the bookshelf, I was pleased to hear an audible gasp.

The picture frame sat on top; front and center. It was a handmade affair that had taken Cameron all week to create. He'd painted it white, so it wasn't noticeable at first that the frame was a collection of rowan leaves. Not that our parents even glanced at it. All eyes were instead locked on the sonogram photo in the middle of the frame, and the border around it that announced her name.

For about thirty seconds, there was zero motion in the room. Then my mom's eyes teared up and she turned to wrap her arms around me. That moment made everything worth it.

Chapter Thirty Six

DRAINING

William had begged me not to do this. If she could kill Edith, what was to stop her from trying to kill me? It was the same thought that had plagued me from the time I had watched it happen. For that reason alone, it was my duty to warn the others. They deserved to know.

In the dark of the new moon, I made my way to the circle. It was not often that we chose to meet during the darkest of nights, but after Edith's death, it seemed appropriate. Thus, when I requested, I heard from every coven member that they would be in attendance. Except Margarite.

As soon as I reached the edge of the circle, I understood why.

Margarite stood in the center of the circle, her back

to me and her gaze directed as if she were seeing her victim once more. This time, I did not run. Crossing into the circle, I moved as close as I dared and erected a shield. As soon as I did it, she began to laugh.

Without turning, she said, "I could feel you. I could not hear or see you, but I could feel your magic pulsing. It feels like the circle. Alive and pure. Power in its most basic form."

Her head lifted a little but she still did not look at me. "That is how I have always thought of you. Magic comes so easily to you. Without any need to coax or cajole it. For you, it is a partner in an intimate dance. Not so with the rest of us."

Shaking her head, she turned to face me at last. "I always thought Edith was a fool to push you away as she has. She saw you as a threat. More than that, she did not trust you to do what was necessary for the coven. I always believed that if she had given you more of a role, you would have taken us to great heights. And your loyalty would always be assured. Is it wrong of me to believe, my dearest Mary, that you might yet prove to be such a treasure?"

"You know why I called the coven, Margarite. You know what it is that I wished to say to them. What they deserve to hear."

"Do you think they are unaware?"

She asked the question in such a simple manner that, for a moment, I wondered if she might not be right.

"Who do you think suggested bringing the children into this? It was I. Not Edith. Why would I do such a thing if I did not wish to see a rise of the witches across this New World? Edith had no vision. She had no thought but to secure us against our husbands and fathers. This was her calling, she said. To protect the circle. That old witch could not comprehend that this circle was gifted to us to be used, not hidden away."

"That is false! We were entrusted with its safekeeping, not given this power to corrupt it."

"How is it corruption? It has given each of us a part of itself because we are worthy."

"The circle gave unto you all a gift so that it would be protected from those seeking to destroy it."

"As you say. I say different. In the end, which of us is to judge? The coven has already chosen its next High Priestess, and it is not you."

"I am sure they feel safe knowing that the woman that chooses to lead them now will merely kill any who oppose her."

"If that were true, you would not now be standing

before me."

"Margarite, the reason I stand before you is because you are not strong enough to kill me."

At once, the wit and banter were at an end. Her eyes narrowed into slits as she glared at me. "You think yourself so powerful. You were not the only one awakened, Mary. I have magic in my veins as ancient and powerful as yours."

"Speak what lies you wish, but we both know well the truth," I sneered. Taking a calming breath, I continued, "I came here tonight to warn the coven against you. This, I will still do. Yet, if your corruption of them proves too great, then this edict I now declare: I am no longer a part of Cedar Creek Coven. I am no longer your friend. I am no longer a sister witch. And our families will never meet again. This is the end of us, Margarite."

"What do you think you are doing, Mary?"

"What do you think you have done? You chose this road for us when you chose to murder an innocent woman for your ambition. There are consequences to your actions, Margarite. This is one of them. And when you go home and tell your children why they will never see Mercy again, you remember that it is because innocent blood stains your hands. And when

your husband asks why his partner has taken all of his shares and vanished, know that this is why. Know that you bring misery to everyone you touch. Know that no one in this life will ever be able to trust you again. Know that I do not love you."

It was draining. After every happy moment in my life, I had to experience one more devastating one from Mary's. Perhaps the only consolation was knowing, somehow, that it was almost over.

I had most of the answers. All that I really needed now was to know what spell Mary had set on her nemesis. What trap had Margarite walked into?

After taking a few deep breaths, I opened my eyes and got my bearings. The garden table stretched before me with three steaming pots of tea residing between the last of the floral displays for the fading summer. It was two days after Rowan's name was revealed to our parents. Two days since Nathan and I snuck through town and dropped the announcements into the other witches' mailboxes. Now we would have a chance to hear Rebecca snap at us in person. Something

I had been looking forward to ... right up until that memory hit.

Talk about a buzzkill.

"That bad?" Nathan asked as he came up behind me, his hands landing on my shoulders. I groaned when his thumbs dug into the knots beside my shoulder blades.

"How long have I been out of it?"

"A few minutes."

Releasing a heavy breath, I explained what I had just witnessed. When I mentioned that Margarite had arranged for the children to play witness, his hands stilled. After I finished the recounting, I turned to look at his face. Even his features were stiff, but his eyes were distant.

"She wanted witches spread across the New World," he murmured. "You were right. Those other covens probably started right here. Because of her."

"The real question is: what happened to the ones that were left behind?"

He shook his head. "Without knowing the names of the witches from Victoria's time, it's impossible to say."

"I only know a handful. No last names. And

I can't get them now because that story's over."

A smile pulled at his lips. "Wasn't actually relying on you for that part," he said with a chuckle. "You're forgetting that research is kind of my thing. I'll start with Alice and Anne and work my way around from there."

Alice. The woman with the ability to know the truth, no matter how unpleasant or justified. And Anne. The twin with the necessity to see justice was done and every account balanced. They were the reason Morgan had been orphaned. They were some of the last witches to make up the Cedar Creek Coven.

If that was the last of the coven.

For a moment, I considered if it might be true. If, somewhere in New England, there was still a group operating under that name. Yet, I knew there wasn't. The deaths of Victoria and Alyssa had broken something integral to the coven. Or maybe it had just been the final blow to a system that had been cracking since the days of Mary and Margarite. Either way, there was no chance that any coven of any strength could escape my notice anywhere close to Cedar Creek.

But for those outside of my particular influence, there was still the matter of forging a bond. The kind of connection that would allow them to rely on me and those like me. Maybe then I could bring into the fold those that belonged here. Those whose lives were inexorably linked to this circle as mine was.

Before Nathan or I could think much more on the subject, the others started their journey down Old Grove Road. I cast a smile on him when his eyes darted to the gate. His magick wasn't on the same level as mine, but he was getting pretty good at listening to his instincts.

No, the circle wouldn't awaken anything in Nathan. But if he let it, I was pretty sure he'd get the biggest shove of his life.

The gate burst open and Rebecca stomped over the line. In her hand was the announcement, raised above her head like a battle flag. My eyes darted to the gargoyles to see their reaction, but since she was allowed to pass, I knew she wasn't too upset.

Not that she wouldn't play the part.

"You guys suck," she snarled as she marched up to us.

"What did we do?" I asked innocently.

In response, she shoved the sonogram announcement in my face. "I had plans for this,
you know."

"Did you?"

Her features darkened. "Yes," she said in a
clipped tone.

I shrugged. "Well, how was I supposed to
know? According to *my mother*, my only obligation in all of this is to show up when and where
you tell me. No one said I couldn't do my own
thing in the meantime."

She looked anything but amused. Then her
eyes dropped back to the announcement and
her nose wrinkled. "Would it have killed you to
make it pretty?"

"Were we supposed to?"

"Hopeless. You two are utterly and completely hopeless." Shaking her head, Rebecca said,
"Now I have to redo all of the invitations."

"Why?" Nathan asked.

"Uh, the name! Look, I know you're not
into everything like this, but the name means ...
everything. Okay, it turns the focus of the baby
shower away from Alex and straight onto Rowan.
It becomes about her, now. Which, no offense, is

way more appealing in the long run."

My suspicion was starting to spike and I leaned closer to her. "More appealing to who?"

Rebecca's eyebrows rose and her entire body became smug all over. "Never mind. Your job is simply to show up when and where I tell you."

"I hate you right now."

"You love that I'm doing it and no one else has to."

"Doesn't mean that I don't hate you."

"It's just because you don't like not knowing things."

There was no way I could argue with that. Out of everything said of me, that was probably the truest statement ever applied.

I was saved a reply by the others moving about the table, setting down dishes, taking their seats, and all of the gossip that came with a witchy gathering. Most of it was about Rowan's name and the sonogram photo. There were a few other remarks that caught my interest, however.

"Where's George?" I asked Basil when I noticed her husband was nowhere in sight.

Her demeanor was casual, but her words were loaded with meaning when she looked at me and said, "He's visiting some friends out of state. Irish family near Boston. You'd like them."

Chapter Thirty Seven

LOST HEIRS

Two weeks into October, I realized it was time to focus back on my spell. When I first started, I had mistakenly thought it would be challenging, but not difficult. I was an idiot. As the most complex spell I had ever created, there were bound to be a thousand dilemmas. Most of it was the fact that the spell wasn't for me.

My eyes once more zeroed in on the plastic bag that held the lock of Grey's hair. I owed him this connection. Magick owed it to him. After what we stole, there was only one way I could think of to give it back. Grey deserved more of his daughter's life than meeting her when she became an adult.

If only I could replicate the bond Nathan and I had.

It had been instinct. A mutual connection forged in secrets and chaos. Our bond had grounded us in ways nothing else could. And neither of us had a clue how it had come to be.

This bond couldn't be created of the kind of turmoil that had strengthened mine and Nathan's. It had to be gentler than that. Something that would grow and bloom and thrive the same way Rowan would. Yes, there had to be instinct involved, but there also had to be guidance. And protection. Two things that I was required to provide, as her mother. I owed it to her.

For some reason, I thought of the blackness. The place where the bond between Nathan and I had evolved into an entity of its own. It was created of our worst fears, and that one bright spot of hope.

It was neutral ground.

That's it!

Maybe it wasn't about creating a bond. Maybe it was about creating a place where a bond could be forged. A place for father and daughter and no one else. Not even Mom.

I was so deep into my new thought process and spell planning, that the time completely shot over my head. When a knock sounded on the door, I shot a foot in the air. Nathan eased open the door. He wasn't smiling.

"What's going on?" I demanded, stepping around the table.

Holding up a thick folder, he asked, "Want a history lesson?"

My stomach knotted and I motioned him to the couch. While I cleaned up my supplies, Nathan sat down and started spreading papers over the coffee table. I couldn't help but remember a similar scene between Grey, Spring, and I. Could Nathan's revelation be anything like learning Azure was a killer?

"Okay, tell me," I said as I sat beside him.

Nathan passed me the top sheet of paper out of his folder. On it was a list of names. Including Alyssa, Victoria, Alice, and Anne.

"The last generation," I mused.

"You can say that again," Nathan said in a hard voice.

My eyes snapped to his. "What does that mean?"

In response, he pulled out a photograph of Anne and Alice. "On paper, Alice LeFayette had one child. Morgan LeFayette. Her sister, Anne, had no children. Neither did their cousin, Elena. Nor her sister, Catherine. Nor another girl named Eve. Guess what they had in common."

My eyes closed. "There were three other girls learning beside Victoria and Alyssa. They were weak, and Alyssa hadn't bothered with them."

Nathan nodded. "Eve, Elena, and Catherine were all between the ages of eight and twelve in 1922. But they weren't the only ones. There are four others near Alice and Anne's ages that were also infertile. Two of them were male."

"Seriously?"

Once more, Nathan set files on the table. This time, they were medical. After a moment of perusal, my wide eyes met his. He nodded.

"The LeFayette family is the only one that survived the ages, and Morgan's not even a real LeFayette."

"You're telling me that the Vaile family is the only one that is still alive?"

Nathan shook his head. "I don't know about from the beginning, but from the last batch? Yes. Lex, they were all infertile. None of them could reproduce. How is that possible?"

Short answer: it wasn't. Complicated answer: because someone else made sure of it. But who would do that? Why? How?

My first thought was Alyssa Rice. I knew she had tried to kill her competition, but had she tried something else, as well? Had she gone above and beyond and eliminated any chance of future competition?

No. At nine, Alyssa was purely goal-oriented. She had a one-track mind and didn't understand that there were things such as big pictures. Victoria, on the other hand, was all about the big picture. Was that why they had wanted to see justice done for Alyssa? Was it because she had laid a spell on all of them that they deemed she had to die for?

Or it could have been Alice. If she knew the road the coven was taking, would she have cut it off where it could do the least damage? Or Anne the justice taker? Would she have done it in order to balance the scales?

"There's too little information," I sighed. "There are too many suspects and too many motives. And why would everyone be singled out except for Victoria? Why allow her genes to pass on and no one else's?"

"She was the only strong one left," Nathan suggested. "Other than Anne and Alice, Victoria's gifts were substantial and no one else's were." He was just guessing, but it was sound deductive reasoning.

"You think someone might have been trying to thin the herd?"

"Or cut out the weak links."

That didn't fit with any of them. But it sounded like someone else I knew. Too bad Azure wasn't a viable suspect considering her not-yet-born status.

"Why couldn't it be easy?" I sighed, leaning back into the couch.

"What?"

"I mean that I was just wrapping up Mary and Margarite. We were getting this whole community project off the ground. Rebecca is all over the baby stuff. And the one thing I thought would be the easiest is now a whole new mystery."

"Sorry."

"Don't be. Not your fault. You were just doing what I asked you to do. Trying to find the lost heirs."

Saying it like that meant something. I wasn't sure what, but the fact that Cedar Creek Coven had depleted so far that only the Rice and Vaile families could produce substantial witches... The coven had had access to the circle for centuries. Their children should have been stronger. Instead, their magick had grown weaker.

"Could this have been Mary?" I asked aloud.

"Why do you think that?"

I barely heard him. My mind was whirling through possibilities. Maybes that could very well be realities. All I needed to do was study the source.

"Come with me," I said as I stood up and headed for the door.

"Where are we going?"

"The circle."

Nathan hesitated. "Why?"

I didn't answer. I was too lost in thought. The more I twisted the idea around, the more I was sure I could lay the blame for the fallen bloodlines at Mary's feet.

When we arrived at the circle's edge, I could feel the memory lingering on the other side of the stones. Without a thought, I crossed over.

At last, I would have my reckoning.

Traveling through the trees, it pained me to feel how dull the pulse was from the circle which had once welcomed me as one of its own. Too much had been taken from it, without anything being given back. Witches created as the coven was had no thought as to what magic required. A price would always need to be paid. The balance would always be restored.

With that, at least, I could be of some assistance.

When I entered the clearing, I was gratified to notice that no other witches were present. As it was a new moon, I could not expect them to gather, but I had also been absent a year. What patterns they had developed could have shifted beneath the reign of Margarite.

It was reason enough to cast the spell while I could, with little risk of discovery.

Making my way to the center of the circle, my magic placed my tools with careful precision. Herbs and stones followed. Then the candles. I drew runes in the earth and crooned a lullaby into the night.

Slowly, the magic rose from the depths of the circle. Roused from its despondent state, it first wrapped around me, trying to determine my worth. When it met with the same strain of magic that resided in me, it decided to give of itself. The magic of the circle delved into me, enhancing what I could already carry. Enough so that I could set the spell that would free us both from the tyranny of witches.

When I closed my eyes and bowed my head, I pushed the magic out. A little at a time, it spread to the edge of the circle, settling deep within the roots of the plants and the very stones that marked its boundaries. Bit by bit, the wall encompassed the mediocre spells already there, absorbing them into its own thick barrier and binding them to what would come next.

Holding the magic at the borders, I called my athame to me. To bind a spell as complex as this, it needed something to ground it. For what I had in mind, nothing would work as effectively as blood. Taking up the blade, I took a breath and held it to my forearm. Releasing the breath, I made a quick slash. As my blood fell to the ground, I sank every reserve I had into the fallen drops.

To free us both, I bound the wall in place.

To pay the price, I breathed into it purpose.

For the sake of balance, I taught it to take back what had been given.

In the name of vengeance, I sought to end those

that had corrupted its gifts.

Drop by drop, I wove the spell into a net meant to ensnare all those who returned to this place. By tying it to my blood, I made certain that I was the only being who could undo what was being done. Should my blood be spilled, the spell would target all those responsible. Not only would they pay, but so would their children and their children's children. For everything the circle had given unto them, it would take back until no more of itself rested in the outside world. Damn Margarite and her ambitions.

There was only one mild regret I had in regards to the spell: it would not work on those who were awakened instead of gifted. Thus, the lines of Vaile, Blake, and Carter were untouchable. Even if it proved necessary to avenge myself on Catherine and Agnus, their line would know no harm.

Hence the necessity of yet another spell.

As the last drops rolled off my forearm and dripped from the blade, I completed my vengeance. It was a vile curse on my own blood. Should it be shed by any being other than myself, so a black stain would be laid upon them. With the magic of the circle steeped with my own, I wrote the spell in the very soul of this place, that whosoever should harm me would sacrifice all of their magic to this place. To kill me was to have their power stripped from them and all camaraderie fade. Without their magic, they severed their connection to the coven, and the coven would sever their lives. Anything to keep their secrets.

Margarite was the object of my vengeance, but the coven would not be spared. The balance must always be paid.

Chapter Thirty Eight

BLOODLINES

When the memory released me, I found myself clinging to Nathan's forearms as he steadied me. As soon as I started blinking, his features relaxed for a moment. Then the worry reasserted itself.

"You okay?" I asked, my voice sounding slow as my mind tried to catch up with the present.

"I should be asking you that."

It was then that I noticed where we stood. Inside the circle. The one place Nathan was afraid of.

This time, my voice was more urgent when I demanded, "Are you okay?"

Without answering, he asked, "What happened? What did you see?"

His body remained a little tense, but I was glad to see some color returning to his face. Despite my reassurances, Nathan had not had good experiences with the circle. To him, more death occurred here than life. But it was also the place he would meet his firstborn, and it was obvious he was trying to come to terms with the locale. Given that fact, I took a deep breath and began to recount the memory.

It must have helped, because his features were considering when he asked, "So, wait, Mary couldn't touch the other bloodlines because their magick was bred into them, not part of the circle?"

"Precisely."

"But she still somehow managed to make Margarite and the other two lose their magick. Explain that to me."

"I would if I could," I sighed, looking out over the circle. Raising one hand, I placed my palm against the solid-feeling barrier that separated the circle from the rest of the world. "Can you feel that?"

Slowly, as if afraid it would bite, Nathan raised his hand and reached for a spot next to mine. The second his eyes opened wide, I knew he felt it as I did.

"Before Mary's spell, the protection on this place was so weak, anyone wandering these woods in daylight could have stumbled across it. The spell Mary put on it anchored it. It gave it an actual will to deny entrance to those it deemed unworthy and it steered others away. And for the sake of itself, she layered the spell so that the circle would always get what it was owed. Not just what it gave out, but any recompense for past transgressions.

"Mary's spell sounds similar to Azure's in that it stripped the magick from them. But it was different in that she used *the circle* to do it. Her spell wasn't about taking it to see if she could. It was about the circle taking it as payment. Without the circle to act as a magnet, I doubt it would have worked."

"I still don't see how that differs from what Azure was doing."

"Magick is all about balance and payment. If Mary had done what Azure did and pulled magick from others with nowhere else for it to go, there would have been consequences. But by making the circle–a place of magick–responsible for taking it, she circumvented the blame. This way, not only was it taken from a witch, it was taken by a place of power that had a distinct right to it. Mary cut out herself as the middleman."

"Fair enough. Now, what about that part about 'the coven would sever their lives' if they didn't have their magick?"

"Remember when we realized there had to be dozens of witches in Cedar Creek, but none lifted a finger to help Margarite, Catherine, and Agnus? That's why. If any of the three confessed to witchcraft and pointed out their sisters, the whole coven would hang. Without their magick, they were no longer assets, but liabilities. To protect themselves, the coven easily would have come to the decision that all three were better off dead. That's why no one saved them or spoke in their defense at their witch trials."

Shaking his head, Nathan sighed, "So that's why we had to rush over here. How did you know?"

I shrugged. "I wasn't certain, but the only other person I knew who would do something as cruel as killing off several magickal bloodlines is Azure. The thing about Azure, though, is that she's not that different from me. Then I realized that it was something that I would do, given the right reason."

"And this counts as the right reason."

"You got it."

"So, by grounding that spell into the protection surrounding the circle, Mary made it so there was no time limit, correct? And to get at the three who were immune to that spell, she placed a curse on her blood. Since the whole coven was responsible for killing her, how come that same curse was not applicable to them?"

My eyes traveled over the circle as echoes of the past seemed to collapse in on me. Then I smiled. "I think it was applicable to them." Raising my eyes to his, I explained, "Maybe that's the other reason they couldn't help Margarite and the others. They had no magick left to stop them, and the only beings with magick enough were too young to know how to use it. That's why the coven became Margie's responsibility and that's why Francesca was able to take others with her and disappear when her sister got to be too much to handle. There was no one left to stop either of them."

There was a moment of silence between us as we looked out over the circle. Then Nathan asked, "Is that it, then? Is that the last piece of the puzzle?"

It was. But it didn't feel like it was over. Though I wouldn't admit it to Nathan, I wanted to see Margarite hang. As Mary, I never got the opportunity. Reading a journal entry claiming the deed was done wasn't good enough. I had to know that this had ended how it was intended.

"We still don't know what happened to the kids," I said aloud. As before, I was less concerned with her son than with Mercy. He'd been left in a loving home. It was Mercy who had to be erased from the rest of the world.

"I'm still working on that. I might have an answer to at least one of them in a couple of weeks."

I didn't ask which one. Instead, I looked about me once more and said, "I didn't see it when Mary told Henry about Margarite. The journal said that Mary had been accused when she left immediately after William's funeral. I wonder what she told Henry when she came back. What had she done to convince him that his wife was a witch?"

"I don't know, Lex, but I doubt the answer is here."

For a few minutes, I'd forgotten how he felt about the circle. While he'd done a great job of pretending it wasn't affecting him, the past few minutes had allowed some of the uneasiness to wriggle back in, and it was getting noticeable. Letting a small smile spread across my face, I nodded in agreement and took his hand. He didn't complain when we reappeared in the cottage a second later.

One of our silences fell as I went back to the table and allowed my supplies to spread out again. Nathan gathered up his files and scribbled a few notes down in relation to his findings. It was nice, being able to work alongside one another on our own projects. He didn't ask me what I was doing, and I didn't question his notes. After a while, he told me he was heading home and I told him I'd see him in a few hours.

There was truly something magickal about Friday the Thirteenth. In the hours since Nathan left, the spell fell together with perfect ease. Then, as I was about to walk out the door, I glanced up at the moon that was appearing over the tops of the trees. At once, I fell into the memory.

The full moon sent bars of white light through the window pane into the room. Below, I could see Margarite ushering her two daughters down the way. They would stop at the church and wait for Catherine Blake and Agnus Carter and their children before all of them made their way to the circle. No time would be better.

Drifting toward the bed, I made myself invisible before I dared to remove the sleeping spell Margarite had placed upon her husband. When Henry began to twitch, I leaned close and whispered, "Where is your wife, Henry? Where are your children?"

I had just moved out of reach when he jerked upright. At once, a hand flung out to the empty spot in his mattress. The second he realized his wife was absent, his eyes darted around the room in search of her. He was still groggy when he pushed to his feet and headed for the door. I stopped him with another whisper.

"Look to the church. See that she gathers."

In his half-asleep, half-panicked state, Henry didn't question it. Instead, he lurched toward the window and almost pressed his face to the glass. There, in the midnight hour, his family was clearly exposed standing beside the steeple. As we watched, Agnus Carter dragged her eight-year-old son toward Margarite. Her other boy was not going to make it this night, it seemed. None of Catherine Blake's brood attended with her as she made her way slowly toward the gathering. Fresh from the birthing bed, she looked far more than weary.

As Henry's breath fogged the glass, I leaned a little closer and murmured, "What women gather in the mid of night? What creatures vanish into the forest as the moon reaches her height?"

His breathing became more labored and I watched as terror filled his eyes. Then, when the group turned and slipped away into the forest, he sank to his knees and began to blubber out a prayer while tears coursed down his round face.

I was able to finish my work with one more word. "Witch."

Chapter Thirty Nine

DEFIANT

It was officially the end of what I would get out of Mary. The story was told, now. Which meant I was finally able to share it.

For some reason, I didn't.

Nathan knew, but we both felt like we were still missing something. It was enough of a deterrent that, come Sunday, I didn't broach the subject with the other witches. So, it was just as well that Rebecca had a different strain of conversation to steer us all down.

"What's this?" I asked as an ivory envelope dropped onto the table in front of me.

"Open it," she replied as she continued to pass them out.

I hurried to comply and my eyebrows shot

into the air as I removed a cream-colored card from the envelope. On the cover was the sonogram picture of Rowan with 'You Are Invited…' written in white cursive above the image. When I opened the card, I was surprised by the formality of the request. What surprised me most was the location.

"Salem, Massachusetts?"

"They're used to witches of all kinds coming out to celebrate, and they have the accommodations for it."

"What kinds of witches did you invite?" I almost growled.

"The kinds willing to build a community," she shot back.

My mouth fell open, giving Nathan the opportunity to ask, "Why December sixteenth?"

"Close enough to Christmas that everyone is already in a gift-giving spirit. Also gives them plenty of notice to come up with something good."

"How many people did you invite?"

"Not people, Alex. Witches. And I invited almost every single one I could find in New England."

"Why?"

"Hey, you're the one that wants this place to thrive on a community mindset. You can't do that and stay out of the action. You're the Witch of Old Grove Road. Use it or lose it."

I opened my mouth to argue some more, but no words came out. Because she was right. This was my idea and I had to put in the same amount of effort as everyone else. George and Basil had reached out. Terry had over a hundred practitioners for friends. Cameron was spreading the word. Everyone else was doing their part. If sharing this small part of my life with the witches of New England was all that was asked of me, didn't I owe them the chance?

That didn't stop my expression from slipping into a pout. At which Rebecca rolled her eyes. "Yeah, yeah, I know, you hate it that I'm right. But cheer up. Do you know how many presents you're going to get?"

Caroline shook her head. "It's not the quantity, but the quality." Throwing me a wink, she said, "You know us witches. We like to make things with our hands."

Which was why naming Rowan had been so important. Nathan may not have understood, but Rebecca had been right when she said it would shift the focus. Instead of the baby shower being about giving me what I needed to prepare, it would now be about giving Rowan things she could use. Not just toys and diapers and clothes, but ritual tools and gifts of power, protection, and knowledge.

"Poor kid is going to have hand-painted tarot cards coming out of her ears," Terry muttered. She would know. She was our resident card reader.

Karrie was chuckling to herself. "How many books do you think they'll get doubles of?"

"Oh, want to take bets on how many have 'Wicca' in the title?"

"Why Salem, though? It's so far away," Olivia grumbled.

Rebecca turned to her and said, "Because Alex doesn't want strangers to know where she lives. It took her this long to warm up to the rest of us. If this place got invaded, she'd kill me."

"Good point," Karrie muttered.

I tried to hide a grin.

The rest of the hour passed in the same manner. At last, the others were gone and Nathan was helping me clean up the last of the dishes.

For some reason, I was more exhausted than normal and was using magick to get most of the work done.

Abandoning the dishes, Nathan sat beside me on the couch and said what I was thinking. "It's not going to be over for you until you see Margarite hang."

"Well, it sounds crude when you say it like that."

"But it's the truth."

I shrugged. "The truth isn't just about making sure she died for this. The truth is that I still can't help but wonder what happened with Mercy and the boy. I don't even know his name, and that's probably what bothers me most."

Shaking his head, Nathan stood up and held a hand out to me. "Come on."

"Where are we going?"

"Just trust me," he said with a sly smirk.

I did.

Leaving an astral behind to finish the cleaning, Nathan and I walked through the woods back to our house. Then we jumped in the truck and Nathan took us toward town. When we stopped outside one of the little churches, I was confused. For about ten seconds.

"Nathan, this is..."

"The church from your vision. Sort of. The original burned down, but this one is a pretty close replica."

"Why are we here?"

Nathan pointed at the middle of the intersection. "Because that's where the tree was that they hung Margarite from. Want to know what happened to the tree? It's part of the floorboards of the church," he said, pointing back at the building.

"You've got to be kidding me. How did you figure that out?"

"In the preacher's journal, it mentioned that they were hung from a towering oak that stood in front of the church. This was the only church erected at the time. Then I found an article about the church burning down in the early 1800s. Cedar Creek was expanding by that point, and the oak was where a nice new crossway could be made. So, they cut it down, sent it to the mill, and had it turned into planks in order to help reconstruct the new church."

"You're telling me that if I step foot in that

church, there might be a memory from the oak in there?"

He grinned. "Don't get struck by lightning."

"Ha ha," I muttered as I climbed out of the truck. Then I marched up to the heavy front doors. I kept my eyes on Nathan as I grabbed the handle. No lightning. Grinning, I ducked into the darkened interior.

The vision hit me full-force.

The first thing I saw was a little girl with braided yellow plaits tied with black ribbon. She stood beside an older girl who looked very similar. One glance at those sharp, crystalline eyes and I knew at once that I was staring at Margie and Francesca. Then Henry Vaile stepped up behind them and placed a beefy hand on their shoulders. He was dressed for a funeral.

Turning in place, I found a crowd of people gathered, all wearing the same grim expressions. While most of the men were of little interest to me, it was the wide, staring eyes of the women that intrigued me. As it was a memory, it was impossible for me to feel if they had their magick or not, but I was willing to bet most of them had been stripped of their borrowed power. Which might have been the reason nine-year-old Margie looked more furious than frightened.

All of a sudden, the crowd ceased its murmuring as a man dressed in the costume of a magistrate stepped forward to stand beside the ancient oak that grew in the center of the village. Behind him, three men marched three bound women into the space. At once, a hiss erupted from the crowd as people crossed themselves and held up signs warding off evil.

Agnus was the first to flinch away as her eyes filled with tears. Her two boys stood next to their father, tears running down their cheeks. Beside her, Catherine Blake stood as tall as possible and stared straight ahead. Neither her husband nor her children were in attendance. Margarite stood the tallest, but her expression was the least satisfying. Defiant until the very end, she appeared as if she would walk away unscathed. As she had walked away from Edith's murder, and William's, and Mary's.

Unconsciously, I took a step forward, determined she wouldn't walk away from this one. But I had no bearing on this moment.

The man acting as magistrate stepped forward and read off the charges and the convictions of all three women. Then he read out the sentence: hanging by the neck until death. In that same moment, three ropes were launched over the branches of the oak tree and three large crates were placed beneath them.

The witches were then led to the crates. Catherine began to cry at last when the rope was secured about her neck, while Agnus dropped to the ground in front of the church and began to spout off the Lord's Prayer. If she was hoping it would save her, it didn't. Two men hauled her to her feet and thrust her up onto the crate. Margarite was almost regal as she strode to her crate and stepped gracefully onto it. Had her hands not been bound, I think she would have held her hair for the hangmen as he secured her noose.

"Agnus Carter, Catherine Blake, and Margarite Vaile, you will now perish for the crime of witchcraft. Have you any last words?"

Agnus was the first to speak, but her words ran together, drowned out by her sobs. With tears leaking from her eyes, Catherine said in a high-pitched voice, "I regret my actions and I hope God has mercy on my family so that they may escape what I have done to them."

When it was Margarite's turn, she looked straight at her eldest daughter and said, "Your will be done, my daughter. Your will shall decide our future."

My eyes shot to Margie and watched as the little girl gave a solemn nod. My stomach twisted as the meaning became clear. Margarite was counting on her nine-year-old child to set her free. She was so determined to have her way, it did not matter to her which lives she would ruin; so long as they were of use to her.

Then, at a signal from the magistrate, the crates were kicked out from under them, one by one. Catherine was the only lucky one. She was small enough that her neck snapped as soon as the rope went taut. Agnus, on the other hand, strangled to death in long, painful moments. Then there was Margarite...

Whatever deal she had made with her child, it wasn't honored. When she reached the end of her rope, it didn't snap. She didn't regain her footing. As she struggled to breathe, her wide eyes sought out her daughter's.

For some reason, it held no joy for me to watch as the betrayal caused her eyes to grow dim with horror. Then the light left them at last, and I turned to find myself watching over two girls whose mother had been killed for being a witch. While it wasn't the real reason that she was hung, it was the reason that would haunt forever two beings bred of magick. I could find no pleasure in that.

Turning back toward the church, a figure in the crowd caused my head to snap around. For a moment, I thought I was staring at Mary's ghost. Then I realized the worn lines in her face and gray hair escaping her bonnet made her someone much more important. Mary's mother turned, pulling on the hand of a little girl no one else seemed to notice.

I ran to catch up to them. They didn't go far. The messenger service that was something akin to the modern post office stood beside the trading store that was Henry and William's work. Mary's mother paused there, removing a sealed letter from her apron. I had just enough time to read the name before it fell into the box.

Chapter Forty

SENTINEL

"May I help you?" asked a kindly-looking man when I opened my eyes.

It took me a minute to get my bearings, but when I did, I laughed aloud. "No, thank you," I managed to gasp before I turned and wrenched the church door wide open.

Nathan's eyebrows rose as I climbed into the truck, laughing so hard that tears were forming in my eyes. "Lex? C'mon, what's going on?"

For a few seconds, I couldn't speak. Then I told him in fragments what I witnessed. None of which he found funny until I told him that I saw Mercy and her grandmother dropping off a letter.

"That's why you're laughing?"

I'd finally gained enough control over my

mirth that I was able to wipe my eyes as I said, "It was addressed to Thomas and Elizabeth ... Rice."

Nathan's hands smacked against the steering wheel as he threw himself against the seat. "You've got to be kidding me," he growled.

I shook my head. "Guess we know what happened to that missing bloodline, hmm?"

Nathan chuckled. "The same thing that happened to the other one."

At once, my mirth was gone. "Excuse me?"

Instead of answering, he started up the truck and headed back to the house. On the way, he remarked, "How much do you want to bet that Mary's son had a son? How much do you want to bet that he had only one child, and it was a son?"

"What are you talking about?"

"Remember that hunch I had about one of the kids? Let's just say that it panned out. If I'm right, Mercy and her brother have a lot of family resemblances."

"What does that mean? You found Mercy?"

We pulled into the driveway and Nathan shut off the truck. Then he looked me in the eye and announced, "I found Mercy."

In an instant, I leapt out of the truck, growling at him to show me what he found. Nothing infuriated me more than when he looked at me, smug as a cat, and said, "Not yet."

"Excuse me?" I snarled.

"Give me a little time to track the Rice family. When I show them to you, I at least want to have his name."

My eyes narrowed into a glare, but an aching in my chest kept me from snapping at him again. Gritting my teeth, I asked him for one detail at least. "Tell me she survived."

Grinning at me, Nathan took a step closer and kissed me on the cheek. "She did more than survive, Lex. She thrived."

Some hard, solid knot that had been with me since childhood suddenly released. For the first time in nine years, it felt like I was taking my first deep breath. Mercy had lived. The spell had worked. I'd protected her. Knowing that was enough. More than enough; it was everything.

"You have until Samhain."

The air was crisp and cool. The way it could only be in the northeastern states as autumn reached her peak. Scarlet and gold were withering into brown and mottled as they fell to the ground. A crunchy carpet of leaves littered every sidewalk and driveway. The entirety of Old Grove Road was coated in the oak leaves as the trees prepared for winter. And the smell of apple cider seemed to cling to the entire town as every coffee shop and café brewed the fall elixir.

It was the first Samhain I spent with others in at least four years. Instead of holing up in the cottage with my spell books, ritual supplies, and cats, I strode along Main Street and enjoyed every aspect of this sacred day. No one was holding back with the decorations.

Skeletons were hung on lampposts while hay bales were set on every corner, boasting wicked pumpkins and creepy scarecrows. *Mystic Manuscripts* had an incredible mummy propped up in the window holding a tome about ancient Egypt. Arrayed in the rest of the window display was a stuffed black cat sleeping atop a collection of occult books. A caged raven was perched atop *The Complete Works of Edgar Allan Poe* and a toad was propping up the latest *Harry Potter* book. The fact that there were candles hanging by fishing line–making it seem as if they were floating–in the windows of *Rook Candle Company* only made it better. It wasn't until I'd seen it all come together that I realized how important Halloween was to Cedar Creek.

"Why didn't they decorate like this when we were kids?" I asked Nathan as we passed by *Basil's Sweet Retreat*. There was a stack of bat cookies arranged in the window next to a fresh-baked pumpkin pie.

"Let me count the witches," he chuckled.

He was right, of course. Like any one of them wouldn't go all-out for Samhain. Considering the number of businesses that catered to the occult, it was fair to say that some of that holiday spirit was bound to rub off on their average neighbors.

"Do we have enough candy at the house?" Nathan asked for the tenth time.

"No, we don't. We only bought out half the store two weeks ago."

More than we needed to, certainly. And we'd spent those two weeks sorting things into little purple bags I'd gotten from the dollar store. I'd even stopped at the craft store and bought a box full of necklace and bracelet charms. Now each bag held a piece that was coated in spells to promote luck, prosperity, health, and things of that nature. My gift to the children of Cedar Creek.

As the afternoon waned, Nathan and I finally drove home. We barely made it through the door before I said, "There, we're home. Now quit stalling and tell me his name."

He chuckled as he kicked off his shoes and hung his coat up under the stairs. "Give me a minute," he said, indicating I should wait for him in the parlor.

I did as he asked and was rewarded with his reappearance a moment later. He held two manila folders in his hand and a wide grin covered his face. Then he handed me the folder with 'Rice' written on the tab. As soon as I opened it, I found Thomas and Elizabeth's names written at the top, along with their birth and death dates. Beneath them was one other name.

"Lucas Rice," I murmured. For a moment, I got a flash of a happy, chunky baby boy with cobalt eyes.

"Keep going," Nathan urged.

I did as he suggested, reading the name of Lucas's wife and their son. And his son. And his son. And his son. On and on it went, each Rice male producing only one more Rice male. All the way down until...

"Alyssa Rice," I breathed, staring at the photograph Nathan had seen fit to add to the file.

"The only daughter, and the only noticeable witch. It's the same with Mercy's side."

At that, my head jerked up and my eyes narrowed. "What's the same?"

"Everything. Son after son after son. And so on and so forth until the line finally comes to an end on an only daughter. The only witch."

He didn't need me to ask. As he finished speaking, he handed over the file. I almost dropped it when I saw 'Ryder' written on the tab.

"That hunch I had? It was you. I figured you might be more connected to Cedar Creek and all of this than just having Mary as your past life. So, I started tracing your family tree. That's how I found Mercy," he explained as I thumbed through the pages of Mercy's lineage. A smile pulled at my lips as I realized my dad was probably the eighth or ninth John Ryder in the history of our family. Starting with Mercy's husband.

When I reached the end of the file, I found

one of my prom pictures. I was sitting at Alyssa's piano with my hands folded in my lap. Silently, I placed the picture of Alyssa beside mine on the coffee table. In my head, I was tallying up the same similarities I'd heard on the TV ages ago. Same initials: A.M.R. Same age when she disappeared and I found her. Even the same bedroom.

Now I could add one more similarity to the list: same ancestors.

"Thank you, Nathan," I murmured. "This is what I needed."

He reached over and squeezed my hand. "I know."

It was time.

Standing in the center of the circle, luxuriating in the autumn breeze, I listened to the circle breathe. Felt every pulse of its heartbeat. And understood what it wanted from me.

Just because it had gone unnoticed for so long didn't mean it would remain a piece of forgotten history. Things were changing, and the chances of it being discovered were rising. If I didn't protect it now, there was no guarantee I would be able to protect it in the future.

I called the witches.

Pulse after pulse shot out of me, seeking them out and drawing them in. Like bees to honey. An hour passed before the first of them pushed through the trees.

Caroline was dazed and confused as she stared through the circle. While she had come, she had no idea where or why she had been called. Slowly, I crossed the circle to reach the barrier. The second I stepped over the dividing line, she jumped almost a foot in the air.

"Alex?"

A small smile pulled at my lips as I said, "Welcome home."

I held out my hand to her and waited for her to take it. When she did, I guided her over the line and took her to the place that marked Fire. Moments later, George and Basil arrived. He was given the place of Earth and she took up the position of Water. Elena and Patrick, the other two energy workers, arrived near the same time. She wandered to the place of Spirit while he took up a station for Air.

These five people were the supports to

any decent spell work. All energy workers. All aligned to certain elements. As if the circle knew it needed them to go forward, it had drawn them to Cedar Creek. As it had drawn Mary and all of the first members of Cedar Creek Coven.

It was as I stood staring at them that four more people drifted through the woods. Then three more. Then two sets of two. Yet, no one was more surprised than me when one other person showed up.

As soon as my eyes met Nathan's, he sent me a wry smile and leaned up against a tree well outside the border. Ever the sentinel. He was here to observe and protect, but not be involved. I shot him a smile and nodded once in understanding before I turned back to station the new arrivals.

Before I could stop myself, I began to hum. It was an old song that skipped and hopped through time, past even the days of Mary and Margarite. It was a lullaby that belonged to the circle. A piece of itself that affected everyone around it. As was proven when Elena took up the song and it traveled through the circle. That was our first bit of magick performed together. We sang a song it should have been impossible for us all to know, but it allowed us to know one another best of all.

When it had ended, midnight had struck, carrying us into November first. It was then that I looked around at the sixteen witches I'd come home to and asked them to sit. In a wave, they sank to their knees where they were and got comfortable. Even Nathan stretched his legs out before him as he leaned back into his tree.

Settling myself in the center of the circle, I looked around at the other witches and said, "Once upon a time, there was a young witch named Mary Sullivan."

Chapter Forty One

EMISSARY

November passed by as a completely unremark-able month. Mom and Anne finished the nursery. My parents managed to sell their house in October, and had bought one outside Cedar Creek. Nathan spent a lot of time in his office trying to track down the descendants of Agnus Carter and Catherine Blake. All the while, I worked on the spell that would offer Rowan and Grey a future.

By the time we got to December, the only thing anyone wanted to talk about was the baby shower. Considering how far it was from home, we were all gearing up for a week-long stay—that Rebecca had already booked for most of us. Those that couldn't make it threw a pre-baby celebration for me at the house. It was by-far the most normality I could hope for, considering I got boxes of diapers and baby toys out of it.

Then it was time. We arrived in Salem three days early and acted like regular tourists for the most part. I kept my magick masked the entire time, because I soon realized that there were a lot more energy workers in New England than I could have imagined. At least five hundred practitioners; one hundred of which landed on a power scale somewhere between Caroline and the Season Sisters.

At last, the sixteenth arrived and I was ushered to the ballroom where this event was taking place. Part of me scoffed at the ridiculousness of it. Who'd ever heard of renting out a ballroom for a baby shower? Then I got to witness the number of witches who showed up. When we reached eight hundred and sixty-three, Rebecca announced that was everyone who'd responded to the RSVP.

"For the record, *Maid of Honor*, the wedding is going to be *small*."

She grinned. "That's fine. But Rowan's first birthday isn't."

I could have killed her, but I didn't have

time. For now, it was all about the guests and making a good first impression. Oh joy.

Three hours later, I'd made it through awkward introductions, a large and lasting lunch, and about half of the games Rebecca had arranged. We were then coerced into decorating onesies with quotes. Famous or otherwise. So far, I'd counted six containing the Wiccan Rede and almost a dozen of the same three Dumbledore quotes. Nathan's was simply 'Once upon a time...' and my mother made her 'Ryder Pride' in electric blue.

Those of us that had finished the onesie decorating invariably made our way toward the food still arranged along the one wall. It was there that I was cornered by a stout older woman with a clever gleam in her brown eyes. "Quite the turn out, eh? I'll admit, I wasn't the only one surprised to receive this invitation. But since I'm only an hour out, I never pass up the chance to get to Salem when it presents itself."

My first instinct all day had been to blame it on Rebecca. Then I swallowed that urge and said, "I wanted this to be something we could all celebrate. It also seemed like a great opportunity to meet the most interesting people."

"Interesting is one word for us, all right," she snorted. "Now, tell me the truth here, what was the point in sharing such a special occasion with so many strangers?"

Automatically, my hand rested on my stomach. "The point is to build the foundation of ... something. I want a better life for my kids than the one I've lived. I think that might start off by proving that we're not alone. It takes a village to raise a child, right?"

Her smile bordered on smug when she raised a glass of fruit punch and said, "That it does. That it does."

When she wandered away, a girl about my age and with a decent chunk of magick slipped up beside me and cast a smirk at the woman's retreating back. "Jenna McKeery. Sly as an eel and confident as a cat. Good friend to have in a pinch," she confided to me.

I turned to raise my eyebrows at her and her grin widened. "The name is Tessa Blake. You must be Alexandria Ryder."

My mouth almost fell open. Then it took everything in me not to ask. After all, Blake wasn't the most common name on the planet, but it wasn't even close to rare, either. Then her smile grew and I knew.

"Where are you from, Tessa?"

"Myself or my family, Alexandria? Myself, I'm from South Carolina. Most of the family is from Georgia. Though I'm pretty sure it started in a small New England town. Not that I remember the name of it."

Her grin said three things at once. First, that she remembered exactly where her family was from. Second, that she knew where I was from. Lastly, she was answering my unspoken question.

She was from Coral Creator; one of the five major covens in the United States. Tessa was an emissary.

Shaking my head, I turned to look out over the room and sighed, "Who are the others?"

"Well, that hottie over there is Charles Devon of Sacred Summit. Looks like Maiden Falls sent Rachael Graine. Blessed Endeavors seems to have played the same hand as us. They sent Abigail Carter. Rumor has it that her family shares a common source as mine."

This much I didn't mind sharing. "The

rumors are true."

Tessa seemed nothing but mildly interested. "Is that so? Dad will be glad to hear it. Huh. I don't see anyone from Crone's Crescent. Do they no longer consider New England neutral ground, I wonder?"

The corners of my lips twitched as I realized the hand that was played. "They'll be here soon. And as long as I am here, Crone's Crescent knows New England will always be neutral ground."

With that, I glided away from Tessa Blake and went in search of Nathan. If there were emissaries from every other coven, there would most definitely be one from Crone's Crescent. Depending on who it was, this whole party could go sideways.

Halfway across the room, a lithe shadow appeared at my side and I heard a familiar voice say, "I've missed you."

At once, I turned in place and pulled Faye to me. For a second, she hugged me just as tightly. Then she cleared her throat and pulled away. It could have been a nice, normal moment ... except that her eyes were wary and her magick was masked.

"He sends you to spy yet again," I murmured.

"Better me than someone else. Did you think something as big as this wouldn't make waves?" As a point, her eyes shot to my stomach before taking in the room.

"First off, this wasn't my idea. I just wanted to build–"

"A defense," she finished with a knowing smirk. "It's a good plan. It'd be better if you hadn't tipped your hand so that every coven across the country didn't see you trying to guard against them. Now it's an open invitation."

"Or a gentle reminder that New England is neutral. In all things," I added with my own, slow smile.

Her eyebrows rose and her eyes darted around the room once more. "Is that why Tessa Blake looks like she bit a lemon?"

"No, I'm pretty sure that expression is because she recognized you. Your mask is slipping."

"Damn," she muttered, her eyes narrowing as she focused just a little harder.

"Better."

"But it won't last long. Which means I've got to wrap this up," she sighed. For the first time, her eyes raised to mine and I got to see a rare tender smile. Then she pulled out a folded bandana from her pocket and placed it into my hand. "This is for Rowan. He said it was so she could find her way back to him."

Unfolding the bandana carefully, I gasped when I found a locket almost identical to the one around my neck. Instead of a clock, however, there was a compass full of Grey's magick. It wasn't pointing due north.

"She will never be without it," I vowed.

"I'll tell him," she assured me. Then she reached into another pocket and retrieved a tiny box. "And this is for you."

Somehow, I knew what it would be before I opened it. Not just because of the familiar magick radiating from inside, but because the bracelet on my left wrist seemed drawn to it. Taking another breath, I removed the lid.

My eyes landed first on the rowan charm. The thin blades of the leaves looked so delicate, I almost worried they'd snap. Somehow, I knew he'd commissioned it the same day he'd named her.

The second charm was of greater surprise.

Though I couldn't imagine how he knew, there rested a tiny silver avens flower, identical to the ones I wore to prom. My throat grew dry even as I allowed Faye to attach them both to the charm bracelet. For a moment, the whole world felt right as they landed against my skin.

"Thank you, Faye," I said, giving her one last hug. Being that close, I dropped my voice so that only she could hear me when I said, "Tell him she'll find him soon. Tell Grey not to fight where his dreams take him."

Pulling back, Fay nodded once. Then she was gone and reality crashed in around me once more.

Chapter Forty Two

SILENTLY

When I imagined myself giving birth, it was at night. It was under a starry sky with the moon shining brightly overhead. Anne, my mom, and Nathan would be the only ones present and we could get through it together. With minimal witnesses and interference.

That's not at all how things happened.

It started in the morning of January twenty-first. At first, it felt like the same constant backache I'd had for two weeks straight. In those same two weeks, I'd been plagued with false contractions meant to help prime my body for the big event. Something that I was more than ready for, all things considered. While I was one of the lucky women that hadn't experienced the world's worst pregnancy, I was still seriously over Rowan's current residency. I wanted my body back.

What was really ironic about everything seeming so normal was that the turn toward real labor happened in the blink of an eye. One minute I was mildly uncomfortable. The next, I understood exactly what Anne meant when she said I would know the real contractions when they hit.

Almost at once, Nathan wanted to call our parents and head for the circle. Given all of the stories I had in my head of Anne's other patients, I refused. Labor was likely to last several hours, and I wasn't going to have everyone camped out in the circle any longer than we needed to be.

For the first couple of hours, they came in steady, almost meandering waves. There was the pressure of the buildup, the sharp crest, and then the subtle ebb as it pretended like it was going away. Then it would come back in the same way. Yet, sometime just after two, they started to draw closer together and I knew that it wouldn't last much longer.

"Call the moms," I gasped.

"Your parents will be here any minute and

Mom said she'd meet us at the circle."

I nodded slowly and continued to pace through the parlor. The faster I dilated, the faster Rowan could have her own room. And all I kept thinking the whole time I was walking was that it didn't hurt as much as the burns.

The second my mom arrived, I grabbed hers and Nathan's hands and teleported to the circle. They both protested for about as long as it took for the next contraction to hit. Then they focused on steering me toward the center. Anne already had her battle station set up.

Then I heard them. The witches had begun to gather. As the first wave of them pushed through the trees and passed through the barrier, I groaned. My eyes shot to Nathan, imploring him to tell them to go. He ignored me.

"Set them all around the perimeter," Caroline instructed a few of the practitioners carrying her candles. They did as she said and we were soon encased in the warm glow of candlelight. Then Caroline passed one to Nathan. When he handed it to me, it was just the right size for me to wrap my hand all the way around it and squeeze.

I would have laughed if another contraction

hadn't hit in that same moment. As I squeezed my eyes closed, I could feel them retreat to their places. Then the lullaby began. Somehow, I knew it would not stop until she was born. It would be the first thing Rowan heard.

From that moment on, things seemed to go rather quickly. At 3:33pm I heard my daughter's first cry.

The second Nathan laid her on my chest, magick happened.

More than anything else in the world, I wanted to put it off. Never in my life had I felt such bone-deep exhaustion. Nor had I felt so gross. Yet, it had to be done.

Which was why, twenty minutes to midnight, I dragged myself out of bed and made my way to the cradle. Remarkably, she seemed wide awake when I picked her up. It was scary how tiny she was, even though Anne had weighed her at seven pounds and six ounces. All things considered, I was more paranoid about dropping her than anything else.

Taking a deep breath, I tapped into the

magick that was still swirling heavily around us. Almost before I thought it, we were standing in the center of the circle. A shiver traveled up my spine as I realized how easy it was. How natural it would always be for her. And this was long before her Ascension.

Creepy and fascinating all in one.

I had to take another moment to focus on the task at hand. This was the most important spell I'd ever created, and I needed it to be done flawlessly. After a moment, I called for my tools. Something this complicated called for the whole ritual. No half-measures.

It started with a lullaby ... it ended with Rowan clutching the lock of her father's hair. Using the charm bracelet imbued with his magick, I was able to form the focus. At last, I built the bridge.

Modeled after the darkness that still held Nathan and I each night, I made something a little more special for Grey and Rowan. It was a field of wildflowers with a massive rowan tree standing in the center. For now. Everything past the immediate area looked as if it were painted in watercolors. That was because, when she got old enough, they'd be able to set the stage themselves. They could go anywhere and experience anything in their dreams. But when they parted, she'd be safe in bed at home. That was what I offered them.

Thirty seconds later, I saw him walking toward us. At once, I smiled and murmured to our baby girl, "Rowan, this is your father, Grey Walker."

He couldn't tear his eyes away from her and he looked more nervous than me when I transferred her into his arms. For several long moments, he was too stunned to speak. I let him enjoy the moment.

At last, I was too tired to wait any longer. "This is your place, Grey. Yours and Rowan's. Nothing can hurt you here, and no one else will be able to intrude. When she's here, you'll know. And when you want to see her, she'll know."

"Lex, how...?"

I smiled widely and said one more word. "Magick."

Then it was gone. The meadow and Grey were all a part of Rowan now. Her buried treasures.

Glancing down at my daughter, I saw that

her eyes were firmly shut and her breathing was deep and even. It was in moments like this that I realized how deeply someone could love. And it seemed so foreign to me that I couldn't feel attached to her at all when our journey first started. Yet, some deep part of me knew that she was Grey's. Rowan wasn't really meant for me, though I got to enjoy her the most. Which was why I owed this to them both.

Not that it didn't cost me. That was a lot of energy used in such a short amount of time. And I needed one more surge to get us home and back in bed.

This time, I had to concentrate more before we reappeared in the darkened bedroom. With a grateful exhale, I deposited the newborn into her cradle and backed away toward the bed. I'd just made myself comfortable when the door opened and Nathan eased into the room. From the sound of things, the grandparents were still celebrating in the parlor.

Nathan took one look at my open eyes, smirked, and went to check on Rowan. For several long seconds, he stood there staring at her. Then he turned and climbed into the bed beside me.

"Is Rowan with him?"

"In their dreams," I said through a yawn.

Nathan pushed my matted hair out of my face. "Think we'll ever dream again?"

"We get to live the dream. What does it matter that our brains mute every once in a while?"

"Fair enough," he said, pulling me even closer.

As comfortable as I was, it was impossible not to fall asleep then and there.

It felt like a short time later that Rowan's sharp cry pierced through the blackness. I jerked awake in the same moment that Nathan rolled out of bed and headed for the cradle. With slow, stiff movements, I sat up in the bed and prepared to feed my child.

It wasn't until I reached for her that I re-alized there was a new weight on my left ring finger. In the dim light, I could barely make out a white band with an emerald stone resting against my skin. Then Rowan was in my arms and my focus shifted.

That was how Nathan proposed, and that was how I accepted.

Silently. As was our way.

EPILOGUE

I absentmindedly rubbed at the valerian scar resting inside of my elbow. It had been twelve years since it formed in my skin, and I seemed to feel the ghost of it every year. Sometimes less, sometimes more. This year, it was more. I blamed it all on the recent bout of nostalgia that hit me ever since Rowan turned nine.

Time had passed too quickly to get us to this point, and it was reflected in the pictures filling up the house and cottage. While I still held to a simple family portrait on my birthday, my father-in-law had made it a point to document almost every other day of the year. Thus, as my eyes traveled around the cottage, I was able to track every brilliant moment of the past nine years.

On the mantel was the first picture taken of me, Nathan, and Rowan on the day she was born. Then came our wedding photo. Right next to it were a few pictures taken three years later, when we'd brought the twins home. Holly Jasmine Ryder was born six minutes prior to her sister and weighed three ounces more. She had a single dimple in her left cheek and brilliant blue eyes. Willow Althea Ryder was considered dainty by all. Where Holly was opinionated and fussy, Willow was patient and accepting. The mirror image of her father. Right down to the emerald irises.

They were supposed to be our last, the twins. Nathan and I had agreed a long time ago that three was a good number. Then came surprise number four.

Reed Richard Ryder was born three days before my twenty-seventh birthday, and so he got to be featured in the latest family portrait hanging above the mantel. At five months, I was glad to have the newborn madness behind us. All the same, I couldn't imagine where the past five months had gone. It felt like he was only a week-old yesterday.

As if he knew I was thinking about him, Reed gave a little snort before he filled his lungs and began to cry. Shaking my head, I was halfway across the room when the door burst open and his sisters clambered into the cottage. Fully ignoring me, Rowan was at his side in a moment. Even though he was almost half her size, my eldest child picked him up in her arms and proceeded to carry him outside.

"He needs fresh air," she proclaimed.

Holly and Willow giggled in pure enjoyment. Then Holly turned on her heel and darted back out into the sunshine. Willow, however, waited on me. When I reached her side, she held her hand out to me. I ignored it and lifted the grinning six-year-old up onto my hip. Once again, I was reminded how it was getting to be less and less likely that I carried the girls around like that.

When I made it outside, Rowan was sitting with her legs on either side of the bench with Reed sitting in front of her, his back against her stomach. Her head was lowered so that she could whisper in his ear as she pointed out the various plants in the garden.

Skipping along the path to the garden gate, Holly was singing to herself. Willow wriggled a bit and I let her slide to the ground. Then she, too, was headed up the path, joining her sister in a chorus. I smiled and took a seat on the other end of the bench. My children all continued to ignore me, immersed with each other as they were. I'd have been lying if I said I didn't enjoy it.

As was the way with children, it was completely unexpected when Holly ran up to me and almost threw herself into my arms. She was laughing up a storm when I caught her. Then I held her close while she pretended to struggle in an effort to get away from me. When she collapsed against me again, she was running her little fingers over the garden on my arm.

"Mommy, where did you get your scars?"

For a moment, my eyes closed and I took a deep breath. I didn't know what to think or how to respond to that. While I'd never planned to keep it from them, I'd also never figured out what to say. Rowan had never asked questions, so I had no experience to draw from. So, I did the only thing I thought I could do.

"Come here, and I shall tell you my story."

I retrieved Reed from his sister even as Holly and Willow dropped into the dirt at my feet, looking every bit enraptured by what I would say next. Beside me, Rowan gave a small smile and an encouraging nod.

This was it. They were old enough now to understand what I had endured, but young enough not to be frightened of it. And we would take this one step at a time. Nothing would be shared before they were ready.

With that in mind, I cast a loving smile on my steadfast Rowan, inquisitive Holly, and gentle Willow. Then I looked at Reed cradled in my arms and began, "The house was the most beautiful I had ever seen."

ACKNOWLEDGEMENTS

Well, this is it. The fifth book in the *Prideful Magick Collection* and the last one in which Lex will be the narrator. It has been an adventure, and an experience. As such, there are some very important people I have to thank for bringing this to an ideal conclusion.

Chrissy is the genius behind most of my ideas. Her work on each of my novels goes above and beyond what any best friend should reasonably have to do. This woman designs my cover, galley, and graphics. All whilst maneuvering around her own hectic life. She is my Wonder Woman and I am in total awe over all of her skills. Thank you for sticking by me!

Connie was a major contributor to the first

draft of *Avens* and she was instrumental in helping whip this beast into shape. With a great deal of her insight, I now feel more comfortable presenting this version of the book to the world. Thank you for all of your editing input.

Mariah ... we did it. We finally made it here to the end of Lex's story. I'm impressed and unconvinced all at once. Thank you for pushing me so hard for so long. We never would have made it this far without you.

Christopher, you'll probably never know how much your love means to me, and that's okay. Being with you is what home feels like to me. And I can't ever read about Nathan and Lex without thinking about you and me. Knowing that I have a love like that just adds to the enjoyment and anticipation I feel every time I read this book. That's what you do for me: enhance all the best moments in life. Love you, Honey.

This part of the acknowledgments always goes to my Nana and Papa. Because of them, I know what it means to always be loved, supported, inspired, and acknowledged. Your love means everything to me and I am so proud to be your granddaughter. Thank you.

Last of all, I have to thank my Big Dude. As many times as I have said it before, I can still say it one more time: this woman is my world. I love you, Mom. Thank you for everything.

ABOUT THE AUTHOR

Hollow Ryan is a Michigan native with thirty years spent too much in her own head, and twenty years putting it all on paper. This obsession with the written word has led her to publish the five-book paranormal series, *The Prideful Magick Collection*. It has also started her on a journey full of *Demon Kin*.

When not working on her ever-expanding Work List, Hollow is dealing with the three most spoiled fur-children to be found in Northeastern Michigan. (Her spouse is absolutely to blame for that.)

For more information, please visit:
www.hollowryan.com